When
Haru
Was
Here

ALSO BY DUSTIN THAO

You've Reached Sam

When Haru Was Here

DUSTIN THAO

WEDNESDAY BOOKS
NEW YORK

This is a work of fiction. All of the characters, organizations, and events portrayed in this novel are either products of the author's imagination or are used fictitiously.

First published in the United States by Wednesday Books, an imprint of St. Martin's Publishing Group

WHEN HARU WAS HERE. Copyright © 2024 by Dustin Thao. All rights reserved. Printed in the United States of America. For information, address St. Martin's Publishing Group, 120 Broadway, New York, NY 10271.

www.wednesdaybooks.com

Designed by Susan Walsh

All emojis designed by OpenMoji—the open-source emoji and icon project. License: CC BY-SA 4.0

Library of Congress Cataloging-in-Publication Data

Names: Thao, Dustin, author.
Title: When Haru was here / Dustin Thao.
Description: First edition. | New York : Wednesday Books, 2024. | Audience: Ages 12–18
Identifiers: LCCN 2024016441 | ISBN 9781250762061 (hardcover) | ISBN 9781250371379 (international, sold outside the U.S., subject to rights availability) | ISBN 9781250762078 (ebook) | 9781250384720 (signed edition)
Subjects: CYAC: Adjustment—Fiction. | Grief—Fiction | Imagination—Fiction. | Reality—Fiction. | LCGFT: Novels.
Classification: LCC PZ7.1.T44725 Wh 2024 | DDC [Fic]—dc23
LC record available at https://lccn.loc.gov/2024016441

Our books may be purchased in bulk for promotional, educational, or business use. Please contact your local bookseller or the Macmillan Corporate and Premium Sales Department at 1-800-221-7945, extension 5442, or by email at MacmillanSpecialMarkets@macmillan.com.

First Edition: 2024

10 9 8 7 6 5 4 3 2 1

For sixteen-year-old me.
You did it.

When Haru Was Here

Fall

BEFORE

Sometimes it's the little things we remember the most. Like the way Jasmine never finishes a book because she's afraid of the ending. Or the way she saves those paper fortunes from the restaurant when she wants them to come true. Or how she never brings an umbrella when she knows it's going to rain. Even the way she borrows my things and always forgets to give them back.

"Isn't this my jacket?"

I'm sitting on the floor of her room, watching her pack up her clothes for college. It's the beginning of fall. In a few hours, she'll be heading to the University of Michigan to start her next chapter. It's a five-hour drive from our house in Skokie, Illinois. I'm supposed to be helping her move the boxes into the car. Instead I'm going through them, wondering what she's taking with her.

Jasmine turns her head. "You said I could borrow that."

"How long are you *borrowing* it for?"

"If you want it back, then just take it," she says, flipping her long hair at me. As the younger brother, you would think my clothes would be safe from her hands. But Jasmine always finds her way into my closet, taking anything she likes.

The smell of lemongrass fills the house. Mom is cooking dinner in the kitchen while Dad watches television in the living room. Once everything's packed and ready, the three of them will be driving to Ann Arbor for the weekend. I wish I could go with them, see where she's spending the next four years of her life, but there's not enough room in the car. I stare at the jacket for a moment. It's a blue plaid button-up I thrifted a few years ago. Honestly, Jasmine wears it more than I do. "No, you can keep it," I say, putting it back for her. It's colder in Michigan, anyway.

I open another box and find a photo of us. We're standing on the front steps of the house, dressed as Lilo and Stitch for Halloween. Jasmine has her arms around me, our cheeks pressed together, her grass skirt brushing against my blue fur. It's hard to believe this was taken seven years ago. Sometimes I wish we could be kids again. Life was so much simpler back then. It's hard to pull my eyes away from the photo, but when I do, Jasmine appears on the floor beside me.

"I went through them yesterday," she says, smiling over my shoulder. Then she reaches into the box, pulling out another photo. "Look at this one—"

The photo is overexposed from the flash. I'm sleeping on one side of the sofa while Jasmine snuggles up with Gracie, our black Lab who passed away three years ago. Her big brown eyes are staring right at the camera.

"Aw, I miss Gracie," I say.

"I miss her, too."

The thought of her always makes me smile. I still keep her favorite tennis ball on top of my dresser. Sometimes I find myself tossing it against the wall when I'm feeling down. I could never get myself to throw it away.

"Here's another one—"

Jasmine hands me the next photo. We're around nine and ten years old, playing on Jasmine's toy piano in our matching pajamas.

The sight of that piano brings back memories. "*Oh my god,*" I say, widening my eyes. "You used to make me sit for hours, listening to you play that thing."

"You got a free concert. Be grateful."

"For what, the trauma?"

Jasmine pushes my shoulder as we laugh. The truth is she's great at the piano. She's been playing since she was seven and even writes some of her own music. Sometimes I'll lie down in her room while she's practicing one of her songs. "How come you're not taking your keyboard with you?" I finally ask her.

She sighs. "I told Mom and Dad I'd focus on classes."

"I thought you were going to major in music."

Jasmine glances at the door, holding a finger to her lips. I know not to ask further questions. Our parents wanted her to stay closer to home, so this must be one of the concessions. But the University of Michigan isn't too far away, so I'm sure we'll see each other all the time. As we look at another photo, my phone vibrates. I glance at the screen, hiding a smile.

Jasmine looks at me. "Who's texting you?"

"Just Daniel," I say casually.

"Don't tell me you're seeing him later," she says. "Is that why you're not coming with us?"

"There's no room in the car."

Jasmine narrows her eyes.

"No one's coming over!"

"Alright," she says with a shrug. Then she checks the time before rising to her feet again.

I send a quick response to Daniel and look for more photos. Peeking out beneath them is a white envelope with my name on it.

To Eric

"What's this for?"

Jasmine tries to grab it from me. "Nothing, put that back—"

I pull it away from her. "It says my name on it."

"I was writing you a letter." She sighs. "But I'm not done yet. So give it back to me."

"A letter for what?"

"I don't know. I just thought it would be nice, alright?" She moves her hair behind her ear, snatching the envelope from me. "I was gonna mail it to you when I'm in Ann Arbor. I figured I'll have more to say once I'm gone."

"You're not moving across the country."

"It's still a five-hour drive," she says. "It's not like I can just come home all the time."

I say nothing. For some reason, I always assumed she

would. That things wouldn't be too different. I glance around the room again, imagining it completely empty for the first time. Our house will be a lot quieter when she leaves. She's like the soundtrack here, her piano music constantly filling every room of the house. Jasmine must sense something, because she sits down again and says, "I'll be back every now and then. And you can always visit me, too."

"I don't have a car," I remind her.

"You can go with Kevin," she suggests. "He's driving up next weekend. The three of us can hang out together." Kevin Park is Jasmine's boyfriend of three years. They've known each other for much longer, so he's sort of family at this point. He's going to the University of Illinois here in Chicago. "I'll ask him to pick you up on the way."

"How often are you guys going to see each other?" I've been curious about their long-distance situation.

Jasmine glances at the door and back at me. Then she whispers, "Don't tell anyone yet, but Kevin is trying to transfer in the spring. We've been looking for apartments."

"*You're gonna live together?*"

"We're still figuring it out," she says, keeping her voice low. "But you have to keep this a secret, okay? Especially from Mom and Dad."

"Jaz . . ."

"*Promise me,*" she says, holding out her pinkie.

I give her another look and hold out my pinkie, too. "Alright, I promise."

We're always keeping secrets for each other. Jasmine was the first person I came out to a few years ago, even though I sensed she always knew I like guys. Hopefully we can still share things when she's gone. Eventually Dad appears at the doorway, reminding us to finish packing. Jasmine and I glance at each other, maybe speaking telepathically.

I'll miss you, I think she says.

I'll miss you, too.

Then we push ourselves up and grab some boxes. I hope she has a good time in Michigan.

The car hums in the driveway. Mom lingers in the kitchen, putting away dishes while everyone's already waiting outside. She left a pot of food on the stove for me, along with cut fruit in the refrigerator. They'll only be gone for the night, but she always worries I'll starve to death. "Ăn xong còn lại nhớ cất vô tủ lạnh," she says. *Remember to put it away later.*

"Yeah, okay."

"Đừng mở cửa cho người lạ." *And don't open the door for strangers.*

"I won't."

Mom kisses me goodbye and locks the door behind her. I watch the car pull out of the driveway before vanishing down the road. Then I turn toward the living room, taking in the new silence of the house. I guess I'll have to get used to this. After a moment, my phone vibrates again. There are several new messages from Daniel.

hii
what are you up to?
stop ignoring me ☹

I smile and text him back.

> sorry I was busy
> you can come over!

Twenty minutes later, there's a knock on the door. Daniel comes inside, wearing a denim jacket over his red sweatshirt. He has been wearing this combo since we became friends at freshman orientation. Daniel hugs me with one arm, removing his jacket with the other. He hangs it on the back of the chair and heads straight for the kitchen.

"What did Mom make us for dinner?"

"It's called *thịt kho*."

"My favorite," he says.

"You've never had it before."

"I love everything she makes."

Daniel lifts the lid from the pot, letting out some steam. I lean against the counter, watching him make himself a bowl. His brown hair seems lighter in the stove light. He takes a bite of pork belly and turns to me with a mouthful. "So what's the plan tonight?"

I shrug. "I don't know. We could watch a movie."

"It's Saturday night. Let's do something fun."

"Like what?"

Daniel pulls out his phone. "Zach texted me an hour ago. He's having some people over tonight. We should go."

"Doesn't he live in Rogers Park?"

"We'll take the train."

I stare at the counter, considering this. "I told my parents I wouldn't go anywhere tonight. They'll probably call to check in."

"Just turn your phone off. They'll think the battery died."

I give him a look. "Are you new here? They'll think *I* died and send out a search team."

Daniel groans. "What else are we gonna do, hang out on the roof again?"

I don't say anything. Because I was about to suggest this. Every now and then, we'll find our way up there, and it feels like we're the only people in the world. But it sounds like he'd rather do anything else tonight. "You can go to Zach's if you want," I say.

"You mean, *without you*?"

"It's not a big deal."

"We haven't seen each other all week."

"We can do something tomorrow." I was looking forward to spending some time together. But I don't want to force him to stay here if he doesn't want to. Especially if he has better plans.

Daniel's phone goes off in his hand. He glances at the screen, reading the text message. "You *really* don't want to go?"

"I can't tonight," I say.

His phone vibrates again. Daniel looks at the door and back at me. A silence passes as he considers his options. For a second, I think he's going to say goodbye. But he lets out a breath and says, "*Alright,* you convinced me. I'll stay."

A breeze rolls across the rooftop, ruffling the trees around us. We've been lying out here for hours, staring at the sky. There's an empty pizza box between us, along with some snacks we grabbed from the store earlier. We decided to come up here after a few episodes of *Twin Peaks*. His red sweatshirt is folded under his head like a pillow. I stare at him for a while. His eyes are moving around, as if he's looking for something. Eventually, he points to the right and says, "There's another one! Tell me you saw that."

"What are you talking about?"

"That star is literally blinking."

I squint at the sky. "Yeah, that's really weird."

"I'm telling you, it's a *glitch*."

"What do you mean?"

"Haven't you seen *The Matrix*? This is all a simulation. I just watched a video about this." Daniel pushes himself up and looks around. "See that orange cat across the street? And the houses around us with all their lights on? Nothing but code."

I take this in. "So you're saying, *everything* is a simulation."

"Exactly."

"Does that include us?"

"*Of course not,*" he says. "We're the main characters." He

lies back down, putting his hands behind his head. "As far as I know, you and I are the only thing that's real."

This makes me smile. We stare at the sky again, searching for more glitches in the universe. After some silence, Daniel turns his head again and stares at me. "What are you thinking about?"

I don't answer this.

"Jasmine?"

"Yeah, I guess."

"Are you sad she's leaving?"

I think about this. "No, I'm happy for her. It's what she really wanted, you know? Move out of Chicago and everything. I mean, my parents wanted her to stay home. Took a lot of convincing on her part," I explain. "But things are really gonna be different now that she's gone."

"You still have me," Daniel says.

I smile again. "That's true."

"And we'll get out of Chicago, too," he adds, folding his arms on his stomach. "Since we're gonna be college roommates, *obviously*."

"Where should we go?"

"Eh, we'll talk about that later." He sighs, waving the thought away. "We still have the rest of junior year to get through. And our trip to Japan, remember?" There's an annual trip that's coordinated by the school's international club. Jasmine went last summer and loved it.

"Jasmine gave us a list of places to visit."

"I can't wait for the food," he says.

As I move my hand, my fingers graze against his. A warmth goes through me, but I keep this to myself.

"*Sorry,*" we both say.

We lie in silence again. Then Daniel checks his phone. "It's eleven eleven. Time to make a wish."

I glance at him. "Do you actually do that?"

He shrugs. "Sometimes. Do you?"

"Never."

"Why not?"

"I don't know," I say. "Seems a bit silly, making a wish every night at the exact same time. You really think it will come true?"

"I figure it's a numbers game," Daniel says thoughtfully. "The more you put out into the universe, the more chances something happens. The challenge is having to come up with good ones, you know?"

"Wouldn't it make sense to wish for the same thing?"

"Depends if there's something you *really* want." He looks at me again. "What would you wish for?"

The question makes me go still. Looking at Daniel, I know exactly what my answer would be. But I look away, keeping it to myself. "I haven't thought about it."

"Yes you have. Just tell me."

"I said I don't know."

"Then I'm not telling you, either."

We sound like kids arguing on the playground, making us both chuckle. Daniel and I stay on the rooftop awhile longer, listening for passing cars and the barking from the neighbor's dog. To keep from shivering, I cross my arms and close my eyes for a moment. When I think Daniel has fallen asleep, I turn my head and find him facing me. We stare at each other in silence. Somehow, his brown eyes shine even in the dark. I don't know why, but he looks even more beautiful tonight. I wish I could run my hand through his hair and pull him closer to me. But I shake the thought out of my head. I try not to think of him this way, because I don't want to ruin things between us. Then he asks me something I don't expect.

"Can I . . . kiss you?"

I swallow my breath. For a second, I think I misheard him. But the way he's looking at me makes me want to move closer. So I lean forward and close my eyes. The next thing I know, his lips press against mine. The touch of skin sends a quiver through me. I've thought about this moment a million times before. My heart pounds inside my chest as his hand moves along my neck. The kiss only lasts a moment. But the feeling of it lingers as we lean back, catching our breaths. Neither of us says anything else. We just lie there on the rooftop for the rest of the night, staring up at the sky.

I wish I knew the ending to our story sooner. Maybe it wouldn't hurt as much.

Summer

BEFORE

Petals fall from the sky as the train doors open, letting me onto the platform. The summer heat hits me like a wall. I spin around, taking in all the foreign signs. I'm supposed to meet Daniel back at the hotel, but I seem to have gotten lost along the way again. We're on the annual school trip to Japan. It's our last day in Tokyo before we head to our next stop. I woke up early this morning to film some shots of the city for my senior project. Jasmine mentioned this café by the river I needed to see before I left. I must have taken the wrong train on my way back. I pull out my phone again, trying to make sense of where I am.

There's a new message from Daniel.

where did you go?

I send him a quick response.

> sorry. ran out to grab some shots. be back soon!

Daniel has a surprise planned for us later today. We're supposed to take a ferry across the water to a place he hasn't told me about yet. But it leaves in a few hours and I still need to get back to the hotel and change. It's been almost a year since our kiss on the rooftop. I thought our friendship would have blossomed into something new. At least, I wanted it to. But we haven't really acknowledged it since the night it happened. I was hoping this trip would bring us closer. There's something romantic about exploring a new city together.

I wipe sweat from my brow and make my way out of the station. The streets are crowded with people. I keep glancing at my phone, confused by the map. None of the buildings look familiar. As I turn my head, someone from the crowd makes me go still. He's taller than everyone else, with waves of black hair falling past his ears. His shoulders are broad, framed nicely in a billowy blue-striped shirt. I take in the rest of this stranger as he comes toward me. For a moment, I forget I'm lost.

The light must have turned green because the crowd starts moving again. I snap back to myself as my phone vibrates in my hand, telling me to cross the street. Another text message from Daniel pops up, asking me where I am.

Maybe it's the glare from the sun that blocks my vision. Or the fact that I'm distracted by the notifications on my phone. Because I don't see the delivery bike coming. It's one of those moments that happens in slow motion. A bell rings as I step off the sidewalk, oblivious to the incoming crash . . . when someone appears from the side, grabbing the handlebar. He must have *squeezed* the brakes, because the bike halts abruptly as the driver flips forward, flying out of his seat—but the stranger catches him by the back of his hoodie, helping him land on his feet.

It takes my brain a second to process the scene. Then relief floods through me as I look around, blinking wildly. The bicycle bell still rings in my ear as his face comes into focus. The guy in the blue-striped shirt stares back at me. The one I noticed a moment ago, standing half a head taller than me, waves of black hair blowing in the breeze of traffic. He says something to the driver, gesturing my way.

The driver nods at me and says, "Gomen'nasai." I practiced enough Japanese last semester to make out the word *sorry*. Then he grabs his bicycle and rides off again. Before I can breathe out a *thank you for saving me,* the guy in blue stripes turns to me and says something else I don't understand.

"What was that?" I ask.

"You should watch out for bicycles," he says.

I let out a breath, nodding graciously. "Yeah, right. I mean, *thank you*. Sorry, I just got lost and wasn't paying attention to—"

"Where are you going?"

"Oh—" I pull up the address on my phone. "Just back to my hotel. It should be around here somewhere."

"Want me to take a look?" He holds out a hand.

"Okay," I say, handing him my phone.

He glances at the screen. "The Asakusa Hotel in Taitō?"

"Yeah, that's it."

"You really are lost," he says, handing me back my phone. "That's in the other direction."

"Wait, seriously?"

He nods. "Taitō is east from here. You're in Asagaya."

"*Asagaya?* I don't even know where that is!" I stare at the map again, wondering how I ended up here.

"Sounds like you took the wrong train."

"How do I get back now?"

"I can take you there," he says.

I look up. "Really?"

He smiles. "I'm actually heading the same way."

"What a coincidence," I say, adjusting the bag over my shoulder. "I would really appreciate that."

"I have a few stops to make first," he adds. "It shouldn't take long, though. You can come with me if you'd like."

"Oh—"

"Unless you have somewhere important to be."

I take him in again. His shirt hangs loosely from his shoulders, sunlight partially seeping through it. I know Daniel is waiting for me at the hotel. But I don't want to go off on my own and get lost again. "No, I have time," I decide.

"Then let's get going."

He turns around, sliding his hands into his pockets. Then he walks off without another word. I hesitate on the sidewalk for a moment. Then I put my phone away and follow him through the crowd. As we cross the street, he glances over his shoulder and says, "I'm Haru, by the way."

"I'm Eric."

"Where are you from?"

"Chicago."

"How long have you been visiting Tokyo?"

"About two weeks."

"Welcome," he says.

We walk another block before Haru turns the corner, leading us into a shopping street. Lanterns hang from canopies of mom-and-pop storefronts. Looks like a festival is taking place. Paper stars have been tied to electrical poles, stirring in the air like parade floats. I take in all the decorations and say, "Is today a holiday?"

"It's the Star Festival."

"What's that?"

Haru glances to the right, where a man is sitting on a wooden stool, painting in the middle of the street. He gestures at him and whispers, "See what he's painting there?" A man and woman in long robes are floating in a starry sky, their hands outstretched toward each other, the moon glowing behind them. "That's Princess Orihime and her husband, Hikoboshi. The two were forbidden to see each other, separated by the stars. Orihime was so heartbroken that her father, god of the heavens, allowed them to meet once every year. It happens on the seventh day of the seventh month. So the festival celebrates their reunion."

"Why were they separated?"

"The two spent so much time together, they forgot their duties to the world. So the gods forced them apart," he explains. "But it's only a story."

I stare at the painting. "Well, I'm glad they get to meet again."

Haru smiles at me as we keep walking. There's a line of carnival-style games, children crowding around them. I glance over their shoulders, wondering what they're playing. Colorful plastic balls swirl inside a barrel of water.

"It's harder than it looks," Haru says, noticing me watching. "The nets are made of paper. You have to catch the balls before it rips."

"Looks like fun."

There's a spinning wheel on the other table. The woman behind it waves us over, speaking in Japanese. "She's giving us a free spin," Haru says to me. "Go for it."

"Why me?"

"It's your first festival. And I have a feeling you're lucky."

I raise a brow. "You're sure about that?"

"One way to find out."

I lean forward, spinning the wheel. The colors swirl together before landing on red. The woman behind the table frowns, letting me know I didn't win. Haru steps forward, handing her some coins from his pocket.

"Try it again," he says encouragingly.

I give the wheel another spin. The colors swirl before it lands on red again. I let out a breath of disappointment. Haru digs into his other pocket and says, "Now that one didn't count." I start to protest, but he hands the woman more change, insisting I give it another go. So I spin the wheel again. This time it lands on yellow.

I glance at Haru. "What does yellow mean?"

"You get to spin again."

I guess that's better than losing. I spin the wheel one more time. The colors swirl before it finally lands on white. The woman claps her hands, then gestures to the basket of prizes on the table.

"I knew you were lucky," Haru says with a wink.

I shake my head, holding back a laugh as we look through the prizes together. It's mostly key chains, erasers, random toy figurines. I find some bracelets with wooden beads braided through them. "These are pretty nice," I say.

"She says we can each have one," Haru says, turning to me. "You can pick yours first."

"Okay."

I decide on the blue bracelet and Haru takes the red one. Then he turns to me and says, "Now let's trade them."

I give him a look. "Why?"

"This way, we'll have each other's," he says, holding his out for me. "And I think red looks better on you."

I smile at this. "Alright."

I hold out my wrist, letting him tie the bracelet around me. Then I tie mine around him, too. It's like this little secret between us. I keep looking at it as we continue our walk together. The streets are lined with food vendors, filling the air with smoke from hot grills. There's so many things I haven't tried before. A woman passes us, holding a stick of round dumplings covered in dark glaze. Haru notices me looking again. "It's called dango," he says. "Have you tried it before?"

"No. Is it sweet?"

"Wait right here . . ."

Haru walks off to the food stands. A moment later, he returns with the skewer of dango. He hands it to me and says, "It's a very popular dessert. I think you'll like it."

"Oh, thanks."

I take a bite of the dango. The texture is chewy like mochi, complemented by a saltiness from the glaze, making it not too sweet. "That's *really* good," I tell him.

Haru smiles. "Anything else you want to try?"

"Oh, um." I take a look around again. Another woman walks past us, holding a rolled crepe in her hand. When I turn to Haru, he's already off to the food stands. I follow him, offering to pay this time. There are a dozen toppings to choose from. We both get matcha ice cream and fresh strawberries. As we're eating in the partial shade of a yellowed canopy, I hear music. A procession of men in gray robes appears from the corner, playing bamboo flutes. Haru and I watch them make their way through the crowd, enjoying the performance.

We finish our crepes and continue on. Some of the boutiques have their doors open, displaying their things out on the street. We walk through them together, smelling candles, looking at some of the clothes. There are robes I've seen people wearing throughout my trip. I run my fingers over one of them. The fabric is almost paper thin, crinkling to the touch. The sleeves billow like the top of a kimono.

"You should try it on," Haru suggests.

I shake my head. "No, that's okay."

"It's called a jinbei," he says, picking it up from the table. "We wear them at summer festivals. So it's very appropriate for today."

"I won't look like a tourist?"

"Not if you're with me."

I smile a little. "Alright, if you think I should."

Haru and I look through the different colors. I decide on the light gray with ocean wave patterns, two red lines running down the shoulders. "The red goes with your bracelet," Haru says, helping me tie on the jinbei.

"You mean, *your* bracelet, right?" I correct him, remembering we switched them earlier.

Haru grins. "Right."

I pay the woman inside and wear it out of the shop. Even though it's humid, the jinbei feels nice against my skin. As we continue down the street, I notice Haru hasn't bought a single thing yet. I'm about to ask where he's leading us when he finally stops outside a stationery store.

Haru turns to me. "Wait out here. I'll only be a minute."

"Yeah, sure."

I watch him disappear inside. Then I glance around the street. Giant paper ornaments hang in the air, streamers fluttering beneath them like the tails of shooting stars. I would have never known this place existed if I hadn't followed Haru. Then I remember my camera. I'm supposed to be filming shots for my senior project coming up. I grab it from my bag, turning it on to record some of the shops, the festival decorations, the sound of flutes in the distance.

A moment later, Haru comes outside. He holds a small paper bag in his right hand. I put my camera away and wipe my brow.

"You're sweating," he says, noticing.

"I think it's the jinbei," I sigh, feeling the hot sun on my neck. "I could really go for a drink right now."

Haru nods. "I know just the place."

There's a used bookstore down the street. Haru leads me inside, where a man is sleeping behind the counter. At first, I think he's here to pick something up. But he heads to the back of the room and opens a curtain, revealing a narrow staircase. We make our way up to the second floor, where another curtain opens to a hidden café. A cool blast of AC hits my face as I look around. Low wooden tables are separated by shoji screens. I take in the smell of incense as I follow Haru to an empty table. There are no chairs in the room. We sit crisscrossed together on the woven mats as a woman comes to take our order.

The moment she walks off, I take in the rest of the room. "What's the name of this place?"

"It doesn't have one."

"Why is that?"

Haru leans into me. "To keep away the tourists."

"That makes sense," I say, nodding. "Thankfully I'm with you, right?"

We smile at each other. A moment later, the woman appears with a pot of tea. Haru gently removes the lid. The pot is filled with loose leaves, sprinkled over ice. "This is koridashi," he says. "It's brewed with ice instead of hot water. We drink it during the summer."

Haru pours me a cup first. The tea is sweet and refreshing, cooling me down instantly. A scroll hangs on the back wall beside a vase of flowers. Haru leans back and sips his tea. His paper bag sits on the floor between us. I'm curious about what he bought. So I finally ask, "What did you get?"

Haru blinks at the bag as if he forgot it was there. He pushes it toward me and says, "Feel free to take a look."

I open the bag and find a single piece of paper inside a plastic sleeve. It's about the size of my palm. There's nothing else in here. "Is this all you got? A piece of paper?"

Haru nods.

"Just one?"

"I only needed one."

I turn it over in my hand. "Is there something special about it?"

"It's washi," he says, leaning forward. "See the fibers inside? That's how you know it's handmade. The process gets passed down from generations. This one was made in the mountains in Echizen." He takes a sip of tea. "My family owns a paper store in Osaka. I work there every summer, with my mom. She said it's important, helping stores like ours. So I always make sure to buy something, even if it's just a piece of paper."

I run my fingers over it, noticing the texture. "You're right, it does feel different. You make your own paper?"

"Not as much these days," he admits. "I mostly help

around the store. But my dad taught me some other tricks. I'll show you." He takes the piece of paper from my hands. I watch curiously as he folds it intricately. Then he slides it back to me. It's an origami star. Just like the ones hanging outside.

I pick it up from the table. "In honor of the Star Festival?"

"Or of us meeting."

I look at him. "It is funny how we just met, right? And now we're here, drinking tea together."

"Hopefully it isn't the last time," he says.

We smile at each other again. Haru runs a hand through his long hair. I take another sip of tea, ignoring the flutter in my stomach. The woman returns to refill our pot and walks off again. Haru pours me another cup and asks, "So how do you like Tokyo so far?"

"It's been a lot of fun," I tell him. "I'm actually here on a school trip. But I snuck away this morning to do some filming on my own."

"What are you working on?"

"I don't really know yet," I say with a shrug. "It's for my senior project next year. I'm still learning to edit things, you know? But I got some shots of the Sumida River. Mostly through the train window, which I think gives it a cool aesthetic. There was this other place I wanted to go, but I didn't realize how far away it was."

"Where?"

I take out my phone to show him. "The Shikisai Hills. My sister told me about them. She was here last summer for the same trip, and said the flowers reminded her of one of our favorite movies."

Haru glances at the screen. "*Howl's Moving Castle,*" Haru says almost instantly. "When he shows her the garden."

"Yeah, that's the scene."

Haru nods knowingly. "I actually haven't been before. It's supposed to be beautiful in the summer." He smiles at me. "We should go together."

For a second, I imagine us walking through the field of flowers and almost say yes. But I can't bail on my plans with Daniel tonight. I let out a breath. "I really wish I could. But my friend is waiting for me back at the hotel." I glance at my phone, realizing how much time has passed. "I should probably get going soon."

"When are you leaving?"

"My flight is tomorrow."

His eyes widen. "*Tomorrow?*"

"I know," I say. "I wish I had a few more days here."

"What are you doing tonight?"

"I have plans with my friend," I say. "The one who's waiting for me. We'll probably meet up with the rest of the group, too. Since it's our last night together."

A silence passes between us. Then Haru nods and says, "That's too bad. I would have loved to show you around. But I'm glad we at least got to meet."

"I'm glad we did, too," I say. "I should try to get lost more often."

Haru leans back and smiles. If only we had met each other sooner. I wish I could stay with him longer, explore the rest of the festival together. It's funny how some people walk into your life. A few hours ago, we didn't even know each other. Maybe we're meant to take the wrong train sometimes.

We finish our tea and head outside. As we step into the street, Haru turns to me and says, "If you have time, there's one more thing I want to show you. It shouldn't take too long."

"You said that a couple hours ago," I remind him.

Haru grins. "I thought you were having fun."

"Yeah, but I really do need to get back."

"The Chūō line comes every ten minutes," he says. "I promise we'll make it back in time."

I think about Daniel again. He's probably wondering where I am. But I'm sure he can wait a few more minutes. "Alright, if you promise."

Haru smiles as he motions me to follow him. We turn down the side street, moving through the narrow space between the shops. Normally I wouldn't follow a stranger like this, especially through unfamiliar alleyways. But it feels like we've known each other longer, maybe in another life or something. I can't really explain it.

Haru leads us across the road and through the trees. There's a stone path lined with red lanterns that look like tiny houses. I keep looking around, wondering where he's taking us. Then the gates of the temple come into view. All the trees have been decorated with colorful slips of paper, hundreds of them, tied up with white strings.

There's a wooden table at the end of the path. Haru walks over and picks up a slip of paper. "This is a tanzaku," he says, placing it in my hand. "During the Star Festival, we write wishes on them and hang them in the trees. I thought you should make one before you leave."

"What are we supposed to wish for?"

"Anything you'd like," he says.

Haru grabs a slip for himself. Then he leans over and starts writing. I stare at the piece of paper, thinking of what I want. It takes a moment for something to come to me. I grab a pencil from the table and write it down. Haru drops some coins into a wooden box, then steps toward the line of trees. I watch as he ties his wish to one of the branches. Then he turns to me, waiting for me to do mine.

As I stare at the trees, a breeze comes through, blowing white petals across my path. I turn toward them, wondering where they're coming from. On the other side of the gate is a wall of white flowers, covering the stones like a curtain. A few wishes have been tied to them as well.

"It's jasmine," Haru says from behind me.

I glance at him and back at the flowers. "Yeah, that's my sister's name," I say. "They're her favorite." I find a spot on the wall and tie my wish tightly to a vine. A few petals fall to my feet. Then I turn around.

"That's a good spot," Haru says.

"I think so, too."

We look at each other again. I notice he's holding something.

"What's in your hand?" I ask.

"Nothing." Haru shakes his head, slipping it into his back pocket.

I give him a suspicious look. Then my phone vibrates in my pocket. There's a few new messages from Daniel.

> where are you??
> You're supposed to be back
> by now
> we're going to miss the ferry

I glance at the time again. Then I turn to Haru, letting him know I have to go. Haru nods and takes out his phone. As he's checking the train schedule, his brows furrow. "That's unusual," he says. "Looks like there's a problem with the Chūō line. The last train it's showing comes in six minutes."

"How often does that happen?"

"Around here? Never."

For a second, I think the universe is interfering. Maybe I'm meant to spend more time with Haru so we can get to know each other better. But the memory of my kiss with Daniel rises to the surface and I feel a knot of guilt. I can't keep him waiting for me longer. "My friend is gonna kill me," I say.

Haru puts his phone away. "You can still make it."

"How am I gonna—"

My voice cuts off as Haru grabs my hand, pulling me down the path. I nearly stumble as we make our way back to the streets, cutting through the crowds. "*Watch out for bicycles,*" he reminds me as we race to the train station, pausing only at the turnstile. My hands fumble around my pockets, searching for my wallet. But Haru swipes me in with his card before following me through.

It's a blur of heads and shoulders, but we make it just in time. The train is still waiting at the platform. We cut through the crowd, rushing toward it. The moment I make it through the doors, I sense something is wrong. Haru doesn't come in with me. He's just standing there on the platform, unmoving.

"*Hurry up,*" I call after him.

"I'm not taking this train."

I give him a look. "You said you're heading the same way."

"I lied," he says.

"What are you talking about?"

"I wanted to get to know you. So I made it up."

I stare at him, unsure what to say. Then the doors start to close. Haru throws out a hand, forcing them back open.

"*Don't leave,*" he says.

"What?"

"You should stay," he says, holding the doors open. "It's your last night. I'll show you around Tokyo. I can take you to the field of flowers." The other passengers are staring, wondering what's going on.

I hesitate for a second. Part of me wants to step off the train. I haven't had this much fun the entire trip. Then my phone goes off again, showing Daniel's name on the screen. I can't keep him waiting on me. Especially since this could be the night things change between us.

"*Stay,*" Haru insists.

I glance at the phone and back at him. My heart pounds in my chest as I consider this. I can't shake the feeling that we are connected somehow. But I let out a breath and say, "I'm sorry, but I have to go."

A bell chimes from the ceiling, followed immediately by a voice, echoing through the platform. Haru reaches into his back pocket, pulling out a piece of paper. The washi he bought from the store earlier.

"I was waiting to give this to you," he says quickly. "My phone number to stay in touch."

The bell chimes again, followed by the voice. As I reach for the paper, another train roars in from behind us, blowing wind up from the tracks. *The paper flies out of my fingers.* Haru spins around, grabbing it from the air. But before he turns back, the doors shut between us.

My heart drops. I press my hands against the glass, trying to open them back up. But it's too late. The train begins to move. I stare through the window, realizing we'll never see each other again. Haru slowly disappears from view. All I have left is a red bracelet and the memory of him.

The train vanishes through the tunnel.

Haru is gone.

I wish I had stepped off the train. Or that the paper never slipped from my hand. How will we ever find each other again?

One

FOURTEEN MONTHS LATER

"Do you want to dance with me?"

A television blinks in the corner of the kitchen. *The Notebook* is playing on low volume as I watch from the sink. It's the scene where they dance in the middle of the street. I've seen this movie a dozen times. He offers his hand, helping her step off the sidewalk. There's no one else around, only the two of them, slow dancing to the music in their own heads. I used to cringe at things like this. But these days, I like to close my eyes for a moment, imagining myself in the movie. It helps me escape from the monotony of—

"Turn that thing off."

Mr. Antonio appears from nowhere, shouting orders at me. I'm a thousand feet above downtown Chicago, washing dishes in the hotel kitchen. Servers come in through the swinging door, tossing plates and spoons into trays that fill up beside me. It's not where I thought I would be after graduation. I imagined myself studying film in college, hanging out with friends on the weekend. But life has a way of sidetracking everything you had planned in your head.

Another hour passes, pruning my fingers. As I'm drying

the silverware, Mr. Antonio reappears in the kitchen, shouting again. "*Stop standing around and get out here!*" He's the owner of the catering company I've been working for over the summer. It's honestly not the worst job in the world. I wasn't exactly picky when I was looking for work. I just needed something to get me out of the house, help save up a little extra money.

I grab a tray of food as I make my way out. When things pick up in the evening, Mr. Antonio occasionally has me serving tables. It's nice being out of the kitchen. It makes me feel more social, even if I'm just refilling people's glasses. Like I'm still part of a storyline, even if I'm just there in the background. It's all I can do when everyone else I know moved away to start new chapters of their lives in college. Meanwhile, I'm stuck living in the same boring episode. I adjust my collar before stepping through the curtain that separates us from the grand ballroom.

The lights blind me for a few seconds. Then everything comes into focus. Draped walls, low-hanging chandeliers, a sea of cocktail dresses. The sound of the jazz band fills the air as I move through the crowd, a tray on one shoulder, careful not to bump into anyone. I'm staffing the dessert table, which means making sure trays are stocked and everything looks presentable. I stand beside the table, hands behind my back, watching the tiramisu go fast.

It's a bit of an older crowd tonight, with men in suits at every corner of the room, drinking casually. But there are some around my age, too. There's a table of college guys to my right, blazers hanging over their chairs. I noticed one of them earlier, dark blond hair with a pinstripe shirt. His sleeves are rolled up to the elbow, a silver watch shining on his wrist. As I'm admiring him, Mr. Antonio appears again.

"Stop standing around."

"But you said to—"

"*Waters.*"

"Yes, sir."

I move between tables, refilling glasses from a pitcher. The guy with blond hair is still sitting with his friends. I take my time as I slowly make my way to his table. He looks a couple years older than me, maybe a senior in college. His friends are chatting away, drinking Stella Artois. As I reach for his glass, he turns his head and says something I don't expect.

"Nihonjin desu ka?"

I blink at him. "*What?*"

"Your bracelet," he says, pointing. "I can tell it's from Japan."

I glance at my wrist. The red bracelet from last summer. The one Haru and I gave each other during the Star Festival. It always reminds me of that day we spent together, giving me a spark of joy from the memory I still keep with me. Sometimes I forget I'm even wearing it. "A friend gave this to me. When I visited last summer."

"Ah. Which prefecture?"

"Tokyo."

He leans back in his chair, nodding. "I studied abroad there. The University of Tokyo, I mean."

"Oh, I heard that's a good school."

"They say it's the Harvard of Japan," he adds, shrugging casually. He looks at me again. "What about you?"

Normally I like to make up a story at these events. Like my dad owns the hotel and I just want to live a normal teenage life before heading back to Paris. But I decide to give an honest answer tonight. "I'm actually not in school right now," I tell him. "Taking some time to figure things out first."

"Like what?"

I'm about to answer this when I notice Mr. Antonio watching me like a hawk from the other side of the room.

"Sorry, I have to go."

I offer a smile before walking off. I wish I could linger a bit longer, maybe get his name or something. But I have to refill the pitcher and get to the other tables.

The evening continues. Lights swirl along the ceiling and more champagne bottles are opened. I'm standing at the dessert table again. As I'm watching people on the dance floor, the music changes to something slow. Then the lights dim, swallowing the room in a dark blue ocean. Somehow, almost naturally, the crowd tunes itself to the piano, separating into couples, cheeks pressed against each other, slow dancing. Almost like a scene from a movie.

When it comes to music, ballads are usually my favorite. But as I stand against the wall, watching the scene unfold, a wave of loneliness falls over me. It's a feeling that comes and goes, reminding me that even in a crowded room, I'm still alone. That no one even knows I'm here. It's like there's a wall between me and the rest of the world. I'm always on the outside, staring through a screen.

Suddenly I don't feel like standing out here anymore. There's probably some dishes to clean in the kitchen. As I turn to leave, someone bumps into me, nearly spilling his drink. "I'm sorry," he says, touching my arm. It's the cute blond I spoke with earlier.

"It's alright." I laugh awkwardly.

He smiles at me. "I was actually hoping to bump into you."

I look at him. "Oh . . . really?"

He takes a sip of his drink, grinning. Then he leans forward and whispers, "I noticed you standing alone all night. I've been building up the courage to ask you for a dance."

For a second, I think he's joking. No one has ever asked me to dance before, especially while I'm working. "I'm sorry, but I can't right now."

"*Just one dance,*" he says, holding out his hand.

"I'm supposed to be working—"

"You're not turning me down, are you?"

The timbre of his voice makes me hesitate. If we hadn't already spoken, I probably wouldn't entertain the idea. But there's something about him that makes me consider the risk. Maybe if we blend into the crowd, no one will even notice. I know I shouldn't do this. But it is my last night on the job. I glance around for Mr. Antonio before I take his hand, letting him lead me out to the middle of the room.

I've never danced with another guy before. He's a little

taller than me, so I'm not really sure where my hands go. He smiles at this, taking me by the side. My cheeks go warm as his arms move around me. It seems strange at first, slow dancing with someone whose name I don't know yet. But once I relax a little, and we move in time with the music, the two of us blend seamlessly into the rest of the crowd. Suddenly, I feel like the main character of the story.

I rest my head on his shoulder, hoping the song doesn't end. After a moment, he lifts my chin with his finger, so we're facing each other. As he gazes into my eyes, his lips only a few inches from mine, I think we might kiss. Then he leans forward, moving his mouth to my ear. He whispers, "*Are there nuts in these?*"

I blink at him, confused. "What did you say?"

"I said . . . are there *nuts* in these?"

The music cuts out. I blink again and find myself back at the dessert table, leaning against the wall, where I've been standing for the last hour. I look around the room, disoriented for a second. The guy I was just dancing with in my head is pointing at the cannoli, a brow raised at me.

"Did you not hear me?" he says. "I'm asking if there's nuts in these."

I swallow air, trying not to stammer. "Oh . . . I don't think so."

Before I can say more, a girl with blond hair appears at his side, looking stunning in a yellow dress. She grabs his arm and says, "*I love this song. Come dance with me.*" Then she pulls him away, laughing as they both disappear into the crowd.

A familiar ache goes through me. It's this flopping feeling

in my stomach, making me wish I could disappear, too. I stand there a few minutes longer. Then I grab some empty trays and head back to the kitchen for the rest of the night.

I clock out at eleven on the dot. Mr. Antonio usually has me working till the end, helping him move things to the van. But I told him I couldn't stay late tonight. It was only a seasonal job and summer is officially over. I'm not exactly heartbroken about this. But starting tomorrow, I'll have to sit down and figure out the next steps of the rest of my life.

As I'm leaving the hotel, one of the cooks invites me out with the others. "It's your last night with us, kid," he says.

"Would love to, but it's my friend's birthday," I say.

"Thought you said it's tomorrow?"

"Yeah, but we always stay up till midnight together."

It's a tradition between me and Daniel. We started it a few years ago when we each turned sixteen. It's always just the two of us, sitting around in our rooms, sharing some pizza, waiting for the clock to change like New Year's Eve. But it's already 11:15 p.m. and I need to get back in time. It's a quiet train ride home. I look through photos of us on my phone to pass the time. Some of my favorites are the ones from our trip to Japan.

I glance at my bracelet again. *Haru*. It's been over a year since we spent our perfect day together. I still think about him every now and then, wondering what could have been if I had stayed. I wonder if he ever thinks about me, too.

I get home at a quarter till midnight. Daniel and I are meeting on the rooftop again. I don't want to wake my parents, so I use the ladder we keep at the side of the house. I make my way up and find Daniel already waiting for me. He has the blanket laid out for us. A tea candle flickers inside a mason jar beside it. The moment he sees me coming up, he throws his arms around me and says, "Where the hell have you been?"

"I left as soon as I could."

"You're lucky it's not midnight yet."

"You know I wouldn't miss it."

"Did you get it for me?"

I frown at him. He's talking about the cupcake from Lily's, a local bakery in the Loop. I make sure to get him his favorite flavor every year. Chocolate coconut, with a caramel crème filling. "Sorry, but the place closed before I could get there."

His eyes flicker with disappointment. But he smiles anyway and says, "That's okay. All that matters is you're here."

11:43 p.m.

We sit on the blanket together, sharing some hors d'oeuvres I swiped from work on the way out. It's one of the few perks I'm gonna miss about the job. Then Daniel lies down, resting his hands behind his head, staring up at the sky. I lie right beside him, moving my hands behind my head, too. There's no one else I'd rather be with tonight. But I can't shake this strange feeling in my chest. That something about tonight isn't quite the same.

Daniel turns his head. "Is something wrong?"

"No," I say.

"Are you sure? You can tell me."

I take a moment to answer this. "I guess I was thinking about when we were up here last year. Some of the things we talked about."

"You mean, our plans to leave Chicago?"

I nod. "Yeah. Here we are, lying in the exact same spot."

"Why didn't you just go without me?"

His words surprise me. "I wasn't gonna leave you here."

A silence passes between us. I glance at the time on my phone. 11:54 p.m. I push myself up, grabbing a small box from my bag. "I have a surprise for you." I hand it to him.

Daniel looks at the box suspiciously. Then he opens it. Inside is the chocolate cupcake from Lily's. His eyes go wide. "*You liar.*"

"It tastes better this way," I say with a smirk.

"You mean, with *deceit*?"

We can't stop laughing. I place a small candle on top of the cupcake and light it for him. Daniel looks at me, a beautiful smile on his face. For a moment, there's no one but us in the entire world. Everything else is a simulation. "*You and I are the only thing that's real,*" he once told me. I check the time again. 11:58 p.m.

"Two minutes until your birthday."

We lie back down again, a little closer this time. The birthday candle flickers between us, casting some shadows on the blanket. I wish I could stop the clock from moving. So we could stay up here for as long as we want. But I know it's too late for us. A breeze rolls across the rooftop, reminding me this is coming to an end soon. I don't want to lose him again. I want to keep him with me forever.

"*I miss you,*" I whisper.

"*I miss you, too.*"

"I wish I could kiss you one more time."

"What's stopping you?"

I swallow my breath as we look at each other. Then I lean toward him, closing my eyes. I *feel* him leaning into me, too.

But our lips never touch.

Then my phone goes off, telling me it's midnight. The moment I open my eyes, I'm alone on the rooftop again. No one is lying there next to me. I stare at the empty side of the blanket as another breeze rolls through, ruffling the trees. A chill in the air sends a shiver through me. Then I lean forward and blow out the candle.

"Happy birthday, Daniel."

I lie there on the rooftop for the rest of the night, wishing he were still here with me.

Two

"You and I are the only thing that's real."

His words echo in my head.

What does this mean now that you're gone?

Sometimes I wake up to the smell of him. As if Daniel has been lying next to me all night. If I reached out my hand, I would feel the warmth of his skin as we lace our fingers together. Then my alarm goes off, forcing my eyes open again. I feel around the sheets, searching for my phone. It's eight thirty in the morning. I'm usually not up this early, especially since I'm not in school at the moment. But I'm growing tired of spending my days in bed, looking through old photos of us on my phone.

It's been nearly a year since Daniel died. I'm still not used to a world without him in it. Sometimes I catch myself checking my phone, expecting a text from him. He was always the first person I heard from when I woke up. Sometimes I pretend he's not actually dead. I imagine he moved away to a remote island, somewhere without signal, making it impossible to stay in touch. It makes things a little easier, pretending he's alive somewhere else, even if we're not together.

Another alarm goes off, reminding me to start the day.

I sent out dozens of job applications a few months ago and finally got an interview. So I have to get there on time and make a good impression. Daniel and I often talked about the future, so I know he would want this for me. He wouldn't want me wasting the day, thinking about him. I take a shower and change into something professional (a dress shirt with a tie from Dad's closet). Mom left breakfast for me this morning. I think she worries I haven't been eating enough lately. I take a few bites for her, along with some coffee to wake me up a little. Then I head back to my room in search of something. There's a white paper bag on my desk. It's been sitting there for the last few days, untouched. I stare at it for a moment, wondering if I should take it with me. I grab it along with my phone as I leave the house.

The trains are crowded this morning. The interview is at Tribune Tower, a thirty-six-floor high-rise that looms over the Chicago River. I head through the revolving glass doors, adjusting my tie. It's a sea of gray suits bustling through a marble-floored lobby, chandeliers hanging from the high ceiling. I read over the email, wondering where I'm supposed to go. The interview is for an assistantship with CHI-23 Entertainment, an indie production company based here in Chicago. I saw one of their films at a festival a few years ago. The cinematography inspired the way I think about light and color. I thought it was a long shot, but I sent in an application anyway. It would be a dream to work in the film industry, even if I'm sorting through mail all day and answering phone calls.

I press the elevator button and step inside. As it begins to rise, I imagine the scene—assistants running back and forth carrying trays of coffee; executives sitting around long tables, pitching ideas behind glass walls. Then the doors open to a small reception room with nobody there. A few boxes are stacked against a plain white wall. I look around, wondering if this is the wrong floor. I expected things to be exciting like the movies. I wander around the office, hoping to find a Stanley Tucci–like character to take kindly to me, offering some words of wisdom. A few turns later, I find a woman with short black hair sitting behind a desk. I walk up and give her my name.

"You're a little early," she says.

"Sorry."

The woman smiles. "Don't be silly. Leon, who's interviewing you, isn't back from lunch. Why don't you sit in his office while you wait." She rises from her chair and motions for me to follow. There is a series of white doors down a narrow hallway. She unlocks the second one on the right, allowing me inside.

"Leon will be here shortly," she says. "My name is Sonny. Can I take your bag?"

I glance at the white bag in my hand. "No, that's okay."

Sonny nods before disappearing down the hallway. I take a seat in the black chair and glance around the office. The walls are lined with movie posters, a few with titles in different languages. There's a bronze name plate on the edge of the desk. *Leon Nguyen.* So he's Vietnamese, too. Then footsteps echo down the hallway. I straighten up as a man in a T-shirt and jeans walks through the door. He's younger than I expected, maybe in his late twenties. He drops his keys in a glass bowl as he steps to the other side of the desk.

"So you're Eric," he says.

I rise to shake his hand. "Yeah, that's me."

"Great to meet you."

"Thank you for seeing me."

I hand him my resume as we sit down. Leon blinks at it and sets it on his desk. He takes a good look at me. "You're quite dressed up for this interview," he says, swiveling his chair a little. "Things are more casual around here, if you haven't noticed. Hope you didn't put on that tie just for us."

I look down at my clothes and back at him. "Oh, not at all," I tell him. "I'm actually going to a wedding after this."

Leon chuckles. "I assume you're joking."

"No, actually, I'm the wedding singer," I add.

"Well, that wasn't in your cover letter," he says, pretending to be impressed, making us both smile. He laces his fingers together on the table. "Anyway, how did you hear about the internship?"

"I found it online," I say, straightening up again. "But I knew of CHI-23 before. I wrote about one of your films for a class assignment."

"Oh, what class?"

"Digital filmmaking. I took it last year."

Leon takes out a pen, jotting something down. "Is that where you worked on your short film?"

"My film?"

"The one about the Star Festival," he says. "In the link you included in the application. I shared it around the office. Everyone here loved it."

"*Really?*" I lean back in my chair, surprised to hear this. The online application said it was optional. But I sent a link anyway, thinking no one would actually watch it. "Thank you, that really means a lot," I say.

"I know this is essentially a mail room position, but we look for skills beyond delivering coffee," he says, leaning toward me. "This isn't the standard assistantship where you'll be sifting through mail all day. We also look for talent. So tell me more about the film and the idea behind it."

My mind flashes to last summer—paper wishes fluttering in the trees, men in robes playing wooden flutes, fireworks lighting up the Sumida River. I ended up stitching shots together for my senior project as I narrated the story of Princess Orihime and Hikoboshi over it, wishing for their star-crossed reunion. It takes me a second to gather my words. "I was visiting Japan last summer," I answer. "I got lost one day and stumbled into this festival. I didn't know what it was at the time. But someone I met that day told me the story." I pause for a second, thinking about Haru. "The festival is about these two people who were separated by time and space, and somehow found their way back together. I guess I never really stopped thinking about it. A few months later, when I looked back at everything I had filmed, that was the story I wanted to tell. So it was kind of an accident."

I remember watching the videos over and over again,

hoping to see him somewhere in the background, a glimpse of his face. I touch the red bracelet around my wrist. I wish I had more than a memory of that day. It's beginning to feel like a dream or something. Of course, I don't mention any of this.

"Some of the best ideas happen by accident," Leon says, nodding. "Sometimes it's just *the process*. So don't sell yourself short." He glances at his computer and back at me. "What else have you been working on?"

I stare at my hands. "Nothing at the moment. I took a little break."

"Are you at least taking film classes?"

I shake my head. "I'm actually not in school right now."

He furrows his brow. "You're not in school?"

"I hope that's not an issue."

Leon frowns as he leans back, tapping his pen on the desk. "I'm sorry to tell you this, Eric," he says, "but this is a college internship. You have to be a student to apply."

I blink in confusion. "Are you sure? I don't remember seeing that online." There has to be some misunderstanding.

"Unfortunately, yes," he sighs. "The university typically funds the program. So there isn't really a way around it. Why aren't you in school anyway?"

I stare at my hands again. Daniel and I were supposed to go together. "I just needed time to figure things out," I say vaguely.

"Did something happen?"

"It's nothing," I assure him. "I'm reapplying this year. I've already started on a few applications."

Leon stares at me from across the desk. Then he reaches for something behind him. "Well, if you're planning on going to school, why don't you apply for this," he says, handing me a folded sheet of paper. "It's a film scholarship. I know several aspiring filmmakers who have won over the years. And I think your stuff is strong enough. Something you can work toward. Until then, why don't you reach out again next year, once you have things figured out." He slides my resume back to me.

I stare at the desk and back at him. The interview has barely started. It can't be over just like that. "But . . ." My voice stutters a little. "Maybe there's something else I can apply for. Is there a different position here?"

"Not at the moment."

"Are you sure?"

Leon scratches his chin, thinking about it. "Well, we might have an opening for an assistant role. But, quite frankly, I don't think you have the experience for that."

"What would count as experience?"

"The internship would be a good start," he says with a straight face. There's a silence as I sit there, unsure what else to say. "I'm sorry about this, Eric," Leon continues. "There isn't really anything I can do. I hope you understand."

At this point, it's clear it's over. I didn't even have a chance to begin with. All because I'm not in school right now. I take the piece of paper and rise from my seat. "Thanks for your time," I say. Then I grab the bag from the floor and head out.

"Good luck," Leon says from behind me.

As I step into the hallway, I stop short. I'm not sure where the burst of bravery comes from, but I have nothing to lose at this point, right? I take a deep breath as I turn back inside, facing Leon again.

I look him right in the eyes and say, "Okay, you're right. I don't have the experience. And I'm not a student in some fancy school that will pay for the internship. But I'm smart, I learn fast, and I will work very hard if you give me a—"

"*Did you forget something?*" a woman's voice interrupts me, pulling me out of my daydream. I blink and find myself still standing in the hallway, staring back at the office door. I turn around. Sonny is waiting for a response.

"Sorry . . . I was just heading out."

I leave through the elevator, hoping Leon realizes he's made a mistake by the time the doors open again. I think of the scene in *The Devil Wears Prada,* the one where the assistant chases Andy into the lobby after Miranda changes her mind at the end of the interview. But nobody follows me down to offer a second chance. I wish this was one of my films I was directing so I could control the storyline. But nothing works out like it does in the movies.

I'm sitting in the garden of the Art Institute, watching leaves fall into the fountain. I didn't really know where else to go. I stare at the blank screen of my phone for a long time. It's one of those moments when I wish I could text Daniel, tell him about the interview. He would know what to say to make things better. But the thought of no one answering makes my chest hurt again. I close my eyes and try to push him out of my mind. I shouldn't let that stupid interview get to me. I knew it was a long shot, anyway.

The paper bag sits on my lap. I'm still not sure why I brought it with me. I'm thinking about opening it when my phone vibrates. Jasmine is calling me. It's feels like a long time since we last spoke. She's been really busy with school these days, double majoring in biology and music. I pick up right away.

"Hey. What are you doing?" Her voice instantly soothes me, like an old song I haven't heard in a while.

"Just sitting around. Why?"

"I just got in," she says.

"Wait, you're in Chicago? Why didn't you tell me you were coming home?"

"It was last minute," she explains. "I got a ride with a friend. And we're only here for a few hours. But I want to see you before I head back. Are you home now?"

"No, I'm in the Loop," I say.

"Perfect. I'm not far. We can get lunch. If you're not busy, I mean."

"Of course I'm not. Where do you want to go?"

Jasmine doesn't visit home much these days. So it's a nice surprise when she drops in unexpectedly. Especially when I'm feeling down. Sometimes I think she has a sixth sense about things. After we decide on the best place to meet, I head for the train and make my way over.

The door chimes as I enter Uncle Wong's Palace. It's our favorite Chinese restaurant in the city. We used to order takeout from here all the time. Red lanterns hang from the ceiling, giving enough light to make out the embroidered dragons along the walls. I walk past the counter and find her sitting by the window, wearing the plaid jacket she borrowed from me. She looks up from her phone as I slide into the other side of the booth.

"Was just about to text you," she says, folding her arms on the table. "I literally just sat down." She stares at my clothes. "Look at you all dressed up."

I let out a breath. "I just came from an interview."

"Was that today? How did it go?"

"I don't really want to talk about it."

"It couldn't have been that bad."

I just stare at the table.

"Hmm."

Jasmine pushes a menu in front of me, picking one up for herself. "Let's order some food. What are you in the mood for?"

I shrug. "Pineapple fried rice sounds good."

Jasmine gives me a look. "You hate pineapple."

"I don't *hate* it," I correct her. "It just makes everything taste so sweet." It's like Hawaiian pizza. That's something I can never get behind.

"Then why do you want to order it?"

"Because you always do."

It's Jasmine's favorite thing here. She gets it every single time.

"Well, if you *insist*," she says, setting down the menu.

I smile at this. The two of us sitting here together. You forget how much you miss someone until they're right in front of you again. Jasmine moves her long hair behind her ear, glancing around the restaurant. "The place hasn't changed much," she says. "Almost feels like it's stuck in time, you know?"

"I like that about it."

"Me, too."

A tea candle flickers between us. Maybe it's the dust on the window, but the light coming through makes the room a little hazy. Piano music is playing in the background. I tilt my head, wondering what song this is. The waitress comes to take our order. A few minutes later, she returns with a pot of tea. Jasmine pours us each a cup and takes a sip. I lean back a little, staring blankly into my cup.

"You're thinking about the interview," she says.

"A little bit," I admit.

"What did they say?"

I shake my head, thinking back to this morning. "Turns out you have to be enrolled in school. Something to do with the funding."

"That's so elitist."

"Yeah," I say, blowing on my tea. "The guy who interviewed me was really nice. He liked one of my films. The one about the Star Festival. I think he would have hired me if it wasn't for the school thing. Or maybe I'm just telling myself that."

"Of course he would have," Jasmine says. "I told you, you're talented. Everyone loves your stuff. I don't know why you stopped."

It's been a while since I touched my camera. I used to bring it everywhere, waiting for inspiration to strike. But it's hard to find that motivation these days. "It's just been hard to focus," I say vaguely. "And it's not like you're around to help with the sound."

"You can't blame me for that," she says.

"I'm not *blaming* you. I'm just saying, you promised to help and you didn't," I remind her. We made all these plans to collaborate. I would work on my films and she would add music over it.

"You know I've been busy with school."

"And I'm busy finding a job right now."

Jasmine leans into the table. "Why are you so stressed about that anyway? There's nothing wrong with taking time off. Especially since—"

"I don't want to talk about it," I cut her off.

Another silence. Jasmine stares at me in thought. "Listen, if you really want to find a job, you should message Kevin. I'm sure he would help."

I look at her. "It's okay to talk to him?"

"Why wouldn't it be?"

"Because you guys aren't together," I remind her. They

broke up in the spring, ending a four-year relationship. I always thought they would move in together, adopt a cat, get married eventually. I think Jasmine did, too. Too bad nothing happens the way we planned.

"We left things on good terms," Jasmine says. "I know he cares about you. You should reach out to him."

There's a knot of guilt in my chest. Kevin has messaged me a couple times. But I never responded to him. I wasn't sure how Jasmine would feel about it. "Okay. I'll text him later."

The waitress reappears, setting down our food. The fried rice is served in a pineapple boat, decorated with a toothpick umbrella. I spoon some onto my plate and take a small bite. It tastes better than I remember. As we're eating, Jasmine's phone goes off. She glances at the screen and places it face down on the table.

"Who is it?" I ask.

"The friend I came with. I have to meet her after this."

"What are you visiting for again?"

"It's a long story."

"Are you missing class?"

Jasmine sets down her fork, taking her time to answer this. "That's actually something I wanted to talk about," she says, straightening up a little. She takes a deep breath and lets it out. "I'm not going back to school."

"What do you mean?"

Her voice is calm as she folds her hands in her lap and says, "I've been focusing more on my music. You know about the band I've been playing with. We've been talking about getting a manager. The friend who drove me is meeting with someone now."

"So you're dropping out of school?"

"I already did."

"You're joking—"

"There's a tour happening soon," she says, leaning into the table. "It's for this band, the Copper Tigers. Our guitarist, Michael, is friends with them, and their opening act bailed. They've asked us to take their place. So we might be leaving soon."

"Leaving where?"

She hesitates. "Amsterdam."

"*Amsterdam?*" I almost shout. "For how long?"

"At least a few months," Jasmine says. "Maybe longer, if things go well. I know it's a long time. But it's a great opportunity to get our music out. Who knows when this could happen again."

"Jaz, you can't just drop out of school."

"I already made the decision."

"Well, it's not a good one—"

"What about you? You're not in school, either," she quickly reminds me. "Did you forget?"

Her words sting. I press my lips together, unsure what to say back. "I told you, I'm reapplying this fall. I'm basically done with all my applications," I lie. "I even applied to a film scholarship and made it to the next round." I remember the one Leon told me about.

"A scholarship? You never mentioned that," she says.

"Well, you don't tell me everything, either."

A silence.

Jasmine stares into her tea, a note of guilt in her voice. "I'm sorry I'm only telling you now. I wanted to do it in person. And I needed the time to make the decision for myself."

"Do Mom and Dad know?"

"Of course not," she says, keeping her voice low. "That's why you need to keep this a secret."

"*Jaz*—" I start.

"At least for right now, okay? Promise you won't say anything."

I stare at her for a long moment. Then I let out a breath. "You know I won't. But I'm not taking the bullet if they find out. You know how they worry."

"They're always worried," Jasmine says, leaning back again. "That's just how they are, especially about me. I haven't felt better in a long time. Staying closer to home isn't going to will me to perfect health. And I know how to take care of myself."

Jasmine struggles with chronic anemia, which isn't uncommon in the family. It causes her body to store too much iron, making her more tired than usual. She has to get blood transfusions here and there, which isn't nearly as bad as it sounds. But my parents constantly fixate on her health.

"I know you can. I'm just . . . surprised." I don't know what else to say.

Jasmine reaches over, touching my hand. "I should have

told you sooner, okay? Who knows. Maybe it won't work out with the music career. But you'll always lose the things you don't go after."

I want to convince her to stay. We barely see each other already. There's a sharp pain in my chest, making it hard to get the words out. "When am I even gonna see you again?"

"I'm not sure," she says, frowning. "We might be going much sooner than I thought. So it might not be for a while." She squeezes my hand.

I stare at my plate, trying not to be upset. I thought she was dropping in for lunch, making up for the time she's been gone. Suddenly, she's heading to another country? And she can't even tell me for how long? I don't want her to go. I want her to stay close to home and visit more like she promised. My heart beats faster, but there's no point in arguing, because it sounds like she's already made up her mind. So I take a deep breath, keeping these thoughts to myself. "It's alright," I manage to say. "As long as this is what you really want."

Jasmine smiles from across the table. Another secret I have to keep for her. I don't ask her more about it. Because I don't want it to ruin the rest of our lunch. But all I can think about is how much I'm going to miss her.

Three

It's chilly when we leave the restaurant. We're standing at the corner, waiting for Jasmine's ride to pick her up. The clouds are thickening above us, casting shadows along the sidewalk. Jasmine tilts her head at the sky. "Looks like it's gonna rain," she says. "You should probably get going, too."

"You really can't stay longer?" I ask.

"My friend is waiting for me," she says. "We have to get back to Ann Arbor soon." She looks at my hand. "What's in the bag, anyway?"

I glance down, remembering I brought it with me. "Nothing." I move the paper bag behind me. Jasmine gives me a suspicious look. I think she's about to ask again when the car pulls up beside us. Jasmine checks her phone. "I have to go," she says. Then she turns to me, hugging me tight. "I'm glad I got to see you."

"Glad I got to see you, too."

"Did you get my letters?" Jasmine has been writing to me since she left for college. I think it's to make up for the fact that she doesn't come home too often. Which is the reason I haven't read them. "I've sent a few of them now."

"Yeah. I did."

"Have you read them?"

"I've been busy."

Jasmine frowns. "Promise you will, okay? I wrote them for you."

"Yeah, I promise."

She hugs me one last time. Part of me doesn't want to let go of her. *What am I going to do without you here?*

Jasmine opens the car door and says, "Text me when you get home, okay?" Then she climbs inside and smiles at me through the window. I wave goodbye as the car heads down the road. I almost wish I could go with her, leave this boring life behind, too. Instead, I just watch her disappear down the corner. A breeze blows in from behind me, bringing the first sprinkle of rain. The train stop is only a few blocks from here. But I don't feel like going back to an empty house. I turn around, heading in the other direction.

Rain continues to fall as I cross the road. I hold the bag to my chest to keep it dry. It's been a while since I've walked through this part of the Loop. Every window display I pass reminds me of Daniel. I wish I could just call him up, ask him to hang out like old times. I thought about visiting his grave today and bringing him some flowers for his birthday. But I didn't want to go by myself. I'm sure he'll understand, though. Sometimes I have conversations with him inside my head. *"Don't worry about it,"* he would say. *"I don't even like flowers."*

The wind picks up, sending a chill through me. I clench the bag tighter as I turn the corner and keep walking. The blue café sign blinks through the mist. I was hoping the place was still open. I cross the street and make my way inside. A bell rings as I push open the door. I don't order anything right away. I find a table in the corner and set my things down.

It's been a long time since I've been to this café. Daniel's dad lives a few blocks from here. He used to spend the weekends with him. This was always our meeting spot when he snuck out of the house. Maybe if I wait around long enough, he'll show up and tell me everything's been a dream. I close my eyes and imagine Daniel sitting across the table.

His voice fills my head. "*Took you long enough. So what did you get me?*"

I place the bag on the table. The one I've been carrying around all day. It's Daniel's birthday present. I bought it for him a few weeks ago. I couldn't stop myself. Inside is the shirt from the Crying Fish tour. Daniel and I went to their concert last spring. It's one of his favorite bands of all time. We waited in line for hours and once we got to the front, it was sold out.

"*We missed half the concert for this,*" he sighed.

"*You could still get the keychain.*"

"*For twenty dollars? Am I Bill Gates?*"

I spent weeks searching for it online. The band is a little obscure, making it difficult to find. I open the bag and place the shirt on the table. Daniel would have loved it. As I imagine the look on his face, it hits me all over again. *I'll never be able to give this to you.* There's nothing but an empty chair where he should be sitting. I run my hand over the shirt, wondering why I'm still doing this to myself. As if it's supposed to make me feel better.

There's a pain in my chest, making me feel sick. When the room starts to spin, I squeeze my eyes shut. I don't know why I came in here. I lower my head to the table as this wave of loneliness crashes over me. I wish someone would come to make everything okay again. But Jasmine is on her way back to Ann Arbor. It feels like everyone is disappearing from my life.

The door chimes as someone enters the café. The bell sounds different this time, like a ring from a bicycle. The sound echoes through me as footsteps approach my table. Someone leans their umbrella against the wall, taking the empty seat in front of me. I don't look up immediately. I need a second to pull myself together.

Maybe Jasmine came back to find me. But how would she know where I am?

As I lift my head slowly, I realize it's not her. Someone else stares back at me, making me think I'm dreaming or something. It takes my brain a few seconds to process his face, the shoulders, the waves of black hair. But it couldn't be . . .

"Haru?"

He smiles at me from across the table, evoking a sky of petals in my head as the memories come flooding back. *A paper card flying through the air, the doors closing between us, the train pulling away*. His dark hair falls gently along the side of his face, and he wears a black shirt. His tanned skin is dewy from the rain.

"It's been a long time, hasn't it?" he says, sitting back in his chair.

I can't think straight. *"Where did you come from?"*

He smirks. "So you remember? Thought you might have forgotten me."

"Of course I remember." I'm trying not to stammer. "What are you doing here?"

Haru glances out the window and says, "I was walking by and thought I saw you. So I came in to make sure."

My head is spinning. The last time we saw each other was more than a year ago. Across the ocean, thousands of miles away. "But what are you doing in *Chicago*?"

"Visiting," he says, so casually. "I remember all the good things you had to say. Had to see it for myself."

"But what are the chances that— I don't— How did you—" I try to speak but can't get my thoughts straight. It's as if he walked out of a dream. I take a deep breath and try to compose myself. "I'm sorry I can't speak right now. I'm just so surprised . . . I can't believe it's really you." Then I remember what I must look like. I wipe my face and straighten the buttons of my shirt. "And I don't usually look like this. I just got caught in the rain and forgot my umbrella—"

"You look great." He winks at me. "Just like I remember."

My cheeks go warm. "I know you're lying, but thank you."

Haru chuckles, running a hand through his silky hair. Then he leans forward, crossing his arms on the table. "I was hoping we'd run into each other again someday."

His words hang between us, sending a flutter to my stomach. "I thought I'd never see you again," I say. "And now you're right here."

Haru smiles. "We have a lot to catch up on, don't we?"

"Yeah, we really do," I say with a laugh. There are a hundred questions running through my mind. I don't even know where to begin. "How are things in Tokyo? What have you been up to?"

Haru places an arm over the back of the chair. "I'm taking some time off to travel. I was working at my family's store in Osaka for the past few months. I might have mentioned it before."

"The paper store." I recall our last conversation. "You said you worked there every summer. When we were at that hidden tea place." We both smile at the memory of this. I still can't believe it's him. *Haru. Sitting right in front of me.* "I'm taking time off, too. Applying to jobs and stuff." Then I glance at the menu on the table. "Did you want to order something? I don't know if you have anywhere to go, but there's food here."

"You read my mind," Haru says.

I hand him the menu. "Order whatever you like, okay? The sandwiches are really good. And this one's on me, since you got it last time."

Haru shakes his head. "I can't let you . . ."

"I want to," I say, remembering all the food he made me try last summer. "You paid last time. And you're in my city now. So just let me get this one, okay?"

"Well, if you're *insisting*," he says.

"I'm insisting."

I can't stop smiling as we look over the menu. It's too late for coffee, so I recommend the strawberry iced tea. Since Haru came in, everything feels lighter. A minute ago, I felt like the world was caving in. Suddenly I'm back in Tokyo, reliving the best summer of my life. "I still can't believe you're here," I say again. "When did you get into Chicago?"

"It hasn't been long."

"How are you liking it so far?"

"I like it a lot more now." He adds a smirk.

"That's good to hear," I say, trying hard not to blush. "Chicago's a lot bigger than people think. I can give you a tour."

"I don't want to *impose*," he says playfully.

"You're not imposing. I'd love to show you around."

"You don't have a train to catch?"

"I . . ."

My voice trails off, unsure what to say. I swallow some guilt, remembering how I left him standing on the platform. Thankfully Haru cracks a smile, running a hand through his hair again. He glances at my arm, noticing something. "You're still wearing the bracelet," he says. He reaches for my hand, making me go still. "I'm surprised you still have it. After all this time."

"Yeah . . . I do."

Then Haru pulls back his sleeve, revealing the other bracelet. The one we switched at the festival. It's as if they've been reunited again, two pieces from an unfinished puzzle. "I have mine as well."

"And we're both wearing them," I say.

"Maybe we knew we'd meet again."

As I look at him, I *feel* paper wishes fluttering around us. Maybe it's the rain tapping against the glass that gives the room a dreamlike quality. But if this is a dream, I don't want to wake up yet. "Maybe you're right," I tell him.

We go over the menu together, ordering things we can share. Eventually I head to the counter, grabbing our food and iced tea. Outside, the rain has calmed a little. We talk for a while, catching up on each other's lives, as people come in and out of the café. Somehow, it feels like no time has passed since we last saw each other. I ask him about the places he wants to visit, the food he wants to try while he's visiting. At some point, the woman from the counter appears at our table, letting us know they're about to close. I hadn't realized how much time had passed. As we head out the door, Haru opens his umbrella for both of us. But I stop short as we step outside.

"Wait, I forgot something."

The paper bag with Daniel's shirt inside. It's on the floor beside the table. I scold myself a little as I turn back inside to grab it. The moment I come out again, I realize Haru is gone. The street is completely empty. I glance around, wondering where he went.

"Haru? Where'd you go?"

But there's no one out here but me. As I turn back to the

café, the door is locked. So he couldn't be inside. I keep glancing around the street, but there's no sign of Haru anywhere. How could he leave without saying goodbye?

I didn't even get your number.
How are we supposed to find each other?

It's like the train doors are closing again. The pain returns to my chest, as if waking me up from a dream. I wait outside the café for a long time, hoping he might return. But Haru never comes back. Eventually the rain picks up. When I realize no one is coming, I make my way to the train station, wondering how I let him slip away again.

Four

My clothes are soaked by the time I get home. I still can't believe what happened. Why would Haru leave without saying anything? Why didn't he just wait for me? We could have at least exchanged numbers or something. I'm supposed to show him around the city tomorrow. How did we end up losing each other again?

I leave the living room lights off as I come in. There's a plate of food on the kitchen counter, wrapped in plastic. I forgot to tell Mom I was missing dinner tonight. I place it in the fridge and head to my room. My wet clothes are sticking to my skin. I throw them on the floor and take a hot shower. My mind is still back at the café. Maybe I should have waited a little longer. What if he got lost and came back looking for me? *How long did you expect me to wait in the rain?* I wonder if it was something I said. I mean, we made all these plans to see each other again. How could he just leave like that? There must have been some misunderstanding. Maybe I'll return to the café tomorrow, leave a note at the counter in case he comes back to find me.

I can't think about anything else. I pace around the room, staring out the window, replaying the last few hours in my head. Why didn't we just exchange numbers? Especially after what happened last summer. At one point, I climb into bed and pull the covers over me. There's nothing I can do to bring him back. The orange streetlight shines across the ceiling, making it impossible to fall asleep. But I'm too lazy to close the blinds. Eventually I just shut my eyes until the rest of the world drifts away.

A sound wakes me up in the middle of the night.

I open my eyes slowly, blinking through the grainy darkness. Someone is sleeping beside me. For a second, I can't tell if I'm dreaming. Then I hear a familiar voice.

"Did I wake you?" he whispers.

Haru stares back at me through the dark. Silence hangs in the air between us. The moment I fully awaken, I'm jumping to my feet, shouting at the top of my lungs. Before I can form a thought, I hear someone coming from the hallway. A second later, my mom bursts in through the door, turning on the lights.

"Bị cái gì vậy?" she says. *What's wrong?*

When I turn back to the bed, Haru is gone. I glance around the room, but there's no sign of him. *Where did he go?* For a second, I think I've lost my mind. Then it quickly hits me. *I was only dreaming.* He was never here. It was all in my head. I let out a breath as I calm down, turning back to my mom.

"Sorry. I just had a bad dream."

"*Nằm mơ thấy gì?*" *What did you dream about?*

It's a question she's asked me before. When I was younger, I used to wake up screaming in the middle of the night. It usually happened after watching a scary movie or if something bad happened. Mom would come in, taking me in her arms, asking me what I'd dreamed about. Sometimes it was a monster under the bed, or something hiding in the closet. Mom would always ward them off for me, staying next to me until I fell asleep again. But my anxieties are not the same monsters from my childhood. They are of a different variety I don't think she'll understand anymore. So I decide not to tell her. "It was nothing. Just a bad dream."

"*Con hét to quá*," she says. *You screamed so loud.*

"I'm sorry," I say again.

She looks at me, concern in her eyes. But she doesn't push me on this. "Okay," she says, nodding. "*Đi ngủ đi.*" *Go back to sleep then.*

"Okay."

This is usually how we speak with each other. Mom will say something in Vietnamese and I usually respond in English. It's not that I prefer it this way. I just don't know how to speak it as well as I used to. But I can still understand a lot of it.

Mom shuts off the lights and closes the door behind her.

I stand in the dark for a moment. Then I check under the bed for good measure. It takes a while to shake off the feeling that someone was here. *It was only a dream*, I remind myself. It's only me in the room. I climb back in bed and pull the sheets over my head. It takes a long time to fall asleep. But eventually the world drifts away again.

Sunlight shines across my face when I wake up. I'm not sure what time or day it is. But I want to stay in bed for a few more hours. It's not as though I have anything worth getting up for. Maybe I'll just go back to sleep. As I turn on my side, my arm brushes against something next to me. It's the warmth of skin that makes me open my eyes.

Someone is sleeping beside me, facing the other way. I blink a few times, expecting to wake up again. This must be a dream, right? I reach out my hand, running my fingers along the arch of their back. But why does this feel so *real*? Then he rouses to life. I pull my hand back as he turns around slowly, and the next thing I know, Haru and I are facing each other again. He scrunches his eyes, as if he's just waking up.

"Morning," he says softly.

Strands of dark hair fall across his face. Time freezes as I take him in. Then I jump out of bed again, barely landing on my feet.

"What are you doing here?"

He pushes himself up, yawning. "I was trying to sleep," he says.

"How did you even get in?"

"Through the front door." He smirks a little. "How did you get in?"

"Seriously Haru, why are you here?"

"I came to see you," he says, brushing his hair out of his

face. "We're supposed to hang out today. Don't tell me you forgot."

"I didn't think you'd show up out of *thin air*!" I say, ignoring that smirk of his. "And we didn't even exchange numbers. How did you know where I live?"

"You told me at the café," he says.

"No, I didn't."

"Are you sure?"

His voice is playful, making me question myself. As I'm waiting for answers, my phone suddenly goes off. It's vibrating on the floor by the bed. I glance at the phone and back at Haru. Then I walk over and pick it up from the floor. *Why is Kevin calling me?* I haven't spoken to him in months. Then I remember my conversation with Jasmine. She kept insisting I reach out to him again. I sent him a text after we finished lunch. For a second, I think about letting this go to voicemail. But I can't avoid him forever. Especially when I texted him first this time. I take a deep breath and answer the call.

"Hello?"

"Eric?"

"Hey, Kev."

"Is this a good time?"

"Uh, yeah."

"I got your text yesterday," Kevin says. "It was really good to hear from you. I know it's been a while. You mentioned you've been looking for a job. This might be late notice, but are you free to meet up right now?"

"Like this second?"

Haru rises from the bed, stretching. I keep my eyes on him as Kevin continues, "I'm at this school event. There's someone from my department who I want you to meet. But I'm not sure how long she'll be here."

"Uh..."

Haru pulls a book from the shelf and opens it. Then sets it down, picking up a different one.

"Do you think you can make it?"

"Sorry, I'm a bit *distracted* at the moment," I say, watching Haru turn to my desk. When he opens a drawer, I walk over and shut it. "*Stop that.*"

"Stop what?" Kevin says.

"Nothing, sorry. What were you saying?"

"The event goes until four. You should come by."

"Well, I'm sort of, I mean—" I start to say something, but Haru has made his way to the closet, looking through my clothes. "Uh."

"It would be good to see you," Kevin says.

There's a knot of guilt in my chest. It's been several months since we've seen each other. When he and Jasmine were together, the three of us used to hang out all the time. Watching movies on the weekend. Taking the train to the lake and walking around the beach. I still have some rocks we started collecting. After the breakup, it felt like I lost him, too. I shouldn't blow him off this time. Especially when he's only trying to help. "Okay. Yeah, I'll come."

"Great. I'll send you the location."

"Thanks, Kevin."

"See you soon."

As I hang up the phone, Haru pulls the jinbei from the back of the closet. The one I bought with him last summer. "You still have this," he says, smiling. Maybe in another context, I would reminisce on this. Instead, I walk over and take it from his hands. "I'm really sorry, but I have to get going," I say, hanging it back in the closet.

"Where?"

"Meeting a friend."

"You're not showing me around?" he asks.

"What do you mean?"

"You promised me a tour."

I think back to last night. "Maybe I did. But I didn't expect you to show up unannounced." He still hasn't told me how he got here. I mean, he practically broke into my house. I should probably be more upset. But I don't have time for this right now. "And someone is waiting for me."

Haru stares at me with disappointment. He slides his hands into his pockets, glancing out the window. "Alright then. I can show myself around." Then he turns toward the door.

The memory of last summer flashes through my head. The piece of paper flying through the air as the train door closed between us. I thought I lost him again last night. I can't let him go like this.

"*Wait.*" I grab his hand. "Maybe we could—"

"You don't have to—"

"I *want* to," I tell him. "Why don't you just come with me? It shouldn't take too long. I can show you around afterward."

Haru rubs his chin, considering this. "I suppose I could do that."

"Okay," I breathe. "Just let me get ready."

I grab a clean shirt from my closet and get dressed. Haru didn't bring any clothes with him. I give him a few options to change into while I brush my teeth. A few minutes later, we're out the door. The Yellow Line comes every fifteen minutes. We wait on the platform as the train arrives. I take an empty seat while Haru stands beside me, holding the hand grip. As we're moving, Haru keeps turning his head, gazing intently out the windows. I watch him do this for a few stops, wondering if he's looking for something.

"What are you looking for?" I finally ask.

"The Bean," he says. "I haven't seen it yet."

"We're heading the other direction."

Haru frowns. "Ah. I see."

"But we can go there afterward," I say.

"Can we also get deep pizza?"

"It's called deep-*dish* pizza, and sure. Any touristy thing you want."

The train drops us off near the University of Illinois, Chicago. Kevin is currently a sophomore there, studying architecture. The directions to the department building are pulled up on my phone. I'm trying to get there fast, but Haru keeps stopping here and there to look at all the sights.

"So this is an American university," he says, taking in the buildings around us. "It's just like from the movies."

A new-student fair is taking place on the quad. White tents line the path as we walk past the various tables. Some of them are giving away free food and pens, inviting people to sign up for their club. There are some games set up, offering different prizes to win. Maybe it's because I'm with Haru, but I'm reminded of the Star Festival last summer. If I close my eyes, I can see paper stars fluttering above us. Haru must be thinking the same thing, because he gestures to a table with a spinning wheel and says, "They're giving away free spins. Should we test your luck again?"

I smile at him. "Maybe on the way out."

Kevin's department building is just up ahead. I must have been too distracted by the memory, because someone bumps straight into me. Her things scatter across the steps of the building, bringing me back to myself. I bend down to help pick them up.

"*Sorry*, I didn't see you," I say.

"It's fine—"

She grabs her bag and walks off. As I turn back to Haru, he's gone. I glance all around me. Where did he go off to?

"Haru?"

For a second, I think we lost each other again. My heart races at the thought of this. Maybe he's already in the building. I make my way inside, hoping to find him. Haru is nowhere to be found on the main floor. He must have followed the signs straight to the event. I head to the elevators and press the button. The doors open up to an atrium on the top floor. Skylights illuminate the room as I head toward the crowd. To my surprise, everyone's wearing button-down shirts and nice pants. Why didn't Kevin mention a dress code? I feel like an outsider as I wander around in a T-shirt and jeans. There's a long table of catering food by the windows. The silver trays remind me of the nights working for Mr. Antonio. Haru must be around here somewhere.

"Eric—"

I turn my head as Kevin appears beside me. He wears a cream silk shirt with a black tie. "I'm glad you made it," he says, hugging me tight. Then he leans back as we take each other in.

"Your hair is longer," I say.

"Yeah, I should get a cut soon."

"No, it looks nice."

We both smile. Feels like forever since we've seen each other. There's an unexpected stir of joy and relief. I didn't realize how much I missed him. Then Kevin turns slightly, gesturing to the tables. "Are you hungry? There's a lot of food here." He steps over and grabs a plate for me. "They have salmon. I know how much you like seafood." He places a few things on my plate.

"What's this event for again?"

"It's a student showcase. I can show you some of my work, if you'd like." He checks his watch and looks around the room. "Let me introduce you to someone first. She's one of my advisers. I think you'll like her."

"Sure." I'm still glancing around the busy room, wondering where Haru is.

"There she is—"

Kevin places a hand on my shoulder, leading me through the crowded gallery. There's a circle of older men in slacks, chatting by the window. Kevin taps one of them on the shoulder. A bald guy in a tweed jacket turns around and shakes Kevin's hand. Beside him is a woman in red glasses, her black hair tied in a bun, a floral scarf wrapped around her shoulders.

"Professor Lin—this is Eric," Kevin introduces me. "I mentioned him earlier."

She adjusts her glasses, taking me in for a second. "A pleasure," she says. "You look a lot like your sister."

I blink at her. "You know Jasmine?"

"Of course," Professor Lin says. "Came to a few of our shows, isn't that right?"

"Professor Lin is the chair of the theater department," Kevin explains. "I helped design some of the sets for class. That's why I invited Eric here. He's looking for a job, if you know of anything."

She looks at me. "What are you studying?"

I hesitate as the other professors turn to listen. "I'm actually not enrolled in school at the moment . . ."

The bald guy in the tweed jacket chuckles. "I should have gathered, given how you're dressed."

I glance at my clothes, the plate of food still my hand. "I didn't know it was a formal event."

Kevin pats my back. "I told Eric last minute and forgot to mention it."

"Always dress for the role you want," the man says, tipping his glass at me. "Especially when you're asking for a job." He takes a sip of his drink.

Someone appears behind me. Their lips are close to my ear as they whisper, "Don't let him talk to you like that."

I turn my head and realize it's Haru.

"*Shhh*," I say back.

"What?" Kevin asks, blinking at me.

I play it off with a laugh. "*Sorry*, my friend just—" I point to Haru—but he's not there. I turn my neck, looking for him. "He was here a second ago."

A few looks are exchanged. One of them must have seen where he went.

"I can always talk to Frank," Professor Lin continues the conversation. "They're usually hiring this time of year."

"That would be great," Kevin says. He nudges me with his elbow. "Eric is very creative. He makes films."

I'm not really listening, though. I'm looking around for Haru. Where did he run off to so fast?

Professor Lin turns to me. "Any experience with the stage?"

"Uh, not really," I say.

"You seem very distracted," says the bald guy, making me

snap back to the group. "I'm beginning to think Kevin wants this job more than you."

The others chuckle.

"Enough from you, Albert," Professor Lin says, shaking her head at him.

I lower my gaze, suddenly embarrassed by myself. Then a hand reaches for my plate, grabbing a bread roll. Haru appears again, whispering in my ear. "*I'm throwing this at him in three . . . two . . .*"

I snatch the roll. "*Don't!*"

"Don't what?" Kevin asks.

More looks are exchanged.

I hide the roll behind my back, laughing nervously. "Sorry, my friend keeps—" But Haru is gone again. I turn a full circle. Then glance at Kevin. "Did you see where he went?"

"Who?"

"My friend. He was right here."

Kevin turns his head. "It is a bit crowded."

How could Kevin not have seen him? Maybe he walked off in the other direction. The fluorescent lights suddenly feel brighter, blinding me a little. The next thing I know, the room is starting to spin.

Kevin squeezes my shoulder. "Are you alright?"

"Yeah, I'm fine," I breathe. "Just need some water."

"I'll go with you—"

I pull away. "No, it's okay."

I walk off immediately. My vision is blurry as I move through the gallery, wondering what's going on. *Why does*

Haru keep disappearing like this? It feels like no one else can see him but me.

There are benches outside the atrium. I toss the plate in the bin and take the seat farthest away from the crowd. I can't seem to think straight. My mind flashes back to last night, when Haru showed up at the café. And again in my bed this morning. I take a deep breath and close my eyes.

It doesn't take long before someone sits down beside me. I don't have to look up this time. I already know who it is.

"Figured you'd be out here."

I turn my head slowly. Haru smiles back at me, the same way he did when we first met. The way the light frames him is like something from a movie. It reminds me of the sunset, when Daniel and I used to watch it from the roof together. As I'm taking him in, a question comes to me. One that's been sitting in the back of my mind.

"Is this all in my head?"

Haru blinks at me. "What do you mean?"

"Why can't anyone else see you?"

He says nothing.

"Did you really show up to the café last night?" I pause, swallowing my breath. "Or did I imagine that, too?" The more I hear myself say it, the less it makes sense. "Why do you keep disappearing?"

"Why does it matter? I'm here right now."

"This doesn't feel real. How you showed up out of the blue."

"It feels real to me . . ."

Haru leans forward, brushing my hair from my forehead. The touch of him makes me go still, pulling me back to the summer before. For a moment, I let myself believe it's him. That we found each other again after all this time. But I can't help wondering how this is possible. I move his hand away and say nothing.

Haru presses his lips together. Then he reaches into his back pocket. "Maybe this will prove I am . . ." He pulls out a slip of paper. I watch as he starts folding it in front of me. Then he places it in my hand. It's an origami star. Like the one he made me last summer.

"The paper star," I say.

"You remember, then."

"Of course I do."

Haru smiles. "Don't let this one fly away."

We look at each other. As I open my mouth to speak, someone calls my name from down the hall, interrupting the moment. I turn my head and Kevin comes toward me.

There's a shift in the light. Like waking from a daydream. I don't have to turn to know Haru isn't there anymore. But I look back anyway. The other side of the bench is empty. All that's left is a paper star in my hand. I run my finger over it as Kevin takes a seat next to me. There's a silence before he asks, "Is everything alright out here?"

I close my hands, hiding the paper star from him. "Yeah, I'm fine," I say.

"Are you sure?"

"Yeah, great."

"You don't seem like yourself today."

I take in a deep breath and sigh. "You don't have to worry about me," I tell him. "Sorry for walking out like that though. I didn't mean to embarrass you."

Kevin shakes his head. "You didn't embarrass me. I just wanted to check up on you."

"I told you, I'm fine."

Another silence. Then Kevin leans in and says, "I know that things are different . . . since Jasmine—"

"We don't need to talk about this," I cut him off. Before he has a chance to say more, I rise abruptly from the bench. "I actually have to be somewhere. So I should get going."

"Where are you going?"

I don't answer this. "Thank you for inviting me."

"Eric, wait—"

I don't stop as I head for the elevator. I feel a pang of guilt for leaving this way. Especially when he's only trying to help me out. But it's not a conversation I want to have right now. I press the elevator button and step inside. As it begins to close, Kevin appears on the other side just in time to say one last thing.

"Text me if you need anything."

That's the last thing I hear before the door shuts between us.

Five

There's a sea of students when I step out of the elevator. Classes must have ended, because I'm bumping shoulders on my way out. I can't remember which way I'm going. There are too many thoughts running through my head. As I'm pulling my phone out, I spot someone through the crowd, making my heart drop.

But it couldn't be him.

"*Daniel?*"

I catch a glimpse of his red sweatshirt, the back of his head. There are too many people walking between us. I move toward him, pushing through everyone in front of me. My heart is racing as I get closer. *Please let it be you.* But the moment I break through the crowd, I realize it's someone else.

What's wrong with me? Of course it's not Daniel.

Haru turns around instead.

"There you are," he says, hands in his pockets. A breeze ruffles his long hair.

We stare at each other as the crowd moves around us. For a second, I'm relieved to see him again. I take a step back, reminding myself this isn't real. That he's only going to disappear on me. But I'm not sure how to wake up from this. It feels like I'm losing my grip on reality. I turn around, heading off in the other direction.

"Where are you going?" he asks.

I don't answer him. I cut through the crowd as Haru follows behind. The student fair is still taking place on the quad. But the tables handing out prizes don't remind me of the festival this time. The magic has vanished now that I know this is all in my head. Haru walks beside me, glancing at one of the games. *But why does he feel so real, then?* I shake the thought away and keep on walking.

A moment later, we reach the train station. As we're waiting on the platform, Haru turns to me and says, "So what's the first stop on this tour?"

I say nothing.

"Is it a surprise?"

"I'm going home," I say.

"You're not showing me around?"

"I can't anymore."

"Why not?"

"I just can't."

Haru stares at me, maybe waiting for an explanation. But I don't even turn my head to look at him. Then he folds his arms and says, "Alright then. Maybe I'll give myself a tour."

"Maybe you should."

For a second, I almost take this back. But the platform begins to rattle beneath us. *He isn't really there,* I remind myself. Because a part of me wants to stay with him. But I have enough problems in my life to deal with. As the train roars into the platform, I turn to Haru one last time. In case I never see him again.

"You don't know how happy I was to find you again," I tell him, the train doors opening behind me. "I really wanted this to be real. But you're not him." I stand there a moment longer. "I still don't know why I can see you, but this isn't what I wanted."

Haru looks at me. "What do you want?"

"Not this."

I step inside the train. As the doors close behind me, I turn around and see Haru looking back at me through the glass. My mind goes to last summer, right before the paper slipped out of our hands and we lost each other. Then the train starts moving, leaving him standing there on the platform. But I don't watch him disappear this time. I just take an empty seat and pretend none of this ever happened.

The house is empty when I get home. Mom and Dad are working late tonight, so it's only me again. Dad is a mechanic at an auto body shop and Mom manages a convenience store on the same block. It makes it easy for them to commute together. I stand at the doorway, taking in the familiar silence. Strangely, I thought it would be more comforting. At least everything seems normal again. I grab a glass of water and head to the living room.

Usually, I leave the television on in the background. But I just sit on the couch and stare at my phone. No missed calls or new messages. Not that I'm expecting to hear from anyone. I think about texting Jasmine and telling her what happened. But how would I even begin to say it? Maybe it's better to keep this one to myself for now.

I keep glancing at the front door in case Haru followed me home. But the hours pass with no sign of him. I take a shower and sit around until my parents come home, offering to help bring in the groceries. Mom makes stir-fry and bitter melon for dinner. I take a plate back to my room where I stay for the rest of the night.

When I wake up in the morning, no one is there beside me. I stare at the empty side of the bed for a while. Eventually, I get up to check around the house. There's no sign of him. I make a bowl of cereal and eat in my room. The day goes by slowly. I play a movie in the background while I work on college applications. As I'm looking up that film scholarship, I remember the lie I told Jasmine. She thinks I made it to the next round, meaning I have to apply, even though I haven't touched my camera in several months. I spend the afternoon trying to come up with some ideas.

My parents bring home Chinese food for dinner. I have beef and broccoli with sweet-and-sour soup. Then I join Dad in the living room to watch the news together. Haru doesn't show up tonight, either. I don't know why I keep expecting him to. Maybe this was all in my head. Maybe he was never really there. Then why can't I stop thinking about him?

The days repeat themselves. I lounge around the house, applying to jobs while something plays in the background.

Time passes without me noticing. I wash the dishes, take out the garbage, play around on my phone. My parents have been working late all week. I make some instant ramen with an egg and bring it to the living room. There's a romance movie marathon on some random channel. *The Notebook* is playing. I've watched it a hundred times, but I leave it on anyway. It's the scene where they're shouting in the rain, just before he pulls her in for a long, passionate kiss.

I turn off the television and stare out the window. It's raining hard outside again. The wind blows against the glass. For some reason, I can't get him out of my head. Haru. I wonder if he's somewhere out there. I imagine him walking around, shivering in the cold. It's been a few days since I left him at the train station. *It wasn't real,* I keep repeating. I push the images away and return to my room. There's still some clothes that need to be washed. As I lift my pants from the floor, something falls out of the pocket.

The paper star Haru made me. I pick it up from the floor to examine it. It's a little bent from being inside my pocket. I stare at it for a moment. If I completely imagined him, what is this doing here? And why does it feel real in my hand? A thought slowly occurs to me. If this hasn't disappeared yet, does that mean that Haru is still out there?

I can't believe I left him at the train station. Especially after I promised to show him around. Maybe it was all in my head. But if I'm being honest, it was nice having someone to keep me company. It's better than sitting home alone all day long. Who cares if no one else can see him? Because I still could.

The next thing I know, I'm grabbing an umbrella and racing out the door. Rain splashes under my shoes as I head to the train station. I don't even know where to start looking. All I know is I have to find him again. I hop onto the Yellow Line, making my way toward the Loop. Haru must be somewhere in the city. Every time the doors open, I hope it's him who wanders inside.

I reach Grand Street, where we last saw each other. Even though it's a long shot, I walk around the platform, looking everywhere for him. Of course he isn't here anymore. But I'm not really sure where to go next. There are eight different lines that run through Chicago, with more than a hundred stops, and he could be anywhere by now. Another train approaches the platform. I head through the doors and continue looking. If I wander around long enough, maybe we'll run into each other. I move between train cars and transfer lines, scanning every platform for him. But hours go by and I haven't found him.

As I'm waiting for the next stop a terrible thought hits me. What if Haru is really gone? Does that mean I'll never see him again? A chill goes through me as I think back to the last time we saw each other. I wish I could take back the things I said. As the last few days replay in my mind, I remember something else. When we were on the train together, Haru kept staring out the window. Wasn't he looking for something? He even asked if I could take him there. The moment it hits me, I jump to my feet. *Why didn't I think of this sooner?*

The second the doors open, I rush onto the platform and switch lines again. It's still pouring when the train drops me off at Lake Street. I hold the umbrella over my head and cross the street toward Millennium Park. The staircase is carved from stone, manicured hedges glistening on both sides like the gardens of a palace. The park is usually crowded with tourists throughout the day. But the rain seems to have cleared the entire promenade.

As I reach the top of the steps, the steel curves of the Bean rise into view. The sculpture reflects the city back like those funhouse mirrors. It looks strange without a hundred people circling around, taking photos beneath the arch. There's something dystopian about it, standing in the emptiness of the park, the rain washing over the steel body. I shiver a little as I take a look around. The Bean was the place he wanted to see most. Maybe he's here somewhere. I wander around the park, calling his name.

"*Haru? Are you out here?*"

It's only my voice that echoes back. I keep walking around, hoping we find each other. But it's only me out here. Maybe this means he's really gone. I never got the chance to tell him I'm sorry. A wave of sadness washes over me as the rain continues to pour. I wish I had one more chance to fix things. But I guess it's too late.

And then I see something in the distance. Someone is sitting on the other side of the park. I didn't notice them before. I'm about to walk off when I realize it's him.

"*Haru?*"

He's sitting alone on a bench, illuminated by the lamplight. A single tree branch from above barely covers him from the rain. His clothes are drenched, long hair slick against his skin. How long has he been sitting out here? I take a moment before making my way over. Then I hold the umbrella above his head. But Haru doesn't bother to look up.

"Hey," I say. "What are you doing out here?"

Haru says nothing.

"I was looking everywhere for you."

Not a word.

"Are you mad at me?"

Haru looks the other way.

I let out a breath, keeping the umbrella over him. "I'm sorry for what I did. I shouldn't have left you like that. I feel really bad about it." But Haru still won't look at me. "I really want to make it up to you. I can show you around Chicago like I promised. We can even grab dinner or something. Anything you want, okay?"

Haru turns his head slowly. There's a long silence before he finally opens his mouth to speak.

"Deep . . . dish?"

Lou Malnati's is the best pizza chain in the city. Anyone who says otherwise probably doesn't live here. It's the first place I think of when someone wants to get Chicago-style pizza.

There are only a few locations, but it's always worth a train ride. Haru and I are seated at a booth in the back of the restaurant. The place is half filled with college students, pouring beer from plastic pitchers.

The two of us are soaked from the rain. Haru runs a hand through his wet hair. His skin is dewy in the fluorescent light. He's quieter than usual, making me think he's still mad at me. I hand him the menu and say, "This is one of my favorite places for pizza. There's a lot to choose from." Daniel and I used to come here all the time. We always split the Chicago Classic and a side of curly fries.

Haru glances at the menu. "It's all deep dish?"

"Yeah, it's what they're known for."

"What do you recommend?"

"I usually get the Chicago Classic."

He nods in approval. "Sounds good to me."

"I'll get us some fries, too."

Our waiter arrives to take our order. Then he heads off again, taking the menus with him. Haru leans back in his seat and looks around the restaurant. Baseball shirts are framed along the brick walls. "This place is very . . . what's the word?" He rubs his chin. "American."

"Very different from the tea place," I say.

His face softens. "You remember the tea place?"

"How could I forget?" It was hidden from tourists in the back of a used bookstore. "After you made us walk all the way there for a piece of paper."

He smirks. "The piece of paper was for you."

"And you *dropped* it."

"No, you didn't hold it tight enough," he says.

"You should have been more careful—"

"You should have stayed with me."

We stare at each other. I'm not sure what to say to this. "I told you. My friend was waiting for me."

"So you don't regret it?"

"That's not what I said."

Haru folds his arms. "That's what I'm hearing."

I can't tell if he's serious. I lean into the table. "I tried to find you online. Do you know how many times I searched your name when I got back?" I didn't even know if it was short for anything. "I looked through tagged photos of the festival, hoping I'd find you somewhere in the background." I stare at my hands, unsure if I should be telling him this. "I even looked up the temple where we made the wishes together. I even thought about coming back to find yours. In case you wrote your last name or something."

"There were thousands of them," Haru reminds me. "How would you have found it?"

"It was the third tree by the entrance, on one of the middle branches," I say. "You wrote on a blue slip of paper."

"I'm surprised you remember that."

"Some memories are hard to forget."

He smirks at this. "I'm glad to be one of them."

I smile back at him. It's a bittersweet moment, the two of

us sitting together again, reliving the past. I've imagined this conversation a dozen times in my head. I'm a little embarrassed to ask this next question. But I can't help myself. "Did you ever try to find me?"

Haru takes a second to answer. "I never stopped looking," he says. "You know, I stayed there for hours, hoping you might come back to see me. But you never did."

"I didn't know," I say.

"It's alright." Haru reaches across the table, taking my hand for the first time. "I found you anyway."

I squeeze his hand, feeling a warmth move between us. There are still a hundred questions racing through my head. But the answers to them don't matter right now. Who cares how this is possible? Maybe it's really him after all. The waiter appears with our order. So I push those thoughts away as we cut into the pizza, enjoying our dinner together.

Haru takes the train back home with me. I told him he could stay over tonight. Dad is asleep on the sofa when we step inside. He left the television on again, but it's not the usual news channel. Then I hear the familiar voice. A home movie of me and Jasmine is playing. We're probably six or seven years old here, running around in the backyard. Since Jasmine moved away, I find him watching them every now and then. Although my dad comes off as stern at times, deep down he's the most sentimental. Jasmine told me that's where I get it from.

I lead Haru to my room and close the door quietly. Our

clothes are still damp from the rain. As I go through the dresser, Haru wanders over to my desk, noticing the paper star he made me.

"You kept this," he says, picking it up.

"Yeah, I did."

Haru smiles to himself as he sets it back down. He looks around the room as if seeing it for the first time. "Where should I sleep?"

"We can share the bed."

"You don't mind?"

"I mean, it wouldn't be our first time," I say.

"I almost forgot," he says with a chuckle. "Hopefully you won't scream at me in the morning this time."

"No idea what you're talking about."

I grab a clean set of clothes and place it on the bed. Then I hop in the shower, leaving Haru to change. The hot water feels nice against my skin. When I return to the room, Haru is staring out the opened window. The moment he turns around, I go still. He's wearing something I don't expect. The T-shirt I bought for Daniel's birthday.

"Where did you find that shirt?" I ask.

"I found it on your desk," he says. "The one you gave me didn't fit. Hope that's alright."

I look away. "Yeah . . . totally."

It's strange seeing it on him. Especially knowing Daniel never got the chance to wear it. But I don't mention this at all. Eventually, I turn off the light as we climb into bed together. It's slightly awkward at first, having someone right next to me. The streetlamp from outside gives off enough light to see his face. We don't fall asleep right away. We just lie there in the dark, staring at the ceiling. After some silence, I turn my head to look at him.

"I'm sorry I left you," I whisper.

Haru runs a hand over my cheek. "Which time?"

"Both," I say. "But I'm glad you came back."

"Always."

We don't say anything else. I just smile as we lie there together, the two of us facing each other, as we finally fall asleep.

Six

Haru is gone when I wake up. Sunlight shines on the empty side of the bed. As if no one was sleeping there the night before. I run my hand across the sheet. For a second, I think it was all a dream. But it all felt so real. The scent of him still lingers. I push myself up slowly and look around the room. *Where did you go again?*

I rub the sleepiness from my eyes and climb out of bed. Maybe he's somewhere around the house. He wouldn't leave without telling me, right? As I step into the hallway, a piano is playing. For a second, I think Jasmine is home. I follow the music into the living room and find the television on. But it's just another home movie. Dad must have accidently left it on again. I watch it for a moment. Jasmine and I are sitting at her toy piano, playing in her bedroom. I can hear Dad's voice behind the camera. He used to film everything when we were younger.

I let the video play for another minute. Then I grab the remote and turn off the television. Maybe I'll watch the rest of it another day. But I'm looking for Haru right now. He has to be around here somewhere. I check every room in the house. I even go to the roof in case he wandered up there. But there's no sign he was ever here. When I return to my room, I find something on my desk. It's another origami star, folded from notebook paper. I hadn't noticed it before. I pick it up and turn it in my hand.

Haru must have left this for me. Maybe this is his way of telling me he'll be back. I wish there were some way to send him a message. I was hoping we would spend the day together. I had it all planned in my head. *How long do I have to wait for you to show up again?* As I stare out the window, my phone goes off. An unknown number is calling me. Usually, I let it go to voicemail. But the area code is from Chicago. So I answer the phone.

"Hello?"

A woman's voice comes through. "Is this Eric Ly?"

"Yeah, that's me."

"I'm calling from the managing office of the Chicago Theater," she says. "We're currently reviewing your application and would like to set up a time for an interview."

The Chicago Theater? For some reason, I don't remember applying there. Then again, I probably sent out a hundred applications over these past few weeks. "Sorry, what job is this for again?"

"A box office associate. Do you have any availability this week?"

"This week?" I pause to think, even though my schedule's completely open. But I don't want to come off as too eager. I clear my throat, trying to sound more professional. "Yes, I should be available. What's the soonest I can come in?"

"The office is open until two."

"Today?"

"Does that work for you?"

"Uh—" I consider asking about tomorrow. But what if someone else comes in today and they end up filling the position? "Yeah, of course I can. I'll be there soon."

"I'll let our manager know. His name is Frank."

"Thank you so much."

I say goodbye and hang up the phone. Then I stare out the window again, watching cars pass along the street. For a moment there, I forgot about the rest of the world. It's like waking up from a dream and feeling the weight of gravity again. I glance at the paper star in my hand, thinking about Haru. Then I set it by the window and get ready for the interview.

The trains are crowded this morning. There's barely room to stand as I google the Chicago Theater on my phone. It's a historic landmark, spanning almost half a city block in the heart of the Loop. Apparently, it opened as a movie palace that premiered films and live events, including the World's Fair in the 1930s. I skim through the shows they're playing before the doors open to my stop.

The marquee shines like a billboard above the street. I've passed by its flashing red-gold lights a hundred times. But it's been years since I've been inside. I must have been a kid at the time. Who was it that brought me here again? As I step through the glass doors, someone takes my hand as the memory comes back to me . . .

"This way."

Jasmine's dress flutters as she pulls me inside. It's like stepping through the looking glass into a strange new world. Marble pillars hold up a vaulted ceiling that stretches seven stories high. I tilt my head, staring at the chandelier as we make our way through the lobby. The theater is nothing like I expected. There's a grand staircase lined with velvet carpet, leading up to a mezzanine.

Jasmine glances back at me and says, "It should be up these stairs." It's our first time at the Chicago Theater. We're too young to afford tickets for the show they're playing. It was Jasmine's idea to sneak inside and give ourselves a tour. "Come on."

"Are we allowed up there?"

"Of course we are."

I give her a look.

"As long as no one finds out. We can do anything."

"If you say so . . ."

As she leads me up the steps, a man in a red vest appears, blocking our way. "Can I help you two?"

"No, thank you," Jasmine says.

"Where are you heading?"

"To see the show."

"It's already started. So doors are closed." He gives us a fake smile like those sales associates who follow you around the store. "Now where are your parents?"

"They're waiting for us. Excuse me—"

Jasmine brushes right past him, pulling me with her. But the man grabs my shoulder and says, "You're staying right here." His fingers press into my skin, making me wince.

Jasmine pulls my hand. "Let go of him."

"You two aren't going anywhere."

Jasmine takes a step down, meeting him at eye level. "I said, let go of him," she repeats.

But the man doesn't release his grip. He just smiles at her, squeezing my shoulder harder.

"I said let go!"

Jasmine lifts her leg up high and kicks him off me. The man goes rolling down the steps as she grabs my hand and motions me to make a run for it . . .

I'm standing at the end of the lobby, staring up at the staircase. The wood details are like I remember, as if nothing's changed after all these years. I wonder what Jasmine would say if she were here with me. If I close my eyes, I can see the ghosts of us running past me. It was one of the secrets we never told Mom and Dad. I smile to myself as I head upstairs, looking for the managing office. There's a series of doors down the halls of the mezzanine. I'm not exactly sure which one leads to the right room. I take a guess and turn the knob anyway. A woman is standing behind a mahogany desk, staring at a bookcase. The moment she turns around, I realize I know her.

"Professor Lin," I say.

"Unless you're my student, call me Angelina." She wears a floral scarf around her shoulders, and her hair is tied into a bun. She points to the chair and says, "Take a seat, if you'd like."

"Is my interview with you?"

She shakes her head. "There's no interview today."

"But the woman on the phone told me—"

"Miscommunication," she says with a wave of the hand. She turns toward the cabinet and grabs some papers, placing them on the desk in front of me. "Just fill this out and leave it here on the desk. Frank will take care of it in the morning."

I stare at the paperwork and back at her. "I'm a little confused. Should I come back tomorrow for the interview?"

"What's there to be confused about?" she asks. "I said there's no interview. A referral from me is all you need."

"A referral?"

"You can thank Kevin for that," she says, pushing up the rim of her glasses. "Speaks very highly of you." She closes the cabinet.

I'm not sure what to say. I didn't expect him to actually get me a job. Especially after my behavior at his event the other day. Not to mention the fact that he's not with Jasmine anymore. I'll have to figure out a way to thank him later.

I grab a pen from the desk and fill out the forms. This might not be the job of my dreams, but it's a step above washing dishes for Mr. Antonio. I mean, the Chicago Theater is a great name on a resume, even if I'm only selling tickets at the box office window. And who knows what other opportunities it could lead to?

Once the paperwork is finished, Angelina walks me to the door and says, "We'll have you start this week. Once Frank takes care of everything."

"I really appreciate it."

When I woke up this morning, I had no idea I would be stepping foot in here. Suddenly I'm starting a new job. I have something to look forward to now. Maybe I'll even make some new friends, too. As I'm heading down the stairs, I think about Jasmine again. I know she would be happy to hear this. If she were still living here, I could take her to see a show or something. Part of me is still mad at her for leaving the way she did. But I have to share the news with her. As I pull out my phone, someone leaving the theater makes me nearly drop it. He's wearing a red sweatshirt, and his hair is a familiar brown that looks just like . . .

"Daniel?"

For a second, I think I've lost it again. But the next thing I know, I'm rushing out the doors as I grab him by the shoulder. The moment he turns around, I realize it isn't him at all. I pull my hand back immediately. "I'm so sorry," I say. Now that I'm standing close to him, he doesn't look like Daniel at all. His hair is a different brown, and the sweatshirt is more of an orange. "I thought you were someone else."

He gives me a weird look.

"Sorry," I say again. I step backward, embarrassed by

myself. *What's wrong with me?* Of course it wasn't Daniel. I wanted to see him so badly, I forgot he was dead. It feels like losing him all over again. I turn around, wanting to make a run for it. As I step off the sidewalk, a bell goes off. I stop just in time as several bicycles race past me, blowing leaves everywhere.

It's not until they're gone that I notice him standing on the other side.

"Told you to look out for bicycles," Haru says. A slight smirk rises on his face.

It takes a second to collect myself. Then relief floods through me as I wrap my arms around him. "*Haru!* What are you doing here?"

"Looking for you."

"Where did you go this morning?"

"I got up early and didn't want to wake you," he says casually. "Did you find the gift I left you?"

The paper star on my desk. "Yeah, I did."

"A thank-you for letting me stay over."

"Of course. You don't have to—"

"Is something wrong?"

Haru runs his thumb over my cheek, wiping away a tear. I didn't even notice I was crying. All because of Daniel. I lower my head and say, "It's nothing. Just something in my eye."

He lifts my chin up. "You can tell me."

For a second, I think about playing it off. But maybe I should be honest. At least a little bit. I take a deep breath and say, "I thought I saw someone I knew . . . But it wasn't him . . ."

"A friend?"

"Yeah. Someone I hadn't seen in a while."

"You must be disappointed."

"Yeah," I say. But I don't want to keep talking about Daniel. Especially now that Haru is here. "Anyway, though, there's something else I have to tell you. I just got a new job. It's at the Chicago Theater."

Haru tilts his brow. "I didn't know you were an actor."

"No, no." I laugh. "I'm just selling tickets at the box office. It's actually right there." I turn around, pointing at the marquee.

Haru looks up. "The famous Chicago sign. It's a lot bigger than I imagined."

"Yeah, it's pretty iconic. You should see the theater."

"Are you offering another tour?"

"Maybe after I start the job," I say. "Hopefully you're still around then."

"I'll be around."

I smile at this. "I'm glad to hear that. Because there's a lot of places I want to take you. I still haven't shown you around the city yet."

"I was just about to remind you."

"Well, let's start now."

I take Haru by the arm, turning him toward the street, facing Chicago traffic. We're north of the Loop, which is basically the heart of the city. There's a million things to do, many of them within walking distance. "The Riverwalk is right across the street. And Millennium Park is two blocks that way, which is right next to the Art Institute, if you're into museums. Is there anything you want to do first?"

Haru rubs his chin, thinking about it. Then he smiles at me and says, "I want to see a movie."

I give him a look. "*A movie?* Really?"

"Wouldn't you enjoy that?"

"Yeah, but we can do that anytime," I say.

"So why not right now?"

"Because there's a million other things we can do."

Haru shrugs. "I want to do something we both like."

I stare at him for a moment. Part of me wants to suggest a museum or something. But I suppose this is his tour. "Well, okay. We'll go see a movie. Was there one you had in mind?"

Haru smirks again. "Surprise me."

The theater is tucked between a laundromat and a yogurt shop. The sign on the box office reads FIVE-DOLLAR TUESDAY. The films are usually a few years older, which Haru doesn't mind. He hasn't seen most of them anyway. We grab some popcorn and a box of Cookie Dough Bites that caught Haru's eye. There's only one other person in the theater, making it feel like we have the place to ourselves. We decided on *La La Land*, one of my favorite movie musicals. Jasmine always had the soundtrack playing in the car. My favorite scene is when they're floating in the planetarium together, stars swirling around them. I turn to Haru the moment it comes on. Purple and blue lights flicker across his face as the music plays. For a second, I imagine it's us dancing through the stars together. Haru glances over at me, making me wonder if he's imagining the same thing. Then he moves his arm over mine, lacing our fingers together over the armrest. Our hands stay like this for the rest of the movie.

The piano music continues in my head as we leave the theater. The streetlamps have come on, illuminating the sidewalk as we head through town together. I notice Haru hasn't said much about the film. He just walks straight ahead, hands in his pockets as we pause at the crosswalk.

"What did you think of the movie?" I ask.

"It was good," he says. "But the ending ruined it."

"What's wrong with the ending?"

"I thought they would end up together." He looks at me. "Didn't you?"

I think about this for a second. "I definitely wanted them to. But you know what they say . . . Better to have loved and lost, right? And it's not like they ended on bad terms. They can always look back and remember what they had. Even if they didn't end up together."

Haru shrugs. "They could have tried harder."

"Maybe you're right," I admit. I slide my hands in my pockets as we keep walking. "But it's still nice, what they had. Someone who loves you back the same way. Even if it was short. It doesn't always work out that way, you know?" I let out a breath. "I'd take someone remembering my drink at a coffee shop, to be completely honest."

"What's your favorite drink?"

"It's not the same if I just *tell* you."

"Then how is anyone supposed to know?" He laughs.

"By getting to know me," I say. "I feel like I'm always the one who remembers, and never the other way around."

Haru stops walking. He holds out a hand.

I turn around. "What?"

"Let's go to the planetarium," he says.

"The planetarium?"

"It's your favorite scene from the movie, right? I figure it's a good place to get to know you better."

A breeze blows across the street, ruffling the dark waves of his hair. I don't say anything else. I just smile as I take his hand. Because at this point, I would go anywhere with him.

Adler Planetarium is a copper dome at the edge of the lake. It's a local gateway to the cosmos, only a few train stops from the Loop. Haru and I spend an hour walking beneath the solar system, looking through telescopes, playing with interactive exhibits about time and space. We missed the sky show that makes you feel as though you're standing on the moon. But as we're walking by the planetarium, Haru notices the doors have been left open. I'm not sure if it's allowed, but we wander inside anyway.

A large projector stands in the center of the room. Rows of seats are circled around it. Haru walks up to the projector and reaches out for a button. Before I can protest, the lights dim as the Milky Way takes shape in the dome above us. It's like staring into a hole in the universe. The cosmos swirls in gorgeous colors over our heads. I wander to the center of the planetarium, gazing at the stars in awe. "It's like the scene from the movie."

"Except we're not floating," Haru adds.

"I never understood that part. Did they imagine it?"

Haru stares above us and says, "I think it's meant to show what it *feels* like to fall in love."

I take this in. "So none of it was real?"

Haru looks at me. "It was real to them."

"Yeah. You're right."

We smile at each other. Then Haru glances around, a mischievous look on his face. He pulls a handkerchief from his pocket.

"Where did that come from?" I ask.

Haru doesn't answer me. Instead, he holds out the handkerchief and lets go. But it doesn't drop to the floor. It just hangs in the air, as if frozen in time. I stare at it, a little confused. Suddenly, it's pulled into the sky by some invisible string and vanishes. We both look up and back at each other. A smirk appears on Haru's face. He holds out a hand and says, "You said you wanted to float around."

I narrow my eyes. "What are you . . ."

"You're not making me do it alone, are you?"

When I don't answer this, Haru steps up on the seat, reaching toward the ceiling. As his feet lift into the air, there's a flutter of a flute, followed by an orchestra filling the planetarium with music. I don't know if it's coming from the speaker or my own head. And then he starts drifting away like a balloon. As I watch the distance grow between us, a sudden fear comes over me. The thought of losing him, too. I swallow my breath, following after him.

"Haru—please—come back here."

But he keeps rising as I stumble toward him, climbing over seats, trying to pull him down.

"Take my hand!" He laughs.

"*How are you even doing that—*"

Haru turns upside down, reaching down for me.

I step on a chair and grab him. The second we lock eyes, a strange sensation moves through me as gravity vanishes, lifting me into the air. The next thing I know, we're floating through a purple galaxy. I don't know how any of this is happening. Maybe Haru doesn't know, either. All that matters is we're together, moving through our own universe. But the scene doesn't last too long as gravity eventually lowers us again.

Haru catches me as we slowly drift down to our seats. He crosses one leg over the other and looks at me. I squeeze his hand as the lights come back on and the universe vanishes.

Seven

The sun is gone when we leave the museum. I don't realize how much time has passed until we're outside again. There are so many places I want to show him. But there's only enough time for one last surprise before the night ends. As the train drops us off at the next stop, I take Haru by the hand, leading him down the sidewalk.

"Close your eyes for a second," I say.

"Is this a surprise?"

"Just keep them closed until we're inside."

Willis Tower stands 108 stories tall, with an observation deck that overlooks all of Chicago. It's been a long time since I've been here. It's sort of a touristy spot, but you can't get these views anywhere else. I press the elevator button and tell Haru he can open his eyes.

A television screen turns on above the doors. As we start to ascend, an informational video plays, narrated by a woman's voice.

"Welcome to the Skydeck," the voice says. "You're on your way to the top of the tallest building in the western hemisphere. Along the way, watch as we pass by some of the tallest buildings, monuments, and structures in the world . . ." Images appear on screen, showing us our elevation in real time.

At the sixth floor, we pass the Great Sphinx of Giza in Egypt. At forty-nine, we reach the height of the Space Needle in Seattle. Ninety floors takes us to the height of the Eiffel Tower. As the number rises, my stomach clenches a little. I forgot how high this thing goes without stopping. Haru turns his head, squeezing my hand. As we pass a hundred floors, something strange happens. The television glitches, scrambling with gray-and-white static as the sound ends.

Then the screen goes black.

Haru and I look at each other, confused.

"I'm sure it's just a technical issue," I say.

The doors open on the hundred and third floor. I breathe a sigh of relief, making Haru chuckle a little. We step off the elevator and head through the exhibit hall. Usually, the observatory is crowded. But for some reason, there's only a few people here tonight, making the place seem larger than I remember. There's piano music playing in the background, growing louder as we get closer to the observation room. Maybe it's just me, but the song is strangely familiar. Has Jasmine played this for me before? I close my eyes for a second, trying to recognize the melody. I can almost see her fingers floating above the keys. But the music fades away before I can finally grasp it.

When I open my eyes, Haru isn't there beside me.

"Haru?"

Where did he go this time? I wander into the observation room in search of him. Floor-to-ceiling windows wrap around the entire floor, giving us panoramic views of Chicago. I've never been here at night before. The lights of the city shine like goldenrods, stretching toward the skyline.

And then I see him.

Haru stands on the other side of the room, hands deep in his pockets, staring out at the city. His silhouette is dark against the window. I make my way toward him, wondering what he's looking at.

Haru points at the buildings below. "You can see the Bean from here."

"*Really?*" I press my face against the glass.

He laughs. "I'm kidding."

"Oh . . . very funny."

Haru smiles, looking out the window again. This side of the observatory overlooks the marina, boats lining the water like little toys. "You should see the views we have in Tokyo. I could have shown you them last summer." Before I have a chance to respond, he turns abruptly. "What's over there?"

I follow his gaze. "Oh, that's the Skydeck. It's what I wanted to show you." It's an enclosed balcony, made entirely of glass, including the floor. "There's usually a long line, but looks like no one's there."

"We must be lucky."

I smile and grab his hand. The Skydeck hangs over the edge of the building. There's only enough room for a few people at a time. I step inside carefully, trying not to look down. But I can't help it. The city stretches out like an ocean beneath our shoes. As I'm staring through the floor, Haru clenches my hand again.

"You're scared," he says.

"What makes you think that?"

"I can feel you shaking."

I take in a deep breath as his fingers lace through mine. Usually, I'll close my eyes and pretend I'm on the ground again. But I feel safe with Haru around. Like nothing bad is going to happen. We take in the skyline, pointing out different buildings, the places we want to go to next. I bet the sunrise would be beautiful from here. I wish we could watch it together. It hits me that I haven't thought about college applications and everything that's been stressing me out. I like having someone to spend the day with. It makes me forget the rest of the world for a moment.

There's a silence as we watch a plane pass. Then Haru turns his head and says, "Can I ask you something?"

"Yeah," I say.

"Why did you leave that time?"

"What do you mean?"

"Last summer when you got on the train, I asked you to stay," Haru reminds me. "Why didn't you?"

I close my eyes as the memory comes back. *Paper wishes fluttering in trees, the two of us running through the train station, the doors closing between us.* Feels like yesterday when we lost each other on the platform. "I made a promise to my friend," I say, staring out through the glass again. "He was the reason I went on the trip."

"You two must be close," Haru says.

"Pretty close."

"Were you in love with him?"

The question catches me off guard. I'm not really sure how to answer it. I stare out the window and say, "Maybe I was. But it doesn't really matter anymore. He passed away almost a year ago."

"I'm sorry," Haru says. "It must have been painful, losing someone you loved."

"Yeah, it was. Especially when he never loved me back."

"How do you know that?"

"It's a long story. And it's not my favorite."

Haru nods. "You don't have to tell me."

We stare out at the view again. Then I turn back to Haru, something on my chest. "I wish I had gone with you, though," I tell him. "I think about it all the time. Sometimes, I have dreams about you. The two of us at the train station again. It all just happened so fast, you know? I really thought you were coming on with me. I didn't mean to lose the slip of paper . . ." My voice trails off.

"It's alright," Haru says, squeezing my hand. "None of that matters anymore. We're together now."

"A second chance," I say. "And I'm not leaving this time."

Haru smiles as he leans closer. There's a flutter in my stomach, maybe from the way he's looking at me. His eyes reflect the lights from the city like a mirror. I wonder if he can see them in mine, too. He moves his thumb gently across my cheek. For a second, I think he's about to kiss me. I shut my eyes, waiting for our lips to touch. But someone taps me on the shoulder from behind, interrupting the moment. I turn around. A girl around my age is standing with a group of friends.

"Do you mind if we come in next?"

I blink and notice other people behind her. The airy silence has shifted to a chattering crowd, like switching radio stations. That's when I realize Haru is gone. I step out of the Skydeck, scanning the room for him. There are more people in the observatory now, holding their phones in the air, taking photos of the view. I circle the floor several times, but there's no sign of him anywhere. But I keep looking. Then I take the elevator back down, hoping to find him waiting for me.

I stand outside the entrance, watching people go in and out of the doors. I wait for a long time, but Haru never appears. It's starting to get late. Maybe he isn't coming back tonight. I give it a few more minutes before I head home alone.

Eight

ELEVEN MONTHS AGO

Lights pulse outside the bars in Boystown. It's a Saturday night during senior year. Daniel and I are heading to some house party in the neighborhood. It's the gay side of Chicago, if the name didn't already give it away, known mostly for its nightlife. We're too young to get into the actual clubs and bars, which is why I don't come here often. But I've heard a few wild stories, making me nervous about tonight. The apartment building is located behind an arcade lounge and a 7-Eleven.

"*Shit.*"

Daniel pauses in the middle of the sidewalk, looking down at his phone. His face is illuminated by the orange streetlight, bringing out the freckles on his cheek. I'm hoping the party's been canceled so we can find something else to do together. Then Daniel turns abruptly, pointing across the street. "Alright, it's *this* way." He's never been good at giving directions. But miraculously we find the right building. It's an old greystone with a few beer bottles sticking out of the bushes. Daniel's phone keeps going off in his hand. I wonder who he's been talking to all night.

"Who are you texting?"

"Someone at the party," he says vaguely. "You don't know him."

I don't say anything. A second later, someone buzzes the door open. I follow Daniel into the building. The wallpaper is peeling from the corners, and there's a weird smell coming from the hallway.

I turn to Daniel. "Are you sure this is the right place?"

"I was here a few weeks ago."

Music carries through the stairwell, amplifying as we head to the second floor. I'm not sure what to expect from this party. At least I get to spend time with Daniel tonight. We don't have any classes together this semester, so I don't see him as much. This is the first time we've hung out in weeks. He's a somewhat bad texter, making him difficult to reach at times. Sometimes we'll go days without talking and then he'll show up to my house with food and a new movie to watch. I don't take it personally anymore, because I've grown used to it at this point.

We pass two guys making out against the wall and find the door marked 2G. It's where the music is coming from. Before either of us knock, Daniel turns to me and says, "Alright, let's go over this one more time. Remember, this is a *college* party. So don't mention where we go to school."

"What do I say if they ask?"

"Just tell them you're from out of town."

I nod. "Out of town. Got it."

What sounds like glass shatters inside, followed by laughter. I swallow down some nerves, feeling completely out of my element. I'm not very good at these social scenes, especially if I don't know anyone there. If it were up to me, we would be wandering around town instead, grabbing some fries, seeing a movie or something. Daniel is the extrovert, always surrounding himself with people. Sometimes I wish I could be more like him, making friends everywhere I go, holding conversations, going to a party without wanting to leave early. We're opposites this way. Maybe that's why he doesn't text me back sometimes.

I turn toward the door, bracing myself. But Daniel still hasn't knocked yet. That's when I notice him facing me. He stares at me for a moment. "You look . . . really good," he says. The compliment surprises me. He holds out a hand, feeling my collar between his fingers. "Is this shirt new?"

"Yeah . . . I just got it." It's a sky-blue polo, his favorite color. I was hoping he would notice it.

Then Daniel leans in, fixing my hair with his fingers. "Just a touch-up before we go in," he whispers. Standing this close, I get a whiff of his cologne. I press my lips together, feeling my cheeks go warm at his touch.

"Thanks," I breathe.

Daniel smiles as he leans back to inspect his work. "Perfect." Then he turns and knocks on the door. A few seconds later, some blond jock holding a red Solo cup opens the door. He takes one look at us and says, "You guys from DoorDash? Where the hell's the food?"

"We're friends with Leighton," Daniel says.

He eyes Daniel, as if deliberating something. Then he turns his head, looking me up and down. "Alright, you two can come in," he says, holding the door open.

I follow Daniel inside, music hitting my ears. I don't know how a room can fit so many guys at once. Everyone's in tank tops and shorts, illuminated under LED strips. The living room is so packed, you can barely make out a sofa. While it's nice being in a gay space for a change, it's hard not to notice we're the only nonwhite people in the room. I wonder what Daniel thinks about this. He's half Colombian, but he usually blends into a crowd because everyone assumes he's white, too.

The guy who opened the door brushes past us, winking at me before disappearing into a hallway. I give Daniel a nudge and whisper, "Did you just see that?"

"Relax, he's just into you."

"How would you know?"

"He let us in here, right?"

"And?"

"They don't just let everyone walk in," he explains. "They turn guys away all the time if they're not hot enough. It's a thing here."

"That's terrible." I shake my head, a bad taste in my mouth. Admittedly, part of me feels some sort of validation from the approval. But it's not something I would say out loud. I turn to Daniel again, noticing him scanning the room, looking for someone. "Who do you know here again?"

"My friend Leighton. It's his cousin's apartment."

"How do you know Leighton?"

"Another party," he says vaguely.

"Which party?"

Daniel doesn't hear the question. Or he's just ignoring me as he keeps looking around for his other friend. Then his eyes widen. "That's him right there—"

I turn my head as he appears through the crowd, wearing an orange polo. Dark blond hair and blue-green eyes, reminding me of the guy from the baseball team Daniel was into. I stand there as the two of them hug each other. To my relief, he's not much taller than me, maybe an inch and a half at most.

Daniel puts a hand on my shoulder. "This is my friend Eric," he says, giving me a squeeze. "Eric—this is Leighton."

Leighton holds out a hand. "Yeah, Daniel's mentioned you before."

He's never mentioned you. I'm not sure what to make of this. "Nice meeting you," I say, shaking his hand. It's a decent grip, but nothing to write home about. He has nice skin, though. I'm sure it's just the dim lighting in here.

"Leighton goes to North Side," Daniel says with an eye roll. They're our school's adversaries. "He's a senior, too. He's also into film."

"Photography," Leighton says. "But I've taken some film classes."

"You guys have a lot in common," Daniel says, nodding. "Leighton's also applying to Indiana."

Leighton smiles. "You're applying there, too? My brother goes there."

"He can help get me in," Daniel says.

"Imagine us all living together." Leighton shoves him playfully.

"That would be sick. But we'd get nothing done."

They both laugh. I say nothing. Daniel and I are supposed to be roommates together. Suddenly he's bringing in some guy I've never met before?

Leighton checks his phone. "I need to grab some ice for Vince," he says, looking at Daniel. "Wanna give me a hand? It's just down the street."

"Sure," Daniel says. Then he turns to me. "Mind waiting here for a sec?"

I give him a look. "You're leaving me?"

"Only for a few minutes."

"It's right down the corner," Leighton adds.

I glance at him and back at Daniel. We just got to the party. I don't know a single person here. But I don't want to appear annoying, especially in front of his other friend. "Yeah, I guess. I'll get us drinks while you're gone."

"We'll be right back," Daniel says. He offers a quick wave before following Leighton out the door.

I let out a breath, glancing around the room. Everyone is chatting in small circles, like their own lunch tables in a cafeteria. I feel like the new kid at school, looking around for an open seat. Maybe I'll get a drink to hold in my hand, so I'm not just standing here awkwardly. I snake through the living room until I find the bar by the window. I don't recognize half the bottles on the table. There's a punch bowl with fresh fruit inside. Are those kiwi slices? As I grab the ladle, someone speaks to me.

"I wouldn't drink that."

I glance up from the bowl. A guy with wispy brown hair stands on the other side of the table, holding a seltzer. He's wearing a gray shirt, and he's on the slim side, making him appear taller at first glance.

"Why not?" I ask.

"I just watched them make it," he says, gesturing at the punch bowl. "Don't let the fruits deceive you. I can't imagine it tasting any good."

"That's too bad." I drop the ladle and glance at the table again. There's a box of seltzer, which seems to be the drink of choice around here. But I've never heard of this brand before. "Any flavor recommendations?" I decide to ask.

"Watermelon is classic," he says.

"Oh, there's one left."

The guy smiles, holding out his drink. "Cheers."

"Cheers—"

Our cans clink and I take a sip. The watermelon hardly comes through, but at least it's carbonated, making it easier to go down. We stand there for a moment, nodding to the music.

"Do you go to Loyola?" he asks.

"No, I go to—" I pause, remembering what Daniel said. "I mean, I'm from out of town."

"Oh, where?"

Think of a random city. "Portland."

"Which one?"

I hesitate. "Maine?"

"That's where I'm from," he says brightly.

"I mean, the other one. *Oregon.*"

"Oh, I've never been there."

"Then *that's* where I'm from."

He gives me a look, as if trying to read me. "I'm Mark, by the way."

"I'm Eric."

"Are you here with someone?"

"My friend Daniel. He just went to grab some ice."

"How long are you in town?"

"Uh, a few days. But I'm back pretty often," I tell him. "I have family in Chicago."

"That's nice," he says, nodding. "Hopefully that means we'll keep running into each other." He smiles, taking a sip of his drink.

I can't tell if he's flirting or just being nice. It's usually safe to assume the latter. Beside us is the living room sofa, facing the television. Two guys are sitting there, playing Mario Kart. Eventually they both get up, leaving the controllers on the sofa.

"I was waiting for them to finish," Mark says, eyeing the television. He looks at me. "Down for a game of Mario Kart?"

"I'm not very good," I say.

He shrugs. "Neither am I. Can't even remember the last time I won."

"Then I'd love to."

Mark laughs. I could kill some time until Daniel comes back. We take a seat on the sofa, grabbing the controllers. I'm a little rustier than I expected, losing the first round pretty easily. Unfortunately, the second round doesn't go much better for me. Mark must have noticed my frustration because he starts slowing down for me.

I turn to him. "Are you letting me win?"

He smirks. "Maybe . . ."

"Don't do that."

"I wouldn't if the stakes were higher," he says.

"What kind of stakes?"

He pauses the game, thinking about it. "How about if I win, I get to kiss you," he says.

I glance at him, wondering if he's serious. "And what if I win?"

"You get to kiss me."

"Mark."

He chuckles again. "Alright. Let me think—" He looks around the room. "If you win, then I'll try the punch."

I glance at the punch bowl and back at him. "That seems fair."

We both smile as we start the next game. Maybe it's the stakes, but I'm a little better this time around. It's a close match, blue shells flying everywhere. But in the end, Mark passes me by a second, taking the win again. He sets down his controller as he turns to face me, one arm on the back of the sofa. I wasn't sure if he was serious about the kiss. When he runs a hand through my hair and leans in, I realize he is. For a moment, I think about letting him. But I turn my face away before his lips reach mine. "I'm sorry, Mark. But I can't."

He frowns. "Why not?"

"I came here with someone."

"Well, where is he?"

"He went to grab some ice."

"Wasn't that a while ago?"

I check the time on my phone. It's been forty minutes since he left. Shouldn't he have come back by now? I glance around the room, wondering if he's here. "You're right, I should probably go find him," I say, rising from the sofa. I feel bad leaving Mark like this, especially since he's been so nice. But I'm sure Daniel is looking for me, too.

The music changes to another Charlie XCX song as I wander through the crowd, searching for him. But I can't seem to find Daniel anywhere. I try calling his phone. When he doesn't answer, my heart rate picks up. I hope nothing happened while he was out. There's so many people in here, it's impossible to move. I wish they'd open a window, because I'm breaking a sweat. Maybe I should go out and look for him. It's supposed to be down the street, right? As I step out of the apartment, there he is.

Daniel's hands are around Leighton's neck, their lips pressed together. My stomach drops at the sight of them. Then he turns his head, noticing me. There's a brief silence as we both stand there, just looking at each other. Two bags of ice are stacked on the floor beside them. I don't know what to say except, "*Sorry—*"

"Eric . . ." Daniel starts.

But I walk off before he can finish his sentence. I don't know how to explain it, but my heart is about to rip out of me. Daniel calls my name again, but my legs move on autopilot. The next thing I know, I'm down the stairwell and bursting out the front door. Daniel clearly followed behind, because I hear his voice as the cold night air sends a shiver through me.

"Eric, where are you going?" he asks.

"Home."

"But we just got here."

I'm not sure what to say back. I just keep on walking, pretending I don't hear him. But Daniel refuses to stop following me.

"Can you stop walking for a minute?"

"You should go back to the party."

"Why are you upset?"

"I'm not. I just have to get home."

"It's only ten o'clock," Daniel says. "Your curfew isn't until midnight."

"I'm not feeling well."

I fold my arms as I cross the street. An hour ago, I couldn't wait to see him. Now I just need to get as far away from him as possible. Another country sounds nice right now. Daniel must sense something is wrong, because he follows me all the way to the train stop. "You should go back," I say again. "I'm sure your friends are waiting for you."

"Why are you acting weird?"

"I'm not acting weird."

"Is this about Leighton?"

I look away as a breeze blows leaves across the tracks. We're the only two standing on the platform.

Daniel sticks his hands into his pockets. "Look," he sighs. "If you really want to talk about this . . ."

"There's nothing to talk about."

"Then why are you so upset?"

I stare at the tracks, unsure what to say. The scene of them in the hallway keeps replaying in my head. Why has he never mentioned Leighton before? I know I shouldn't let this bother me, but I want to know. "How long have you been seeing him?"

"A few months."

"So you kept him a secret all this time," I say.

"I wasn't keeping him a secret," he says, shaking his head. "I just didn't know what it was. We were just friends at first. It wasn't a big deal."

"Then why didn't you mention him?"

"Because I wasn't sure how you would react, okay?"

A silence passes. I stare at the ground, feeling like a complete idiot for not seeing this coming. We've spent so much time together these past few years. What did it all mean to him? Did I misunderstand everything? I can't stop myself from asking this. "Why did you kiss me that night on the rooftop?"

Daniel lets out a breath and says, "I just wanted to. But it wasn't supposed to mean anything."

"Then why did you do it?"

"Maybe it was a mistake."

I wish I'd never asked the question. There's a terrible pain in my chest, making it hard to speak. "Yeah. Maybe it was," I say back.

I turn away, wanting to disappear from all of this. For some reason, Daniel stays with me on the platform. It feels like an infinity before a beam of light shines through the tunnel. I look at Daniel one last time, hoping he tells me none of this was true, that he's always been in love with me, too. But he doesn't say another word. So I step onto the train, letting the doors close behind me.

I wish I hadn't come here tonight. I wish I'd never even met him.

Nine

The marquee lights shine like a carousel. It's been a few days since I last saw Haru. I keep staring at the street, hoping he shows up again. Every bicycle that passes makes me think he's somewhere close. I've been visiting the places we went in hopes of running into him. I even stopped by the café we met at on the way here. But he wasn't there again. Now I'm just standing outside the theater before work. I wish there were a way for me to call him. Ask him when we're going to see each other again. *How much longer do I have to wait for you?*

I give it a few more minutes before I head inside. It's my first week working the box office. I'm dressed in the standard uniform, a white collared shirt with the same bow tie I wore from my last job. But instead of serving hors d'oeuvres, I'll be selling tickets from behind a glass window. I spent all of yesterday onboarding with the assistant manager, learning about their new show that's opening this week. It's called *Mr. and Mrs. Eloise,* about this couple who fake their wealth to climb up the social ladder in Manhattan.

The box office is located to the right of the lobby. Long marble counters are sectioned off by marble pillars. As I head through the back, I see two people around my age sitting at a table by the wall. A girl with blond streaks and a guy with jet-black hair and blue eye shadow are chatting, sharing a bag of M&Ms. I've been curious about who else would be working today. As I set my things under the counter, they both turn their heads in my direction. Their blank stares make me go still.

"*Are you supposed to be in here?*" Blue Eye Shadow asks.

For a second, I question it myself. "I think so. I just started this week." Some blinks are exchanged, but no one says anything. Maybe I should introduce myself first. "My name is Eric."

"Eric *who*?" he asks.

"Ly."

"Do you go to the Art Institute?" asks the girl, crossing her legs.

"No."

The guy tilts his head. "What's your sign?"

She smacks his arm. "Enough with your astrology."

"*If he's a Gemini, he can't work here—*"

"Of course he's not a Gemini. Look at those shoes."

"I can hear you guys," I say.

They whisper intently to each other. Then the girl rises from her chair, moving her hair behind her ear. "Sorry about that," she says, extending her hand. "I'm Alex. And the Jimin impersonator there is Simon."

"Nice to meet you guys," I say.

"Same," she says, still holding my hand. She looks at me for a moment. "You have a very symmetrical face. Has anyone told you that before?"

"I don't think so . . ."

"I'm a makeup artist, so I notice these things," she says, nodding thoughtfully. "The bow shape of your lips is a sign of loyalty."

"*You made that up,*" Simon scoffs.

Alex shoots him a look. "I've read articles on this."

"If you believe that stuff, I have some snake oil I'd *love* to sell you." Simon laughs, rising from his chair. He grabs a box from the floor and carries it to the counter. I notice the color of his nails. They're a midnight blue with flecks of gold, looking like stars.

"I really like your nails," I say.

Simon holds out his hand, admiring them himself. "Thank you. I painted them last night." Then the phone rings beside him. He sighs before answering it. "Hello?" A pause. "Yeah, can you hold?" Simon covers the receiver and turns his head. "Alex, where are those cast tickets?"

Alex shrugs. "How should I know?"

"Because you were in charge of them last week."

"No, *you* were in charge of them."

"Are you gaslighting me?"

A voice mumbles through the phone. Simon lifts his hand from the receiver and shouts, "*I said hold!*" He presses a button and slams the phone down.

I stand there for a moment, wondering what I'm supposed to do. "Can I help with anything?"

Simon gives me an exasperated look. "Listen, Eric. They don't pay me enough to train the new hires, okay? Besides, we have a pretty tight system running at the moment." The phone rings again. Simon picks it up and slams it right back down.

Alex sits on the counter. "We do need someone to work the box tonight," she says.

"What happened to the old man?" Simon asks.

"He sprained an ankle."

"*Another one?* How many ankles does he have left?" Simon shakes his head, then turns back to me. "Alright, Eric. Looks like your services are needed. Congratulations, you'll be staffing the box tonight."

"You mean, the one outside?" I glance at the entrance. There's a little box office window that sits between the glass doors.

"Technically, it's still inside," Alex says, grabbing another bag of M&Ms.

"It's not that bad out there," Simon says, waving away all concerns. "And the glass is bulletproof, so you'll be fine."

I blink at him. "Is that something to worry about?"

"There've been *incidents,*" Alex whispers.

"*You'll be fine,*" Simon repeats. He grabs the cashbox from the counter and hands it to me. "Here—I'm going to assume you know what to do with this. Remember, no public bathrooms! And if you get any weird questions, just tell them you don't speak English."

"How long do I have to be out there?"

"We're supposed to take turns," Alex says with a shrug. "So, it won't be all night."

"Should I come back after—" I start.

"No, we'll get *you*," Simon says, patting me once on the shoulder.

I glance at the door and back at him. I was looking forward to working inside, enjoying the view of the lobby. "I guess I'll head out there then."

"Have fun," Simon says with a quick wave.

I stand there a moment longer, hoping for more instruction. But they both turn back to the counter, chatting casually as if I'm already gone. So I grab my things and leave through the door.

The box sits between the entrance doors, in the awkward space that keeps leaves from blowing into the lobby. It's a small shrine of glass, made to fit a single person, like those fortune teller machines at a carnival. I set my things down and take a seat in the chair. There's still plenty of daylight out, giving me a clear view of the street. Crowds pass back and forth, snapping pictures under the marquee lights. There's not much to do but sit like an old guard, giving directions to strangers here and there. The hours tick by slowly. I keep checking the time, wondering when the others will come get me.

There's a broken desk bell in the drawer. I've been tapping away at it to pass the time. I can't seem to get it working again. The dull sound of metal fills me with a strange emptiness. What are Simon and Alex doing? It's been a few hours with no word from them. By the time daylight fades to a night sky, no one has taken my place.

People start trickling out the doors, signaling the end of

the shift. I guess that means it's time to close up. I'm still figuring out which key works with the lock. That's when I notice them through the window. Simon and Alex are leaving together, already changed out of their work clothes. They're loud with conversation as they walk right past me. I almost call their names, in case they forgot I'm in here. But they don't even turn their heads as they vanish through the doors.

I can't help taking that personally. So much for making friends on the job. I let out a breath as I reach down for my bag. A shadow moves over me, accompanied by the sound of a bell as someone approaches the window.

Isn't the desk bell broken?

I lift my head up. Haru stands at the window, smiling back at me. He's wearing a light gray jacket over a white shirt. I shout through the glass as I drop my bag, "*Haru? Oh my god. You're here!*"

"Surprise," he says with a smirk.

"*When did you get—*" I pause, realizing there's a better way to do this. "Wait right there—" I turn around, stumbling as I open the door. I take a quick look around before I rush to Haru, throwing my arms around him. "I'm so glad to see you!"

"I would have come sooner had I known you missed me this much," he says.

"Where have you been?" I ask. "You left the Skydeck without saying anything. I didn't know if you were coming back."

"Sorry for taking off," he says, moving the hair out of my face. "I didn't mean to keep you waiting."

I breathe a sigh of relief. "It's alright. As long as you're back now."

Haru smiles, moving his hand along my shoulder. "Of course I am." Then he turns his head, glancing back at the box office. "So this is where they have you working?"

"Yeah. For tonight, anyway."

"Mind if I take a look?"

"Sure."

Haru opens the box office door and sticks his head inside. "It's very . . . small," he says, looking around. "Small but charming."

"The glass is bulletproof."

Haru gives me a look. "Bulletproof?"

"Theater can be rough," I say, narrowing my eyes. "I'm really putting my life on the line out here."

Haru cracks a smile. "Well, glad to know you're protected." Then he glances at the floor, noticing my bag. "I see you brought your camera with you. What are you working on?"

"Nothing really." I let out a breath, picking it up from the floor. "I actually haven't touched it in a while. But there's this film scholarship I'm applying to. You have to submit a short film." I leave out the part where I told Jasmine I already made it to the next round.

"What's it about?"

"I haven't decided yet," I admit. "But I have a few weeks to figure it out. I was thinking about getting shots of the theater. But I can do that another time."

Haru shrugs. "Why not tonight?"

"Because you're here. I figure you want to see more of the city."

"We have plenty of time," Haru says. "Besides, you promised to show me the theater."

I consider this. "I guess I can give you a tour."

The lobby is practically empty, making it a good time to show him around. I could get a few quick shots while we're inside. I glance around for security guards. Then I lead Haru through the entrance doors, making a sweeping motion with my hand. "Welcome to the Chicago Theater," I say in my tour-guide voice. "This is the grand lobby, modeled after Versailles."

Haru looks around, appearing impressed by the architecture. "Imagine working in here, instead of that little box."

"Don't remind me." I shake my head and sigh. "Anyway, this is the main box office. And on the opposite side is where you get refreshments." I continue walking, motioning him to follow along. "See the grand staircase behind me? It's a replica from the *Titanic*. I learned about it during training."

"That's a bit dark, don't you think?" Haru asks me. "Modeling something after a tragedy."

"Some of the best love stories are born out of tragedies," I say.

Haru runs a hand along the wooden rail. Then he continues up the staircase. "And what's up here?"

"The mezzanine," I say, following him upstairs. The marble balustrade wraps around the entire floor, giving us a full view of the main floor. It feels like we're standing on a palace balcony, glancing down at an empty ballroom. This would be a great place for a scene in a movie. A princess observing her guests from above, wondering who her prince is.

While Haru is looking around, admiring the paintings on the walls, I take out my camera. I play with the settings, adjusting a few things before I hit record. The lights are dimmed, offering a moodier effect. Someone is wiping down the counter, giving some life to the shot. I move around the mezzanine, trying out different angles, getting a shot of the stained-glass windows. One of the sconces is flickering, adding drama to whatever this will be. This is just practice, getting me back into the swing of things. I only film a few minutes' worth of video before putting the camera away. That's when I notice I'm alone.

"Haru?"

I'm about to call out again when I hear his voice.

"Over here."

It doesn't sound like he wandered too far. I follow his voice, hoping I don't run into anyone. Thankfully, no one else is around when I find him. He's standing beside the entrance to the theater.

"They left it open for us," he says.

"What do you mean?"

Haru smiles as he turns the knob, pushing open the door. Looks like they didn't lock it properly.

"We can't go in there," I whisper.

"But you promised a tour . . ."

"I'm gonna get in trouble."

"You won't get in trouble."

I fold my arms. "And what makes you so sure?"

He smirks. "As long as no one finds out. We can do anything."

We can do anything. Someone else said that to me before. In this very theater, right? Then my mind flashes to Jasmine. The two of us running up the staircase as children, hoping to sneak into the show. Too bad we never made it inside. "Alright, a quick look," I say. "But we have to make it fast, okay?"

Haru holds opens the door, letting me go in first. It's very dark inside, making it hard to see the seats in front of me. A single beam of light shines from the stage.

"How do we get down there?" Haru asks.

"There's probably a staircase."

It takes a second to find it, but eventually we reach the lower level. It's strange being alone in an auditorium, surrounded by rows of empty seats. I wonder what it's like to see a show in here. As I'm looking around in the dark, I realize Haru isn't beside me. I almost panic before I see him on the stage.

"What are you doing up there?"

"I want to look around," he says.

"You're gonna get me in trouble—"

Haru ignores this as he wanders behind a set piece. I glance at the steps at the side of the stage. Then I make my way up to get him. There's enough light to make out the set of an apartment. Two glass doors are open to a faux balcony, overlooking a backdrop of Manhattan. There's a grand piano at the center of the stage. I wander toward it, wondering if it's real. It's been a while since I sat down at the piano. I run a hand along the keys.

"You play the piano?"

Haru appears at my side, startling me a little.

I shake my head. "No, I don't," I say. "My sister does, though. She taught me a few songs when we were younger. But I doubt I remember any of them."

Haru touches my back. "You should try to play one," he says.

I look at him and back at the piano. Then I set my camera down and take a seat on the bench. My fingers rest on the keys as I try to remember the chords. Maybe if I start playing, something will come to me. I close my eyes, letting my fingers move on their own. The sound of the keys rings through me, sweeping me away to another memory . . .

I open my eyes to Jasmine's bedroom. I am eleven years old, sitting at her piano as sunlight streams through the window. She's sitting right beside me, trying to teach me a new song.

"Keep your fingers like this," she says, positioning them for me. She makes it look so easy when she plays, her movements as fluid as water. But I can't seem to follow her, no matter how many times I watch her do it. "Try it again," she says patiently.

We've been at this for hours. But I haven't gotten any better. Finally, I pull my hands back in defeat. "I don't want to do this anymore," I groan.

"You're doing fine, Eric. It just takes some practice, that's all."

"I don't want to practice."

"Then you'll never learn how to play."

"I don't care anymore." I rise to leave, but Jasmine puts a hand on my shoulder, sitting me down again.

"You can't give up like that," she says. "Do you think I learned to play overnight? Just give it one more shot. We'll try something different this time. Here—" She positions my hand again, keeping hers on the piano, too. "You play the left-hand part, and I'll play the right."

"Fine . . ."

It's a little confusing at first, trying to keep in time with each other. But once I find the rhythm, it becomes easier to follow along. Since there's only one hand to focus on, I don't stumble quite as much. I hold the low notes, grounding the song, as Jasmine's fingers dance across the keys to the melody. It's like this intricate dance between us, filling the room with our music.

The door opens behind us as Mom comes in with a laundry basket. She looks at me and says, "Đừng làm phiền chị con nữa." *Stop bothering your sister.* As she walks over to get me, she notices my hands. "You colored your nails?" she says. "Ai cho con sơn móng tay vậy?" *Who let you do that?*

I fold my arms, hiding my hands from her. I painted them last night with Jasmine's nail polish while we were watching a movie. I didn't think it was a big deal. But Mom grabs my hand, taking a closer look at them.

"Who let you do that?" she repeats.

"I painted them," Jasmine lies.

"You shouldn't let him do that."

"It's not a big deal," Jasmine says back. "I know a lot of boys that do it, too. And Eric is helping me practice, okay?"

Mom stares at my hand, shaking her head. "Đừng làm điều này nữa," she says. *Don't do this anymore.* Then she leaves the room, closing the door behind her.

Jasmine leans into me. "It's okay," she whispers. "I like your nails like that."

I don't say anything. I just lower my head, hiding my hands in my lap.

After some silence, Jasmine asks, "Do you want to keep practicing?" But I don't answer her. She doesn't push me on this. Instead, she smiles and says, "How about I play you something instead, okay?" Her hands return to the piano. I close my eyes for a moment, listening to her song until . . .

"You shouldn't be in here."

A deep voice pulls me back from the memory. I look up from the piano as Jasmine vanishes, along with the music. I blink a few times and find myself in the auditorium again. Someone is standing in one of the aisles. But it's too dark to make out a face.

"I said you can't be in here," the voice repeats.

I rise immediately, nearly knocking over the bench. "I'm sorry, I was just looking around." I stumble through the dark, making my way down the stage. That's when I notice Haru is gone. I glance behind me, wondering where he could be. But I can't stay to look for him. The guy is still watching me from the side door of the theater. I can't make out who he is from the silhouette. Hopefully he doesn't recognize me, either. I hurry down the aisle, leaving through the double doors, hoping I don't get in trouble and lose my job on the first day.

Ten

Haru is waiting for me outside. The marquee lights are bright against his face, bringing out the warmth in his skin. For a second, I thought he might have disappeared again. The moment I break through the doors, he smiles at me. Then he glances at my hand.

"Where's your camera?"

I touch my shoulder, sensing the strap is gone. "*Shoot,* I left it inside." It must be somewhere in the theater.

"Let's go get it," Haru says, turning to the door.

I grab his arm. "That guy's still in there!"

"I'm not scared of him."

"No, it's cool," I say, pulling him back. "I can just get it tomorrow."

"Are you sure?"

"Yeah, it's no big deal." I hate the thought of losing my camera. But we only have so much time left tonight. I don't want to waste it looking around the theater. I'm sure it will still be there tomorrow. "There's somewhere I want to take you," I say. "It's only a few blocks from here."

"Another surprise for me?"

Haru smiles as I grab his hand, pulling him across the street.

There's a mile-long waterfront that cuts through the city. High-rises stretch from both sides of the water, offering gorgeous views of the Chicago River. It's a public space filled with cafés, bars, and wineries, with art pieces displayed along the way. People are sitting under patio umbrellas, having dinner along the water. It's a nice place to bring someone for a walk. I'm keeping Haru close to my side tonight. I don't want him to disappear out of the blue again.

Haru looks at me. "So you bring all your dates here?"

"Who said this was a date," I say playfully.

"My mistake . . ." He looks away, pretending to be hurt. We both chuckle at this. Then he glances at the water. "How long does this go?"

"A little over a mile," I say, keeping my eyes on him. "There are a few restaurants here, too, if you want to sit down."

"I'm enjoying our walk."

"Me, too."

We smile at each other. There's a slight chill in the air, but no winds tonight. A river vessel passes along the water. You can see people dining through the wraparound windows. Haru stares at it and says, "There must be a hundred people in there."

"It's one of those dinner cruises."

"I wonder what they're having."

"I wouldn't know. I've never even been on a boat."

"Really?"

We lean against the railing. Lights from the high-rises swirl in the river like an oil painting. Jasmine and I used to come here all the time, watching boats pass by. "I've always wanted to go on one of those boat tours. Just once, you know? I heard it's a lot of fun, seeing everything from the water. My mom would never let us do it. My sister said she'd go with me someday. We never did, though."

"How come?"

"She's really busy," I tell him. "And she doesn't live in the city anymore. But it's not a big deal."

I turn away from the railing and continue walking. But Haru lingers behind a little. "Well, look at that," he says. "Someone left a boat for us."

I turn around. A small wooden boat is tied along the dock. Was that there a moment ago?

"Where did that come from?" I ask.

"You walked right past it," Haru says. He looks up and down the path, as if to see if the coast is clear. "Do you think we could take it for a ride?"

"Of course not."

"I'm sure they won't mind us borrowing it."

Before I have a chance to object, Haru steps inside the boat. Then he turns around, holding out his hand to me. "Plenty of room for two."

"We can't just take someone's boat!"

Haru smirks. "You're not making me go alone, are you?"

"We could get in so much trouble!"

"We'll be back before anyone notices. I promise."

I press my lips together, glancing around the dock. There's no one else around but us. I stare at Haru for a long moment.

The way he looks at me makes it hard to say no. I breathe out a sigh of defeat. "Alright, but not too long, okay?"

Haru takes my hand, helping me into the boat. Then he unties the rope, letting the currents slowly pull us away. I take a seat, trying not to be nervous. I mean, what if someone catches us? For some reason, Haru seems completely unfazed. He picks up a paddle, dipping it into the water.

"I can't believe we're doing this," I say.

"You said you've never been on a boat before."

"I didn't say I wanted to steal one!"

"We're only *borrowing* it," he reminds me, giving me a look. "And you're ruining the moment."

"Sorry." I sit up straight, folding my hands in my lap. The streetlamps look like floating orbs in the distance, casting ghostly lights along the river.

"I told you no one would notice," Haru says, keeping the paddle moving. "Bet you wish you had your camera."

"And document our crime? I don't think so." I lean to the side of the boat, dipping a finger in the water. "I have enough shots of Chicago already. More than I even know what to do with."

"You could make a documentary," Haru suggests.

"About what?"

"Your life here in the city."

"My life isn't interesting enough to be a documentary," I say. "A film about me would more likely be a tragedy."

"Some of the best love stories are tragedies, remember?"

I can't help smiling. As we continue down the river, I take

in the view of the high-rises, the squares of light from their windows. It really is a beautiful night for a boat ride. I'm glad I get to experience this with Haru. I've lived in Chicago my entire life. But it sort of feels like I'm seeing it for the first time. Maybe the view changes when you're looking at it with someone else. I start to think about the film I need to work on. "Maybe a documentary isn't the worst idea. Something like a love letter to the city. I'm sure I'll appreciate it when I'm gone."

"Where are you going?"

"I don't know yet."

"New York City?" Haru asks, raising his brow at me. "I saw it written down in your notebook."

"You went through my stuff?"

"I needed paper to make your gift."

I laugh a little. "It's only a thought," I say, staring out at the water again. "I'm not sure that's in the cards anymore. It becomes a lot harder to get in when you take a year off for no reason."

"But there was a reason," Haru says.

"I still wish I hadn't," I admit to him. I think back to last spring, when everyone started receiving their college acceptance letters. "Daniel and I were supposed to go together, you know? I didn't like the thought of going without him. I never even opened the acceptance letter. He would probably be disappointed if he knew."

"I'm sure he'd understand."

"Can I tell you something else?" I look at Haru. "I never

wanted to go to the University of Indiana. They don't even have a real film program."

Haru blinks at me. "Then why apply?"

"Because Daniel was going. I didn't really care about anything else."

Haru leans back in thought. A breeze ruffles his hair as he nods at me. "I don't blame you," he says.

"You don't think it was stupid of me?"

"That would just make me a hypocrite."

"How so?"

"Because I came all the way here for you," he says, looking at me. "I had no idea if you would remember me. All I knew was I wanted to see you again."

"Of course I remembered. I wanted to see you, too."

Haru places his hand on my knee. "I wish I had gone looking sooner."

"That's okay," I say, feeling the warmth of his skin. "It just makes this moment more special."

We both smile.

As we continue along the river, Haru suddenly leans forward, making me go still. When his hand softly grazes my cheek, I close my eyes for a moment. That's when I feel the first sprinkle of rain. Haru must have felt it, too, because he leans back again, staring at the sky. I probably should have checked the weather tonight. Because the next thing we know, it's pouring.

I grab the other paddle, helping us get back faster. We're completely drenched when we finally reach the dock. Haru climbs out first and holds out his hand for me. Then we run under a bridge for cover, hands over our heads. Rain pours down in sheets, walling us in from the outside. We'll have to wait it out for a while. It's not so bad, though, feeling separated from the rest of the world. I'm secretly happy that we're stuck here together.

But I get a strange feeling Haru might disappear again. I put my arms around him, holding him close to me. "Don't leave yet, okay? I don't want to be alone."

"Who said I was leaving?"

"Just promise me."

"I'm not going anywhere," he says. "Otherwise, I couldn't do this."

Haru lifts my chin with his hand, taking me by surprise. Then he leans in and says, "In case I disappear . . ."

The next thing I know, his lips press against mine. I feel a warmth moving between us like electricity. I close my eyes, ignoring the vibrations of passing cars from the bridge overhead. The rain continues to pour around us. But all I can hear is the sound of my heart beating in my chest. For a moment, there's no one else in the world except us. *You and I are the only thing that's real.*

The rain has calmed by the time we get home. I grab some clothes from the closet and toss them to Haru. I insisted that he stay the night again. As I'm changing out of my shirt, Haru glances at my desk, noticing the paper things he's left me. He doesn't say anything about them. He just smiles to himself as he walks around the room. There's a little Bluetooth speaker on my dresser. Haru picks it up and asks, "Is this for your music?"

"Yeah, it's my—"

Haru presses a button, turning it on. I don't realize it's connected to my phone until music starts to play. *What was the last song I was listening to?* Before I can grab my phone, Brandy's wistful voice fills the room, singing:

Have you ever loved somebody so much,
it makes you cry

I take the speaker from Haru and shut it off immediately. The room goes silent again. "Sorry. I don't want to wake my parents up." "Have You Ever" is the best unrequited love song there is, and no one can convince me otherwise. But it's meant for late nights when you're alone, looking to feel something.

I put the speaker away and check the time. It's almost midnight. Haru still hasn't changed out of his clothes. His damp shirt clings to his skin, showing the lines of his chest. "Do you want a different shirt or something?"

"It's actually warm in here." Haru pulls his shirt over his head. Then he looks at me again. "I hope it's okay that I sleep like this."

I take him in for a second. His skin glistens from being in the rain. Then I pull my eyes away. "Uh, sure," I stutter.

We dry ourselves off and climb into bed. Haru takes the

right side again. Even though I'm feeling tired, I don't want to fall asleep yet. I lie on my side, keeping a close watch on him.

Haru looks at me. "What is it?"

"I'm just surprised you're still here."

"What do you mean? We came back together."

"No, I mean, I thought you would have disappeared by now."

Haru moves the hair out of my face and says, "I told you, I'm not going anywhere."

"What if I fall asleep? Will you be there when I wake up?"

"I'm not sure."

"How come?"

Haru thinks about this. "I don't really control when I go. But I wish I could."

I press my lips together. "Then I won't. I'll just stay up all night."

Haru kisses my hand. "I'll stay up with you then."

I lean in closer to him. Rain lightly patters against the window as we lie awake together. Neither of us says much. We just stare at each other, making sure the other doesn't fall asleep. But it gets harder and harder to keep my eyes open. The second I start to drift off, I squeeze Haru's hand, making sure he's there.

"I'm here," he whispers.

"Just making sure."

"You seem very tired."

"Not at all. Just resting my eyes."

"Whatever you say."

"In case I fall asleep, though. Can I ask you something?"

"Anything."

"If you disappear again, how will I find you?"

Haru kisses my forehead and says, "Don't worry about that. Just know that I'll find you. I promise."

I hope he keeps this promise. Because I would spend the rest of my life looking for him. I don't say anything after this. I'm too tired to keep my eyes open any longer. It's not until some light creeps through the blinds that I realize the sun is rising. I squeeze Haru's hand one last time before I allow myself to drift off. The last thing I remember is feeling his fingers slipping through mine before everything goes black.

Eleven

The sound of a piano fills my head, pulling me into a dream. Light filters through a dusty window, revealing the empty tables of Uncle Wong's Palace. I'm sitting at a booth in the corner, wondering where this music is coming from. I look around the restaurant, my vision a little blurry. Someone reaches across the table, touching my hand.

"I have to go soon."

Jasmine's voice echoes through me. I blink until her face comes into focus. She's wearing the jacket she borrowed; her long hair is tucked behind one ear. The pineapple fried rice sits on the table, untouched. It's her favorite dish. We order it every time we're here.

"Eric, did you hear me?"

I blink at her. "What was that?"

"I said I'm leaving."

My mind goes back to our last conversation. She's moving out of the country to tour with her band. But I don't want her leaving me behind this time. "Why can't you just come back home?" I ask.

Jasmine shakes her head. "I have to go."

"No, you don't."

"I'm sorry."

Sunlight fades from the window, painting a shadow along the table. The piano music keeps playing. But I still don't know where it's coming from. Jasmine glances outside, a distant look in her eyes. Then she rises from the booth.

I grab her hand. "*Jaz, wait—*"

"Please don't make this harder."

"*Then don't go.*"

"I have to—"

Jasmine pulls her hand away and heads off. I get up from the booth, following after her. For some reason, I can't seem to catch up. The floor keeps stretching between us, making it impossible to reach the door. The faster I run, the farther she moves away. The piano music continues, drowning out my voice as I call after her. It's the same song I've been hearing everywhere. Why does it follow me in my dreams?

I keep calling after her, hoping she turns around. But she vanishes through the door without even saying goodbye. The moment I finally touch the door handle, the music fades as I'm swallowed by complete darkness.

I wake up in bed alone again. My eyes slowly adjust to the light as I take in the emptiness of the room. For some reason, I thought things might be different this time. That I might wake up with his head against me, our arms tangled together. But all that's left is the scent of him, along with the memory of the night before. I run my hand over the sheet, wishing he was still here. Maybe it's my fault for falling asleep. At least he promised he'll find me again. I keep his words with me as I push myself out of bed.

I grab my phone from the side table and check the time. There's a new message from Jasmine. I haven't heard from her in a while. Maybe she had a dream about me, too. We've always been somehow connected this way. I'm sure she knows I'm a little mad at her.

> Haven't heard from you in a few
> days. Hope everything's alright
> Will try to see you before I leave

I send her a quick response and stretch my arms. That's when I notice something on my desk. I get out of bed to pick it up. It's a paper rose, folded from light blue paper. I turn it in the window light. Haru left this here for me. Another reminder that we'll see each other again. I stare at it for a long moment. *I hope I don't have to wait too long.*

I take a shower and head to the kitchen. I usually skip breakfast in the morning. But there's this emptiness in my stomach. I decide to fill it with a bowl of cereal. As I head to the kitchen, I find Dad sitting at the dinner table, mail spread out in front of him. He usually works weekday mornings, so I'm surprised he's home.

Dad looks up at me. "Going to work?"

"In a little bit."

He nods.

I open the fridge. There's a plastic bowl, wrapped with foil.

"Your mom made miến," he says, leaning back in his chair.

"I'll have some later."

"Take it with you."

Our family doesn't often make breakfast in the morning. It's usually leftovers from dinner the night before.

I grab a bowl from the dishwasher.

"Mom told me about your new job," Dad says, sipping his coffee.

I've been meaning to update him on things. We haven't spoken much these last few weeks. Especially since I've been coming home pretty late. "Yeah, it just started. But I already like it better than my last one."

"Good."

I pour some milk into my bowl and head to the table. Dad is going through some papers, his forehead furrowed. It's easy to tell when he's frustrated with something. I glance over his shoulder, wondering what he's reading.

"What are you working on?"

"Insurance," he says. He points to a section in the letter. "But I don't know what it means."

"Do you want me to read it?"

Dad looks at the table, thinking. Although he's lived in the US for more than twenty years, his English isn't perfect. He speaks mostly Vietnamese around the house, especially with our family. "If you have time," he says.

I take a seat next to him and look over the letter. The language is a bit jarring, some legal words even I don't understand. Jasmine has always been the one to translate these things. Phone bills, tax forms, etc. It's one of those moments her absence is really noticed. Sometimes I wish my parents would ask for my help more often. I have this feeling they don't want to bother me. That's probably my fault for keeping to myself these days. But I hate knowing they're struggling alone. We spend the rest of the morning reading through letters, filling out paperwork together. It's a good feeling to be able to help out once in a while.

I miss the train on my way to the theater. The paperwork took longer than I expected, but thankfully I'm only twenty minutes late. I nearly slip on the marble as I hurry through the lobby to clock in. Simon and Alex are in the main box office, sitting casually on the counter, sharing a bag of Twizzlers. They're turned toward each other, giggling about something. The moment they hear me, Simon straightens up, crossing one leg over the other. "Well, look who's fashionably late today," he says. "Another homeless guy jump on the tracks on your way here?"

Alex smacks his arm. "That's not funny, Simon."

"Who said I was making a joke?"

"Sorry," I say breathlessly, setting my things on the floor. "I was helping my dad with something and forgot—"

Simon waves it off. "*Relax,* nobody cares you're late."

"Oh."

"Did you lose something?" Alex asks me.

"What do you mean?"

Alex reaches behind her, sliding something into view. "The house manager found this in the theater."

"*My camera!*"

I must have left it on the piano last night.

"It had your name on the strap," she says, handing it to me.

"You're lucky it didn't end up on Marketplace," Simon says, taking a swig from his water bottle. "Almost traded it for concert tickets."

"Thanks for keeping it for me," I say. I'm surprised they're even talking to me today. Especially after how they treated me last night.

"It's the least we could do," Alex says, a note of guilt in her voice. "We felt bad for making you work out there all night. It was Simon's idea."

Simon shoots her a look. "*Don't throw me under the bus.*"

I shrug it off. "Honestly, don't worry about it."

Alex shakes her head. "But you won't have to tonight. The old man is back. And he *always* works the box."

"We think he's living out some childhood memory," Simon says with an unbothered shrug. "That or dementia. Either way, who's complaining?"

I glance around the box office. Music is playing from someone's cell phone. It's a K-pop song I don't recognize. I notice a white box on the counter. Inside is a green-and-blue sheet cake, two forks sticking out of it like chopsticks. "That's a really big cake," I say.

Alex smiles. "Do you want some? There's strawberries inside."

Simon leans back, grabbing a fork. "Please *spare* us the calories," he says.

"Yeah, I'd love some."

Alex hands me a plastic spoon. "We're out of forks. And paper plates."

Simon waves it off. "Bad for the environment anyway."

"Where did you guys get it?" I ask.

"Oh . . . you know, that one bakery around the block," Simon says vaguely.

I take a closer look at the cake, reading the cursive writing. "Why does it say *Congratulations, cast and crew*?"

Simon and Alex exchange looks. A silence passes. Then Simon throws up his hands. "Alright, you caught us. We stole it. You solved the murder. Are you happy, Sherlock?"

"They delivered it here by mistake," Alex says, taking another bite. "It happens every once in a while."

Simon narrows his eyes. "You better not tell on us. Or we'll *ruin* you," he says in a low voice.

"Of course I won't." I laugh. I lean forward, taking a bite to prove myself. The frosting is a rich buttercream. "That's really good. You sure no one will know it's missing?"

Simon offers a sly smile. "Sweet, sweet Eric. You have so much to learn around here." He pulls open a drawer, revealing two bottles of champagne. "These are from opening night. What's left from it, anyway."

I pick up one of the bottles. "Veuve Clicquot? We served this at my old job. It's pretty expensive." To be honest, I always thought about sneaking home a bottle. But I chickened out at the end of the night. "What other perks does this job have?"

"First of all, I *love* your energy right now," Simon says, smiling proudly. "And second, there's actually something a little more *interesting*." He glances at Alex. "It's what we were discussing before you came in."

Alex leans forward and whispers, "There's a cast party tonight. At some fancy apartment in River North."

"You guys got invited?"

Simon laughs. "Of course not! But we're going anyway."

"They don't invite us to those things," Alex says.

I take another bite of the cake. "How did you guys hear about it?"

"I have my ways of obtaining information," Simon says, pressing his fingers together like a movie villain.

Alex rolls her eyes. "He's hooking up with one of the chorus boys."

Simon shoots another look. "I told you, he's an *understudy*!"

"You should come with us," Alex suggests.

"To the party?"

Simon looks at me. "Do you have something better to do?"

I think about this. I was hoping to see Haru again tonight. I was planning on waiting outside after work in case he showed up. There's no way I can explain that to them. But I don't remember the last time I was invited to a party. Maybe I should go. "No, I don't have other plans."

"Then you have to go," Alex insists.

"As long as you have something to wear," Simon says.

I glance down at my clothes. "What's wrong with what I have on now?"

Alex's eyes widen. "Eric, *no*. Your work uniform?"

I shrug. "I mean, if I take off my vest, who will notice?"

"*I'll notice*," Simon says, appearing sick. He shakes his head at me. "If you're coming with us, you'll need to change into something else."

"I didn't bring anything else," I say.

Simon and Alex look at each other. Something must have been communicated telepathically, because they nod in unison. Simon clasps his hands together and says, "Alright, here's the plan. We're taking you shopping after work. There's a few department stores we can hit on the way there."

Alex's eyes light up. "Yes, a makeover."

I hold up my hands. "You guys really don't have to—"

"Eric, *hush* . . ." Simon holds a finger to my lips to silence me. "We've already made the decision for you."

Before I can say something, the phone rings. Simon stares at it, groaning. Then he picks up the receiver and says, "Who is it and what do you want?"

"It's gonna be so much fun," Alex whispers to me. She grabs my arm and walks me to the counter. "I'll show you the dress I'm wearing."

We spend the next hour on Instagram, looking up different styles for me. Alex says a warm spring palette would best complement my skin tone. During our lunch break, Simon introduces me to the girls at the concession stand for free snacks. "Nothing with too much sugar or we'll get bloated," he says to me.

Our shift ends around eight thirty. The old man agrees to close up, letting us head out early. We find a department store a few blocks from the theater and go shopping. Simon and Alex lead me straight to the men's section, pulling different looks together. I try on a few jackets in different colors. There's a dark suede bomber that fits me particularly well. Alex says it accentuates my shoulders. When I check the price tag, I nearly choke. I turn to the others to let them know. "This is almost three hundred dollars. I can't afford this."

"Relax," Alex says, handing me a belt to try on. "We're not exactly buying anything."

I lower my voice. "Are we *stealing* it?"

Simon smacks my arm. "Don't be ridiculous. You want us to go to jail? We're simply trying things out and taking them back."

"What do you mean?"

"You see, this place has an *amazing* return policy," he explains. "You have sixty days to basically try anything. Just don't remove the tags."

I look at him. "Is this . . . legal?"

Simon rolls his eyes. "Eric, people are committing *murders* out there. Is the world going to end if you borrow a jacket?"

"And if you really like it, you can always keep it," Alex adds.

I glance at myself in the mirror. "I guess that's true."

A moment later, a woman rings me up at the counter. I keep the jacket on, placing the receipt in my wallet. We stop by the beauty department where Simon grabs a curling wand, giving my hair some waves like his. Alex spritzes me twice with cologne on our way out. "I feel like a fairy godmother," she says, taking my arm. "Now make a wish."

I look at her. "What kind of wish?"

"I don't know. Something you want to happen tonight."

I think about this during the train ride over.

I wish for something special to happen tonight.

Twelve

The Red Line takes us to River North, a wealthier neighborhood of Chicago. Simon has his app open, leading us toward a high-rise building near the water. His sequined blue jacket sparkles in the traffic lights. Alex is wearing a backless white cocktail dress with pearl earrings. There's a doorman at the entrance of the building. "*Act like you live here,*" Simon whispers over his shoulder. Thankfully, no one stops us as we head through the lobby. As we step into the elevator, Simon presses the button PH. The second the doors close, he turns to me and says, "By the way, Eric, don't go around telling people we work the box office."

I almost ask why, but the reasons are pretty obvious. We're not exactly high on the theater hierarchy. "What should we say instead?"

"It's our moment to be anyone we want," Alex says, adjusting her dress in the elevator mirror. "Tonight, I'm a makeup artist for *Good Morning America*."

"That's not even filmed in Chicago," Simon sneers.

Alex clicks her tongue. "Whatever."

The elevator opens to a beautiful hallway, adorned with silver sconces. I follow Simon and Alex toward a set of double doors. My stomach clenches, maybe from the nerves that are building. Simon doesn't bother to knock. He pushes the doors right open, letting the music pour into the halls as we head inside. There's a sea of silk shirts and glittering dresses. It's like something out of *The Great Gatsby*. Art deco walls, floral arrangements, hands holding martini glasses. The apartment connects two great rooms, taking up half the floor of the building. A server passes in front of us, holding a tray of what looks like smoked salmon on toast.

"The rent for this place must be *ungodly*," Simon says.

Alex leans into him. "See anyone we know?"

He looks around. "Jesus, there's Brian."

I squint through the crowd. "Who's Brian?"

"The *other* chorus boy Simon's hooking up with," Alex whispers to me.

"I told you, he's an *understudy*!"

Alex rolls her eyes. She pulls a compact from her bag, checking her makeup again. More people flow in through the door behind us. I swallow my breath at the mingling crowd, the sound of music filling the air.

Simon takes another look around. Then he turns to us and says, "Alright, ladies, let's split up."

I give him a look. "*Wait . . . what?*"

"We didn't come to hang out with each other all night," he says, rolling his eyes. "We came to *meet* people. You know, rub shoulders with the social elite. Maybe make out with a producer in the bathroom."

"A class act," Alex says.

Simon turns to her. "And what's your plan?"

"I'm here to find my rich husband," she says, putting her compact away. "My strategy this time is playing damsel in distress, so I should probably be on my own."

Simon laughs. "Damsel in distress? That should be easy for you. You're helpless by nature."

I glance between them. "I'm confused. Are you guys *friends*?"

Alex lifts her chin. "Eleven o'clock."

"*What?*" Simon spins around. "*Damn it,* Brian's coming over," he says through gritted teeth. "*I have to go, I have to go.*" He covers his face with one hand, storming off in another direction.

The moment he disappears, I turn to Alex. Her eyes are scanning the crowd, searching for someone. Then she looks at me and says, "Don't be so nervous, Eric."

"You can tell?"

Alex places a hand on my shoulder. "Just try to have some fun. Maybe your future rich husband is out there, too."

"Maybe," I say.

"I think it's good to have goals," she whispers in my ear. "I'm all about manifesting. Putting things out into the universe, you know? You just have to be sure what you *want*."

I think about this. *What do I want tonight?*

"I'll see you in a bit," Alex says with a wink. She turns again, adjusting the strap of her dress. "Off to find someone to pay my loans." She takes a meditative breath and closes her eyes, as if getting into character. Then she wanders off, one hand clasping her shoulder, looking around like she's lost in some enchanted forest. It only takes a minute before some Prince Charming–like fellow appears at her side, offering his hand.

And then there was one.

I take another breath and let it out. If I knew I would end up alone, I might have turned down the invite. I glance around the room again, wondering where to go first. There's an open bar in the corner, a line of people waiting for drinks. Another group comes through the door behind me. I should probably move out of the entryway. The place is even bigger than it looks. There's a spiral staircase leading to a second floor. I wonder how many people are living here. A server walks by, carrying a tray of mini sausage rolls. I take one as I wander into what appears to be a library room, books lining the wall.

A few people are standing beside a grand piano, drinking champagne. If I knew the song, maybe I could join the conversation. Everyone looks a few years older than me, at least. There's a small group mingling by the bookcase. I think I recognize some of them from the theater. Maybe they recognized me, too, because a woman in an emerald dress smiles at me and says, "Are those any good?"

"I think they're vegan," I say.

She nods. "Good to know. I'm Ariella. Have we met before?"

It takes a second to recognize her face. She came to the box office the other day, asking for cast tickets. But Simon specifically said not to mention we work there. So I shake my head and say, "No, I don't believe so. My name is Eric."

"Delighted," she says, offering a hand. "And who do you know from the show?"

I think about how to answer this. "Uh, Angelina."

"Lovely. Are you one of her students?"

"Not exactly. I sort of work for her," I say vaguely.

"Who else do you know here?"

"No one really..."

She nods. "I see."

It's obvious she's bored of this, because she glances around the room and says, "Excuse me. I think I see a friend of mine." She walks away before I can add to the conversation. Maybe she would have stayed longer if I said I was Andrew Lloyd Webber's grandson or something.

Twenty minutes later, I'm in the bathroom. At least it's nice in here. There's art on the walls and the sink is made of handblown glass. I wash my hands and dry them with a fancy towel. Then I stare at myself in the mirror. Maybe I should drink something to loosen up. But that never ends well for me. I wonder what Haru is doing right now. I wish I had waited for him outside the theater instead.

Suddenly there's a knock on the door.

"Someone's in here," I shout.

Another knock.

"I said, *someone's in here.*"

Then comes Alex's voice.

"Eric, is that you? Open up!"

I unlock the door for her. Alex comes inside, holding a drink. She takes a look around the bathroom and says, "This is the size of my entire studio. What are you doing in here?"

I lean against the sink and sigh. "Taking a break from the party . . ."

Alex frowns. "Are you not having a good time?"

"I just don't know anyone at the party," I say.

"And you never will if you stay in here all night." She sets her drink on the counter and takes me lovingly by the shoulders. "You know what? I think we should give you a goal," she says, eye shadow glistening. "Something you need to do by the end of the night."

"What kind of goal?"

She taps her chin in thought. "You should ask for someone's number. That's always an easy one. It doesn't even have to be romantically driven. As long as you meet someone new."

The thought of this makes me more anxious. I'm not very good in those situations. "What if they say no?" I ask.

Alex gives me a squeeze. "The point is you put yourself out there and ask anyway. Do you know how hot you are? You might be surprised by the outcome."

I consider this. "I guess I can try."

"*I believe in you,*" she says, squeezing my shoulders again. "Now please get out. I really need to pee."

"Oh, sorry."

"Good luck—"

Alex locks the door behind me. I stand in the hallway for

a moment. Then I gather myself and head back to face the crowd. I wish I were naturally social like Simon and Alex. I swear there's more people here than there was a half hour ago. Maybe it's the jacket, but it's getting stuffy in here. There's a glass door that's opened to what looks like a terrace. I make my way outside and breathe in the cold air.

For some reason, there's nobody else out here. I wander toward the railing and look out at the river. I forgot how high up we are. I close my eyes for a moment, letting the nice breeze cool me down.

Footsteps approach. A figure leans on the railing beside me.

For a second, I think it's Haru. I turn my head and see someone I don't recognize. "Nice view out here," he says without looking at me.

"Yeah, it is."

"A little chilly, though."

I take him in a little. His black hair is brushed to the side, almost windswept. He wears a cream suit jacket, slightly matching the furniture in the apartment. A silver watch shines on his wrist. He looks a few years older than me, with a side profile that's straight out of a men's fragrance commercial.

He turns his head. "Do you live in Chicago?"

It takes a second for my brain to respond. "Yeah, I'm from here. What about you?"

"Moved here about a year ago," he says, staring out at the view again. "So it's all still new to me."

"Where from?"

"Manhattan," he says.

"Oh, I think I can tell."

He laughs at this. "Is that so?" He turns to me, holding out a hand. "We haven't officially met, have we? I'm Christian."

"I'm Eric," I say.

He has a nice grip. "I don't think I've seen you around. Did you come here with someone?"

"I came with my friends," I say, glancing back at the door. "They're both in there somewhere. You?"

"I know a few people here," he says casually.

Christian turns back to the railing, looking out again. A silence passes as I stand beside him, staring out at the view, too. I can see the Riverwalk from here, the boats passing along the water.

"There's my favorite restaurant," he says.

"Which one?"

Christian points to a rooftop below. "The ones with the umbrellas. Right along the river," he says.

"I haven't been there before."

"The cocktails are very good."

The music grows louder from behind us. We both glance at the door and back at each other.

"Sounds like the band has arrived," Christian says. "Shall we head back inside?"

I consider this. "I might hang out here a little longer."

"Not a fan of the penthouse?"

Penthouse. So that's what PH stands for. "No, it's really nice. A lot bigger than I expected. Not exactly my taste though, if I'm being honest."

"What don't you like?"

I lean toward him a little. "Between you and me, the decor is a bit tacky. Especially all of the gold."

"Not a fan of gold?"

"It's nice in moderation," I say, shrugging. "But they're definitely pushing it. Especially with that statue by the staircase."

Christian frowns at this. "I love that statue. I brought it with me all the way from New York."

My brain completely freezes. "Wait a minute, is this *your* apartment?"

He nods. "Unfortunately, yes."

"Oh my god, I'm *so* sorry. I didn't know you—"

Christian holds up a hand. "Eric, relax . . . I'm not offended," he says with a laugh. "Except maybe the part where you called me *tacky*."

"I didn't mean that—" I start.

"*I'm kidding.*" He stops me again. "You can call me whatever you like." He glances back at the apartment for a moment. "To be completely frank, I appreciate the honesty. Sometimes I think people only tell me things I want to hear."

"So, you're not kicking me out?"

"That's still up for debate," he says with a smirk.

Some cheers from the inside. Christian checks his watch. "I should probably get back in there. But I'm glad we had a chance to chat."

"Yeah, me, too."

Before Christian goes, he pulls something from his pocket.

It's his phone. He hands it to me. "Here—put in your number." He doesn't even ask. He just tells me to do it.

"Uh, okay."

Christian puts his phone back in his pocket. He looks at me one last time. "Nice jacket, by the way," he says with a nod. "I'll see you around." Then he heads through the door, disappearing into the apartment.

It takes a moment for it to process. That means he wants to see me again, right? I mean, why else would he ask for my number? But I've been completely wrong about these things before. I'm sure he was only doing it to be nice. He probably won't even remember meeting me tonight. At the very least, this has to count toward the goal Alex gave me.

I linger on the terrace for a few more minutes. Then I head back inside in search of the others. The lights have been dimmed; flashes of blue soften the room as I move through the crowd. A slow song has come on, changing the mood of the party. Some people have paired up, eyes lost in each other's as I try not to bump into them. I've never been a fan of these slow dances. It triggers a specific memory, filling me with a sense of loneliness. I know it's still a bit early for a Saturday night. But I don't feel like lingering around longer, waiting for someone to talk to me. Especially since I can't find Simon or Alex anywhere.

I leave through the front door and take the elevator to the lobby. There's a slight chill in the air as I come outside. As I turn down the sidewalk, someone is there at the corner, facing the passing cars. It's not until they turn around that I realize it's—

"Haru . . . what are you doing here?"

"Was just out for a walk," he says, brushing his hair back. He's wearing a plaid jacket and dark gray slacks. "Didn't expect to run into you." He smiles a little, then glances at my clothes. "Looks like you're heading to a party."

"I was just leaving one," I tell him. If I knew he was out here, I would have left sooner.

Haru pretends to check the time. "This early? Must have been a boring one," he says.

I let out a breath. "It just wasn't my vibe. That's all."

"Where are you going now?"

"Probably home," I say, placing my hands in my pockets. "You can come with me, if you'd like. We could watch a movie or something."

"And let that outfit go to waste?" He glances around us and says, "It's Saturday night. Don't you want to do something?"

"Like what?"

He rubs his chin. "Something spontaneous."

Any other night, I would steal another boat with him. But I'm not exactly feeling myself at the moment. "Okay. I'm spontaneously going home," I say. Then I walk off, hoping he'll follow me.

"*Eric,*" he says.

"Sorry, I can't stop, my phone is dying."

Haru sighs from behind me. Then he steps out into the street, forcing me to turn around.

"Wait, where are you going?" I ask.

But Haru ignores me as he lies down in the middle of the road.

"*Are you trying to get run over?*" I glance up and down the road for cars. Then I hurry over to help him up. But he remains unmoving, keeping his arms at his side. The streetlight blinks above our heads. It takes a second to realize what he's doing. A scene from another movie.

I sigh. "You're not Ryan Gosling, you know."

Haru doesn't say anything. He taps the ground as if it is an empty seat. I look up and down the road one more time. "Okay, fine." Then I take my jacket off and lie down next to him. Haru smiles at me as we stay there a moment.

"You know a car could come at any second," I say.

"Nothing bad will happen," Haru says, laying his hands over his stomach. "I promise."

I stare at him. "How can you promise that?"

"You just have to trust me."

I consider this. "Okay . . . I'm trusting you."

We stare at the sky together. For a second, I enjoy the silence of the night. Then headlights flash down the road, followed by the sound of a car coming toward us. Haru and I jump to our feet, moving out of the way as it comes zooming past us, honking furiously. My heart is pounding like a drum, but for some reason, I can't stop laughing. Maybe it's the rush of adrenaline that's moving through me.

"That was a close one," I breathe.

"I told you you could trust me."

He offers his familiar smirk. Then he holds out a hand. "The scene isn't over yet."

"You're not serious . . ."

But Haru keeps his hand extended. I hesitate before taking it, letting him lead me back to the middle of the road. He puts one hand on my side, pulling me close to him. It's a little awkward at first. As we continue our dance, music begins to play. A jazz song, maybe from an old radio. But I can't see where it's coming from. I wonder if Haru can hear it, too.

I rest my head on his chest. "This is nice," I say.

"And you wanted to go home," Haru whispers.

I smile again. Then I look at him. "Can I tell you something?"

"What is it?"

"I've never danced with anyone before."

"Not even at a school dance?"

I shake my head. "No. But I almost went once."

Haru looks at me. "What happened?"

"It's not my favorite story," I say.

Haru pulls me a little closer. "You don't have to share it tonight," he whispers. "But I'm honored to be your first."

We continue our dance in silence. Not a single car passes down the road to interrupt us. It's like we're the only two people awake in the city. But I have to ask him something. "Haru . . . where is the music coming from?"

He tilts his head, listening. "Does it matter?"

I don't have to think about it. I already know my answer. "No. It doesn't."

I keep my head against his chest, wishing the song would last the rest of the night. For a brief moment, I think about something else. If someone came down this street, what would they see? Maybe the answer to that doesn't matter, either. Because I can feel him here with me.

Thirteen

ELEVEN MONTHS AGO

Headlights flash through the kitchen window. I keep turning my head, wondering if that's him.

"Can you stop moving? I'm trying to tie this."

"Do I really have to wear it?"

"I told you, it goes with your shirt," Jasmine says.

Daniel should be here any minute now. It's homecoming of senior year. I've never been to a school dance before. Jasmine came home for the weekend to help me get ready. She tightens the knot of Dad's tie around me and straightens my collar. "Okay, there," she says.

I check my phone. "I knew he would be late."

"Are the others waiting at the restaurant?"

"No, it's just us."

Jasmine smiles. "Glad you guys are talking again."

Daniel and I haven't spoken much lately. Things have been different since I saw him kissing Leighton at the party a few weeks ago. They became official recently, posting stories together on Instagram. I thought I wouldn't hear from him for a while. But he texted me the other day, asking if I would be his date tonight. Leighton is in Florida with his family this weekend. I know we're only going as friends, but I can't help thinking something more could happen. Maybe this is my chance to show him we're meant to be together.

I send Daniel another message.

> text me when you leave

I grab some water and head to the living room. Headlights shine through the window. But it's just the neighbor's car again. I take a seat on the sofa, waiting for Daniel to arrive. He was supposed to be here at seven. That was half an hour ago. At one point, Jasmine comes to check on me.

"Is he almost here?"

"He should be on the way," I say.

Jasmine lingers a moment before heading back to her room. I keep checking my phone, expecting a text from him with an ETA. His mom is supposed to be driving us there tonight. Daniel said she wants to get some photos of us together, which is sweet. They must have stopped somewhere along the way.

I glance out the window and sit down again. Why hasn't he said anything yet? We're going to miss our reservation at the restaurant. At one point, I go outside and wait on the front porch. It's a little chilly tonight. But I don't bother to head back in to grab a jacket. I'm sure he'll be here any second now. I just sit on the steps until Jasmine comes outside looking for me.

"What's taking him so long?" she says.

"He's just running late."

"You should try calling him."

The last text from him was a few hours ago. Maybe he fell asleep or something. I wait for Jasmine to head back inside before I give him a call. The phone rings, but he doesn't answer. I try a few more times but it keeps going to voicemail. A dozen scenarios play through my head. What if Leighton came back to surprise him? What if they went together instead? As my mind races, I hear piano music coming from inside. Jasmine must be practicing in her room again. Her music usually helps me relax a little. But time keeps passing and he still hasn't shown up yet.

I head back inside and sit on the sofa again. How could he make me wait this long? I get that we're not on the greatest terms, but I'm still his best friend. He must know how much I was looking forward to this. The least he could do is let me know if he's changed his mind. I'm about to call again when the piano music stops. The house goes quiet for a second. Someone must have called Jasmine's phone, because I can hear her speaking softly in her room.

For some reason, there's this strange feeling in my stomach. I'm not really sure how to explain it. A minute later, Jasmine comes into the living room. There's a long silence as she stands there, the phone held to her chest. The look on her face makes me think something is wrong.

"What is it?" I ask.

"Mom just called me," she says in a low voice. "She just heard from Daniel's dad."

"What did he say?"

Jasmine doesn't answer this right away. "There was an accident," she says. "Someone hit their car earlier . . ."

"You mean Daniel? Is he okay?"

"I'm not sure," she says.

"What do you mean you're not sure?"

When she doesn't answer this, I rise immediately.

"*Where is he now?* I'm going to find him."

My heart races as I look around for my keys. But Jasmine comes to the sofa, sitting me down again. She kneels beside me, taking both my hands. Her voice is calm when she says, "I need you to listen to me, okay? I don't know how to tell you this, but Daniel is not in the best condition right now." She swallows her breath. "They don't know if he's going to make it through tonight."

My body goes still for a moment. I must have heard her wrong. But the look in her eyes scares me even more. There has to be some terrible mistake. "What are you talking about? He just texted me a few hours ago."

"I'm only telling you what they said."

"Then where is he?"

"I'm not sure."

I rise from the sofa again.

"Where are you going—"

"I need to go find him."

"Eric, come back—"

Jasmine tries to grab my hand. But I pull away and throw open the front door. My hands are shaking as I step outside, hoping to see his car parked at the curb. That this is all some prank that's being played on me. But the street is completely empty. The next thing I know, I nearly trip on the lawn as I break into a run. My button-up shirt is tight against my shoulders as I'm racing down the block. I don't even care if the hospital is seven miles from here. I'm not waiting for Mom and Dad to bring home the car. I have to find Daniel immediately. He must be so scared right now. I need to make sure he's okay. We were supposed to have our first dance together. There's no way he would leave me like this. Especially after the fight we had. I never officially told him I'm sorry.

My heart pounds in my chest as I turn down the street. I'm running so fast I don't see the curb in time, and my body goes crashing to the ground. There's a blur of light, followed by a terrible pain spreading through me. I must have hit my head on something hard. Because all I feel is an ache in my skull as Jasmine appears beside me.

"I'm right here. It's going to be okay . . ."

Her voice is the last thing I hear as I close my eyes, and everything goes black again.

I wish I could have made it to you in time. I wish we could have danced together.

Fourteen

The envelope flutters in my hand as the train roars in. It's a cold Chicago morning, the winds blowing in through the tunnel. I'm standing on the platform, staring down at the unopened letter. Jasmine sent me another one this morning. I always assumed they would stop coming at some point. We haven't seen each other since she dropped in for lunch a few weeks ago. I know she's busy with her music and everything. But it's hard to pretend like it doesn't bother me. She hasn't even told me when she's leaving yet. Are these letters supposed to make up for that?

Jasmine used to call me every day. When Daniel died, she went out of her way to come home every weekend to comfort me. I would lie in her bed as she played me songs on the piano to help me feel better. But she rarely visits these days. Now all I get are these letters that appear every once in a while. For a second, I think about tossing it in the bin next to me. But then I stop myself. Because I promised I would read them eventually. I place the letter back in my pocket and head up the stairs.

The streets are quiet this morning. I linger outside the theater a moment, watching cars pass along the road. There's something else inside my pocket. A paper rose I found on my desk this morning. Haru left it there after he disappeared again last night. For some reason, I still have hope that he might be there when I wake up. It helps me fall asleep at night, thinking things will be different this time. But all that's there is another folded piece of paper. At least I know it means he's going to find me again. I hope I see him tonight. I hold on to the rose as I head into the theater.

Simon and Alex are in the box office, sharing a bag of Hot Cheetos. Their eyes follow me to the counter as I set my things down.

Simon clears his throat in my direction. "And where the hell were you last night?"

"What do you mean?"

"You left without saying goodbye," Alex says. "We looked everywhere for you."

"*We?*" Simon says, crossing his leg over the other. "I hardly noticed you were gone, to be completely honest. Did you go off with someone from the party?" He wiggles his brows at me.

"No, I just went home."

Simon sighs. "*Boring.*"

Alex leans forward, eyeing me curiously. "Did you at least have a good time?"

I think back to the party. "Sort of, yeah."

She blinks at me. "What do you mean, *sort of*?"

"There was this guy who asked for my number," I say. "But I didn't ask for his, so I don't know if that still counts toward my goal."

"Of course it does," Alex says.

Simon scoffs. "Rookie mistake. You probably won't hear from him again, so don't get your hopes up."

Alex hits his shoulder. "You don't know that. He was the one who asked for your number, right? That means he's into you."

I smile at this. "You think so?"

Alex nods. "Of course. What was his name?"

My mind goes to the terrace, the image of him in his suit jacket. "His name was Christian," I say.

Simon and Alex look at each other. Then Simon says very slowly, "Do you mean, Christian *Chan*?"

"He didn't give me his last name. But he told me it was his apartment."

Simon's eyes widen. "*Eric* . . . you know who he is, right?"

"I mean, not really," I admit.

Alex leans forward. "Eric, he's the lead in the show. How did you not know that? He's kind of a big deal here."

"*Kind of?*" Simon says. "Everyone's obsessed with him. What did you two even talk about?" He grabs my shoulders. "Tell us *everything*."

"He just asked where I'm from," I say. "And he hasn't texted me yet, so I doubt he even remembers me."

"People *never* text the day after or they'll seem desperate," Alex says. "There's a three-day rule. So you might hear from him soon. But who knows if those rules apply to people with his reputation."

"What reputation?" I ask.

Alex presses her lips tight. She gives Simon a look, as if turning the question over to him.

Simon leans against the counter, lowering his voice. "If you really want to know, I've heard some *things* about him."

"Like what?"

"Let's just say he has a certain *type,* one you don't exactly fit into," he says vaguely, looking me up and down.

I give him a look. "So what's his type?"

Simon shakes his head. "Honestly, forget it. I don't even know if it's true."

"Wait, just tell me," I say.

"No."

"Why not?"

"Because it's probably just a rumor," Simon says, waving a hand in the air. "So let's just drop it, okay?"

Before I can push him on this, the phone rings. Simon picks it up right away, ending the conversation. I wonder why he won't just say it. But maybe it doesn't matter. I probably won't hear from Christian again, anyway. I take a seat at the counter, moving my bag to the floor. Alex appears next to me, glancing at my things.

"Did you go shopping again?" she asks.

"It's the jacket from yesterday. I was gonna return it after work."

"But it looked so good on you," she says, pulling it out of the bag. "Have you thought about keeping it? It could be an investment piece."

"It's three hundred dollars," I remind her.

"Yeah, but if you wear it three hundred times, it's really just one dollar each time," she says. "It's basic girl math. And how often do you splurge on yourself?"

"I really can't justify that . . ."

"At least wear it *one* more time," Alex says.

"I don't have other penthouse parties lined up."

"Then find one. It's all about manifesting, remember?" She smiles as she hands me back the jacket, taking the other seat.

I think back to the party last night. I did feel more confident wearing it. The fabric is smooth to the touch, different from everything I own at home. I really wish I could afford to keep it. But I'm trying to save up for college, among other things. So I put it back in the bag and push it beneath the counter as a line begins to form.

It's been raining all afternoon. But the sidewalks have mostly dried up by the time my shift ends. The first thing I do is check if he's waiting outside for me. I was hoping we could spend more time together. But no one is standing beneath the marquee. Maybe he isn't coming today. Then I glance at the other side of the street.

"Haru!"

He's leaning against the crosswalk sign with his arms

folded. I had a feeling he would be out here. His lips curve into a smile as I cross the street.

"Caught you just in time," Haru says, wrapping his arms around me. Then he glances at the bag in my hand. "Did you bring me a gift?"

"No, it's just this jacket I bought," I say, holding it up for him. "The one I wore last night."

"How could I forget. You looked impeccable."

"I'm actually returning it."

Haru frowns. "That's a disservice to the rest of us."

"It's too expensive to keep." I laugh. It's always a great relief to see him. Like rain during a drought. "How long have you been waiting out here?"

"Not too long," he says, sliding his hands into his pockets. "You came out at the perfect time. I have the rest of the day planned for us."

"Where are we going?"

"I was thinking we could catch a movie at Millennium Park. We could grab a bite to eat along the way. If that sounds good to you."

I smile at this. "Sounds like a perfect date."

"So it's a date?"

Haru takes the bag from me, lacing his fingers with mine. It feels so natural, the way our hands fit together. Strings of lights blink from above us as we head down the street. As we turn the corner, my phone vibrates in my pocket. There's a new text message. But the number is unknown. I open it anyway.

> What are you up to tonight?
> It's Christian btw

I let go of Haru's hand, nearly dropping the phone. "*Oh my god, he texted me.*"

Haru looks at me. "Who?"

"Someone I met last night," I say. "I thought he wouldn't remember me."

"What did he say?"

"He wants to know what my plans are tonight." I take a moment to think about how to respond.

> Hi! I just got out of work
> What about you?

Christian responds almost instantly.

> About to grab a drink.
> You should come by

I text him back.

> You mean right now?

A few seconds later, he sends the location to a restaurant in River North. I pull up the address on my phone. Is that the place he pointed out from his rooftop last night?

Another text from him.

> I'm heading out soon. I hope
> I see you there

I turn to Haru. "He wants to meet up."

"When?"

"Apparently right now."

A silence.

"And you want to go?"

I hesitate. I've been looking forward to spending more time with Haru. But I wasn't expecting this text from Christian. It's not often someone like him asks to see me again. What if I don't get a second chance? Haru and I can see the movie another time, right? I turn to him and say, "They play movies at the park all week. Maybe we can catch one tomorrow. I mean, if you're okay with that."

Haru stares at me for a moment. Then he shrugs. "That's fine. Do what you want."

"You won't mind?"

"I'm not going to stop you."

"Well . . . okay."

I send Christian another text.

> Sounds fun. I'll be there
> soon!

Traffic lights blink around us. I look at Haru again. "I promise to make it up to you. Maybe I'll see you after the movie ends?"

Haru smiles. "Have a good time."

Then he turns down the street and walks off. I shout goodbye, but he doesn't glance back. I wouldn't normally cancel plans like this, but who knows when Christian will invite me out again? I drop my bags off at the theater before I head to the train stop. I can return the jacket another time.

The Red Line drops me off in River North. The rooftop bar is located in the London House hotel. It's only a few blocks from Christian's apartment building. He sends another message, letting me know he's already inside. I still can't believe he wants to see me again. It's not like our interaction was very long. What if he has me confused with someone else he met at the party? I push the thought away as I head into the elevator. The doors open to the twenty-first floor where a piano is playing in the corner.

I wish I had brought the jacket. Everyone is dressed like they came from the country club. I make my way down the bar, looking for the terrace. Christian is sitting at a table alone, dressed immaculately in a beige shirt. He spots me as I come outside, rising from his seat.

"You found me," he says, making room for me on the rattan sofa. "Glad you could make it."

"I was in the area." I sit down next to him. The matching table reminds me of the patio furniture in his apartment. A glass railing runs along the length of the terrace, giving stunning views of the river. "So this is the place you told me about."

Christian smiles. "How could I talk it up when I know you've never been here before?" He picks up a menu from the table and hands it to me. "I hope you haven't had dinner yet. I've been craving oysters all day. Do you like oysters?"

"I'm open to trying."

As I scan the menu, my eyes widen at the prices here. Christian might have noticed because he smiles and says, "Don't worry, just order whatever you like."

"Oh . . . okay."

"Admittedly, the wine selection could be better," he says. "Was thinking of getting a bottle of something, if you have any preferences."

"I actually just turned nineteen," I admit.

Christian chuckles, leaning into me. "They never card at this place. You should get one of the cocktails. They're all good."

"Okay . . . what do you recommend?"

When the waiter comes, Christian orders for the both of us. A dozen oysters and some scallops to start us off. The oysters feels weird to swallow, but the taste isn't as bad as I expected. Our conversation is nice. Christian turned twenty-three a few months ago. He graduated from the Yale School of Drama. When he asks about my education, I consider lying to him. It wouldn't be a stretch to say I go to the Art Institute, since I basically work down the street. But I decide to be honest, despite the advice of Simon and Alex.

"I actually work at the box office," I say.

"I know," Christian says casually.

"You do?"

"Was it supposed to be a secret?" He smiles, taking a sip of his drink. "Apparently, you're the newbie there. Heard you've been taken under the wings of those friends you came to my party with. I hope you didn't have anything to do with the infamous missing cake."

I nearly choke on the bread. "I swear, that wasn't my idea."

Christian laughs. "Relax. We ordered another."

"I'm glad it doesn't bother you," I say.

"Of course not. I prefer chocolate."

"No, I mean, the fact that I work in the box office."

He shrugs. "Why would that bother me?"

I smile to myself. Maybe the rumors Simon heard about him are wrong. The waiter brings out the rest of our food, along with a bottle of wine. I don't really drink very much, but I want Christian to like me, so I let him pour me a glass. We share a tiramisu and crème brûlée for dessert. I stare out at the river, watching a ship pass. Christian must have noticed this because he asks, "Have you been on the water before?"

I think back to the other night, when Haru and I took a ride on the river. "I mean, I've been on a boat. But nothing like one of those."

His lips curve into a smile. "Would you like to?"

There's a two-story yacht docked at the water, a few blocks away from the hotel. It belongs to his friend from Yale, who happens to be hosting a small gathering tonight. I follow Christian up the steps of the stern as someone hands me a champagne flute. The next thing I know, we're moving along the water. It's a bit windy out tonight. Christian must have seen me shiver a little, because he places his jacket over my shoulders. "It's Valentino," he says. The leather smells of vanilla and musk. I wear it for the rest of the night. The views of Navy Pier are stunning from the water. At one point, Christian's friend even lets me hold the helm.

We return to the dock a few hours later. The moment we're back on the sidewalk, Christian turns to me and asks, "Would you like to come back to my place?"

"Are you having another party?"

He smiles at this. "I was thinking of something quieter. Just the two of us," he says.

"Oh..."

I stare at the water, considering this. Although I'm enjoying our time together, I'm not sure if I'm ready for more to happen. "Maybe another night," I suggest. "I have to wake up early for work tomorrow."

Thankfully, Christian doesn't push me on this. "Of course," he says kindly. Then he takes out his phone. "Let me call you a car."

"You don't have to do that—" I start.

He holds up a hand for a moment. "It's already on the way," he says, returning his phone to his pocket. "Should be here in a few minutes."

"Oh, thank you."

Christian walks me to the pickup spot and waits with me.

"I hope you had a good night," he says.

"Yeah, it was a lot of fun."

"I'm glad," he says, leaning into me a little. "Because I want to see you again."

I smile. "Me, too."

A moment later, a black car arrives. Christian opens the door for me. "Text me when you get home," he says.

"Okay."

The door shuts. Christian stands at the sidewalk, watching us drive off. I lean back in the seat the second he's out of view. There are still butterflies in my stomach. It was like something right out of a movie. I can't stop smiling as I stare out the window. At home, I take a shower and get ready for bed. I don't think about anyone else for the rest of the night. I fall asleep easily, wondering when I'll see him again.

Fifteen

I wake up to nothing on my desk. No paper star or roses for me. I haven't seen Haru in a couple of days. I thought he would have shown up by now. We're supposed to see a movie in the park together. But he hasn't been there when I get out of work. I hope he isn't mad at me for leaving the other day. I remind myself to make it up to him when he's back.

I'm a little anxious this morning, checking my phone every few minutes. It's been three days since my date with Christian. But I haven't heard from him since then. His last text was at 11:14 that night, asking if I made it home safely. The jacket he let me borrow hangs on the back of my chair. I still have to return it to him. I texted him the morning after, letting him know I had a great time. But he hasn't responded yet. I'm sure he's just really busy at the moment. Maybe I'll text him again tomorrow.

I couldn't help looking him up online. He has a lot of photos on Instagram, lounging around on the beach. Most of them in different countries. When I googled his name, a few articles from his school came up. He was on the varsity swim team at his private school before going on to Yale. He double majored in political science and theater, graduating with high honors. There's a few pictures of him with some other guy from his swim team at Yale. Maybe that's the type he's into. Someone who went to an Ivy League and spends summers at their country house in the Poconos.

I sit at my desk and turn on my laptop. It's been a minute since I looked at college applications. The portal to University of Illinois is already opened. I'm still planning on applying there again. But I decide to add more schools to the list. Particularly ones I think would impress someone like Christian. Places like Northwestern or the University of Chicago are viewed as Ivy Leagues around here. Though my chances of getting in either are a long shot. My grades aren't too bad, but I don't have a resume like Christian's.

Winning the film scholarship would make me stand out. But it's due in a few weeks and I still haven't started on it. All I have are some random shots of the city. I still can't believe I lied to Jasmine about making it to the next round. At least it's motivating me to pick up my camera again. I spend the rest of the morning thinking of ideas before work.

I arrive at the theater around noon. Alex is sitting at the counter, eating a celery stick from a vegetable platter beside a plate of sandwiches. I set my things down, picking up a radish that fell on the floor. "Where did this food come from?"

"It was here when we walked in," Alex says.

I raise a brow at her.

"Simon found it in the dressing room."

"But we're not allowed in there."

Alex tosses her hair and says, "There's so many rules around here. How are we possibly supposed to remember them all?" She dips the celery stick in hummus and takes a bite.

I pick up the bottle of wine beside her. "Maybe we should ease up on the free stuff. I think they're starting to catch on."

"What makes you think that?"

"Because they know about the cake."

Alex gasps. "*No.*"

"And some other things, too . . ."

"Stop it!"

Simon walks in through the door, holding his latte. He tosses his keys on the counter and says, "What are you ladies gossiping about?"

Alex turns to him. "They *know,*" she says tensely.

Simon blinks at her in confusion. Then his eyes widen with what looks like fear. "What? That's not possible. Nobody else was there that night. And we burned all the evidence!"

"*Not that!*" Alex throws her celery stick at him. "They know we've been taking stuff around here."

"Oh, that?" Simon waves his hand, fanning away her concerns. "Nobody here suspects us for a second. You know I run this place like the navy."

"Eric says they know about the cake."

Simon gives me a look. "And how would you know that?"

"Christian told me," I say.

Alex blinks at me. "Christian Chan? Did you see him again?"

I've been debating whether or not to tell them. "Yeah . . . He asked me to hang out the other night."

"*And you didn't say anything?*" Simon scolds me. "Who said you could keep secrets from us?"

"It happened a few days ago," I say. "I wasn't sure what you guys would think. I mean, given the *rumor* about him. You know, the one you haven't told me."

Simon rolls his eyes. "I told you, it's probably not true. Especially knowing he asked *you* on a date."

"What's that supposed to mean?"

He shakes his head. "I said, forget it!"

Alex leans forward. "Tell us about your date."

"I don't know if it was a *date*," I say, shrugging. "But it was a lot of fun. He took me to dinner at this restaurant near his place. Then we went on his friend's boat around the river, which was pretty cool."

Alex smiles. "A boat ride on the river? How romantic. Will you see him again?"

"I hope so," I say.

"Have you texted him?" she asks.

"Yeah, but he hasn't responded yet."

Alex presses her lips together. "It's only been a few days. I'm sure you'll hear from him soon."

"Unless he ghosted you," Simon adds.

Alex grabs a carrot from the tray, throwing it at his arm. "No one needs your pessimism."

"I'm just being realistic," Simon says defensively. "And stop wasting the food!"

Someone approaches the box office. It's a delivery guy, holding a slender white box. He reads his scanner and says, "Excuse me, is there a—"

"*I'll take that off your hands,*" Simon says, grabbing the box from him. He scribbles his name and turns back around.

Alex and I give him a look.

Simon sighs. "Okay, fine, I have a problem. I'm not afraid to admit it." He holds the box to his ear, shaking it slightly. "Feels like nothing's in there."

"Let's open it," Alex says, grabbing it from him.

"*Alex,*" I say.

"Sorry, I'm weak."

They set the box on the counter, ripping it open. Inside is a single red rose. Simon rolls his eyes. "It's just a stupid rose. Probably for someone in the cast."

"What's the name?" Alex asks.

Simon unfolds the card. Then his eyes go wide again. "*Eric Ly?*" He turns to me. "Did you order yourself a rose?"

I blink in confusion. "*What? No.*"

Alex snatches the card. "Someone must have sent it to him," she says, turning it in her hand. "But it doesn't say from who . . . unless . . ." She pauses to think. Then she looks at me. "You should check your phone."

"Uh, okay."

I pull out my phone. There's a notification on the screen. "Christian just texted me." I gasp.

> Hope you liked my gift
> Let me know if you're free tonight

"*What did he say?*" Simon moves my arm, glancing at the screen. "The rose is from him? He wants to see you tonight? This is getting serious."

"What are you gonna say back?" Alex asks.

I stare at the box on the counter. No one's ever gifted me flowers before. "I don't know . . . But I definitely want to hang out again."

"You totally manifested this," she says, clasping her hands together.

For the next few minutes, Simon and Alex help draft a response. "Keep the message simple, but a little playful, and no exclamation points," Simon says. "You don't want to seem desperate." Alex advises me to wait half an hour before sending it.

> The rose is beautiful, it was very sweet of you.
> Would love to see you again tonight

We get back to work at one point, waiting for his response. Christian texts me an hour later, along with an invitation link. One of his friends is hosting an art gallery opening. Simon and Alex insist I leave early to go to the department store and pull together another outfit.

"Send us photos of options," Alex says.

"You better tell us everything tomorrow," Simon says.

I take the rose with me on my way out. It takes longer than I expected, but I pick out a blue button-down that Alex approves of. Then I hop on the next train toward Hyde Park, transferring lines halfway through. Christian is waiting for me outside the hotel. He's dressed in all white this evening, the button of his collar undone, hair flowing in the breeze. He's as perfect as the sculptures in his penthouse apartment.

"Don't you look sharp this evening," he says, putting his arm around me.

I smile. "Same to you."

Christian glances at the rose in my hand. "You brought it with you."

"Yeah, I came straight from work."

He holds out a hand. "Give it here."

I hand Christian the rose. He snaps off the stem, which startles me a little. Then he takes out his wallet, removing what looks like a pin. "Do you mind?" he asks. I shake my head, letting him attach the flower to the pocket of my shirt. "A boutonniere. It's not *perfect*, but—"

"No, I love it," I say. "Thank you."

Christian smiles at me. Then he gestures toward the hotel entrance.

"Shall we?"

There's a fireplace in the lobby. Christian walks us to the elevator, taking us to the third floor. The doors open to a ballroom where the art gallery opening is taking place. The walls are full of paintings, but Christian walks right past them as if he's seen them already. We grab drinks from the bar and find his friends. A blond guy in a small circle of suits waves us over. He squeezes Christian's shoulder, then turns to me and says, "You must be Eric. I've heard *all* about you."

"This is my friend Nick," Christian says, placing his arm around him. "We know each other from Yale. He showed me around Chicago when I first moved here."

"*Charity work*," Nick whispers to me. "You do them one favor and you can never get rid of them."

"Be nice," Christian says.

"I'm always nice." Nick sips his drink, amused with himself. Then he turns to me again and says, "I heard you went on a boat ride the other day."

"Yeah, with Christian."

"How was it?"

"Really cool. I've never been on a yacht before."

"Well, isn't that *endearing*."

I give him a look, wondering what he means by that. Nick spins back to the group. "Let's get another drink." He looks around. "Where on earth is that server?"

"They've been terribly slow," says one of the others.

Nick shakes his head. "You'd think they were making the food themselves. Ah, there he is—" He snaps his fingers. A young server from the other side of the room turns his head and hurries over.

"Sorry, can I get you something?" the server asks. He looks around my age, maybe a year or two older.

"Some service would be nice," Nick whispers to us, as if the guy can't hear him. "We'll take two Negronis and a dirty martini, my boy." He slips a bill in the server's pocket. "And quickly, alright?"

"Thank you, sir." The server turns and leaves.

"Was that a fifty?" another friend asks.

"Let's hope it speeds him up," Nick says, waving it off. "Probably what he makes for the entire night."

Everyone laughs at this, including Christian. I wonder what they would say if I mentioned I worked as a server, too. That was a little over a month ago. I keep that to myself as their conversation continues. Most of them work in finance, the rest in some kind of art collecting. It doesn't take long to realize how different we are. I listen actively, trying my best to contribute a word here and there. "Oh, interesting." "Wow." But once they get into real estate investments, I feel myself fading into the background. I keep nodding along, smiling occasionally. It's like they're speaking a different language, making it feel like I'm not really here.

As the server appears with the drinks, a bell goes off from somewhere in the room. But no one else seems to have heard it. I glance around, noticing the sound of a distant piano. There's something familiar about the song. I close my eyes for a second, trying to remember where I heard it before. When I think no one is paying attention, I step away from the conversation, wandering toward the music.

There's a piano on the other side of the gallery. Then I notice the person sitting behind it.

"*Haru?*"

I wasn't expecting to see him here. He's wearing a white button-up that fits him beautifully as he plays the piano. If other people weren't around, I'd throw my arms around him, hugging him tight. Instead I walk over casually, taking a seat on the bench beside him. Haru doesn't turn his head. His eyes are focused on the piano. But I can sense he knows it's me. For a moment, nobody else is in the room but us.

"I didn't know you could play," I say.

He doesn't say anything.

"What are you doing at an art gallery?"

Haru keeps his eyes on the keys as he keeps playing. "I'm also interested in art. I saw you with your friends earlier, but I didn't want to interrupt."

"They're Christian's friends," I tell him. "I just met them today."

"They don't seem very friendly."

"You don't even know them."

He looks at me for the first time. "So, I'm wrong then?"

I don't answer this.

"Nice flower, by the way."

I glance at the rose on my shirt. "Christian gave it to me earlier."

"He must really like you." Haru turns back to the piano, continuing his song.

I listen to him play for a moment. "He's been really nice to me. It's just his friends I'm not the biggest fan of. But they're not the worst people in the world."

"Is that why you're sitting here with me?"

I don't say anything.

"You know you don't have to stay."

"What do you mean?"

Haru pauses the song and says, "We could leave right now. The two of us. I bet we could still catch that movie in the park."

"I can't just leave," I tell him. "Christian will think I ditched him."

"You had no problem doing that to me."

We look at each other.

"Is that what this is about? Why you've been gone these past few days?" Someone passes behind me, making me lower my voice. "We could have watched that movie yesterday. You knew I was waiting for you. But you're choosing *right now*? When I'm with someone?"

"So I'm an inconvenience."

"That's not what I said."

Then my phone vibrates. It's a text from Christian.

Where did you go?

I let out a breath. "Christian's looking for me."

"Then you should go find him," Haru says, turning back to the piano.

I don't get up immediately because I hate to leave things this way. And maybe a part of me wants to go with Haru. I imagine us leaving through the back door, running down the stairwell together. But I couldn't possibly do that to Christian.

"I can't blame you, though," Haru says, somewhat out of the blue. "He can give you a real rose while I can only give you a paper one."

"Haru . . ." I start to say something. But my phone goes off again. It's another text from Christian, asking if I'm alright. "I have to go. But hopefully I'll see you again soon."

"Enjoy your evening," he says.

He resumes his song on the piano. I feel a sting of guilt as I'm walking away from him. It doesn't take long to find Christian. He's on the other side of the gallery, staring at a sculpture. "There you are," he says, smiling at me. "Thought I lost you for a second."

"Sorry, I was in the bathroom."

"What do you think of this piece?"

Christian turns to show me. It's a sculpture of a woman bathing herself. I think it's made of stone.

"For your apartment?" I ask.

"Possibly."

I rub my chin. "It's interesting. But I don't know if it's *you*."

Christian looks at me. "What makes you say so?"

"It isn't gold."

"You're mocking me."

"Only a little bit." We both smile. I look around the gallery. "Where did all your friends go?"

"They weren't as impressed with the art," Christian says.

"So they relocated to a bar on another floor. We can always join them, if you'd like."

"I mean, only if you want to."

"I'm not exactly up for a crowd tonight," he says.

"Same, honestly," I admit. "I only came to see you."

Christian smiles at this. "Then what do you say we head out of here? Somewhere less crowded."

"Where do you want to go?"

"We can go back to my place and decide from there."

I had a feeling he would suggest this. Especially since he asked the last time we were together. I can't possibly say no again. I really want him to like me. "Okay, sure."

"Perfect."

Christian takes the last sip of his drink and sets it on the table. Then he walks us to the elevator. When we go outside, a car is already waiting for us. It drops us off at the entrance of his building. A doorman tips his hat as we pass him. "Good evening, Mr. Chan."

"Good evening, Richard."

The elevator doors open on their own. It feels strange to be back here, especially since I snuck in last time. The hallway is longer than I remember. Christian waves a key over the knob and opens the door. The lights come on automatically as we step inside. I look around the apartment. Somehow, the place seems bigger with only the two of us here. Like a museum after closing hours. Our footsteps echo on the marble floors.

Christian steps behind his bar. "Can I make you a drink?"

"Yeah, that would be great."

"What would you like?"

"Uh, whatever you're having."

I take a seat on the curved white sofa. The fabric curls like the wool of a sheep. I keep running my hand over it.

"It's bouclé," Christian says. "The sofa."

"I could fall asleep on this."

Christian smiles from behind the bar. "Don't tell me you're tired," he says. A moment later, he comes into the living room with two drinks. A square block of ice sits in amber liquid. I take the smallest sip, burning my throat.

"What is this?" I cough.

"Bourbon," Christian says. "It tastes better with time. Just let the ice melt a little." He takes out his phone. A second later, music fills the apartment. Something classical.

I hold my breath as I take another sip.

"Did you want some water?"

"I'm fine," I say, clearing my throat. Then I glance around the apartment. "Your place is really big for one person. Do you really need this much space?"

Christian chuckles. "It is on the bigger side," he agrees. "Especially compared to my place in the city. I guess I just fell in love with the view."

"Yeah, it's incredible," I say, glancing at the terrace. "You can see the whole city. I remember from the last time I was here."

"Have you seen the bedroom yet?"

"No, I haven't."

"Would you like to?"

Before I can even answer, Christian rises from the sofa anyway. I take another sip, burning my throat again. Christian smiles as he holds out a hand, helping me to my feet. He leads me up the stairs, taking us to the door at the end of the hallway. He doesn't bother with the lights when we come in. But he doesn't really need them. The glow from the floor-to-ceiling windows illuminates the room, showcasing the city like an art piece.

I wander toward the window for a better view. The drink is cold in my hand. Maybe it's the bourbon talking, but I say, "I can't believe you get to see this every day."

"The view is even better from the bed."

I go completely still. Then I turn around slowly.

Christian is sitting at the side of his bed. His sleeves are rolled up, showing his arms. He runs a hand over the covers, as if to say, *come here*. I take another sip, hoping it does something for my nerves. Then I walk over and sit down next to him. Christian studies me for a moment. Slowly, he runs a finger over my cheek, circling down to my jaw. His hand feels nice against my skin. "You're really beautiful, Eric."

I quiver a little as he leans in closer. His voice is smooth as he whispers, "Can I kiss you?"

I swallow my breath. "Yeah."

The next thing I know, our lips are pressed together. His mouth is sharp with the taste of bourbon. He takes the drink from my hand, moving it to the nightstand. I'm a little numb from the alcohol. I almost don't feel his hands as they grip me. The linen of his shirt scratches my skin; his chest presses against mine. I run my hands through his hair as he kisses my neck. Then he moves to my ear and whispers, "You know, I don't usually bring back guys like you . . ."

"What does that mean?"

"You know," he says vaguely.

He continues to kiss me, his lips warm against my neck and shoulders. Even though this feels nice, I'm still focused on what he said. "I really don't," I say.

Christian looks at me. "I guess you can say I have a preference. Someone more like Nick, if that makes it more clear."

I think back to the gallery. He was the blond friend who kept making jokes about the waiters. "Blond?"

"Not necessary blond," he says.

"Works in finance?"

Christian sighs. "You really need me to say it?"

"I'm just curious."

He takes a moment to answer. "I'm not into Asian guys. You're actually the first."

This catches me off guard. I don't know what to say. "But you're Asian," I remind him.

He laughs a little. "Let's not complicate things," he says. "Just consider yourself the exception." A smiles curves on his lips. As if he just offered a compliment.

Christian starts kissing me again. But it doesn't feel the same as it did a moment ago. I run my hands along his shoulders as he slowly unbuttons my shirt. That's when I notice his is unbuttoned, too. Eventually I close my eyes, pretending I never asked the question. Pretending he's the same person I thought he was before it ruined the moment.

Sixteen

I wake up to a missed call from Jasmine. She left me a voicemail.

"Hey . . . I thought I'd give you a call. I guess it's a bit early for you. Sorry I didn't call back sooner. I've just been busy with the move and everything. There was this issue with my passport. I'm hoping to book the flight this week. It's been a headache, figuring out all the logistics. But I hope everything's okay at home. Your last few texts had me a little worried. What have you been doing up so late? And who are these new friends you've been hanging out with?

Text me when you wake up, okay? Things are still hectic, but I'm gonna try to see you before I leave. I promise. Anyway, I'll talk to you soon."

The voicemail ends.

I've been thinking about Jasmine all morning. Sometimes I wish I could go to her room and find her writing at her desk, or playing a song on the piano. She always knew something was bothering me before I even told her. Everything's different since she moved away. It's like we're living separate lives these days. I wonder what she would say about Christian. It's been over a week since I was at his place. We haven't seen each other since then. He's been extra slow to respond lately.

I think about sending him another text, but I don't want to seem annoying.

I read my last messages to him.

> hi! What are you up to this weekend? I still need to return your jacket
>
> lmk if you want to do dinner or something

No response yet. I'm sure he's just busy, though. Simon told me it's auditioning season. I think back to our last night together. *"Consider yourself an exception."* I know I should probably feel a certain way about this comment, but I try not to overthink it. I hope he texts me back soon.

I climb out of bed and check my desk. I was hoping to find a paper rose from Haru. I haven't seen him since the night of the art gallery. We've never gone this long without talking before. He can't be that mad at me, can he? I wish there was a way for me to apologize. I wait for him outside after work, but he hasn't shown up yet. Maybe I'll stop by the café again.

I've been helping Mom around the house. She sprained her wrist a few days ago and has to stay home from work. Instead of relaxing like the doctor said, she's having me move furniture so she can vacuum the living room. For lunch, she makes scrambled eggs with bitter melon, topped with a little scallion oil. I pull up a seat at the table beside her. A curtain separates the dining room from the entryway. Mom asked me to help hang it up yesterday. Apparently, a dining table should never face the front door. "Để như vậy thì nhà sẽ được hên," she said. *This will keep good luck from leaving.* Mom is constantly rearranging the flow of energy in the house. When anything bad happens around here, she blames the furniture.

Mom places a dishcloth on the table, setting a hot pan on top. We eat in silence for a moment. Bitter melon is an acquired taste that I haven't acquired yet. But she says it's good for me. "Con có một lá thơ. Nữa nè của Jasmine gởi." *You got some mail yesterday. There's something from Jasmine.*

I just nod.

"It's her birthday soon," she says.

There's a knot of guilt in my chest. Because she doesn't know about Jasmine. That she dropped out of school and is moving to another country. But I'm not going to be the one to tell her. Especially since I promised to keep it a secret.

"Con nên đến thăm chị." *You should go visit her.*

"I can't . . ." I say, shaking my head. "I have a lot of work this week." Maybe that came out a little rough, but I'm not sure what else to say. Once I finish eating, I check the time and rise from my seat. "I have to go now. Do you want me to pick anything up on the way home?"

Mom grabs a pencil and writes down a list of things from the store. Then she hands it to me, along with Jasmine's letter.

"Đừng đi chơi về khuya quá," she says. *Don't stay out too late again.*

I bring Christian's jacket to work with me. I texted him again this morning, letting him know I have it in case he stops by the box office. Maybe we can grab dinner afterward. Simon is already there when I arrive. He usually comes in late, so I'm a little surprised to see him. I set my things down and pull out a chair. My mind is too far away to hold conversation. I fold my arms on the counter and rest my head for a moment.

"Aren't you a ray of sunshine today," he says, putting his phone away. "What's bothering you?"

"Nothing," I say.

Simon nods knowingly. "Boy problems, I see." He leans forward, patting my knee. "Tell me everything . . ."

I sigh. "Alright, it's Christian."

Simon pulls his chair closer, crossing one leg over the other. "*Go on.*"

"He invited me back to his place last week."

"*And?*"

"We hooked up, if that's what you're wondering."

Simon gasps. "Oh my god, how was it?"

"It was . . . nice."

"*Just nice?*"

I think about how to answer. "It's not that I didn't enjoy it. It's just, he sort of said something that threw me off. I don't know what to think of it."

"What did he say?"

I hesitate. "He told me he's not into Asian guys."

There's a long silence. Simon leans back in his chair, crossing his arms. For some reason, he doesn't seem surprised by this information. He just sighs and says, "Well, I guess the rumors are true."

"You knew about this?"

"Unfortunately," he says, shaking his head. "He's known to date white men exclusively. You know, blond hair and blue eyes. Typically six feet tall with shoes on. It's always a red flag when they hashtag #wasian on an Instagram post. I thought maybe he matured since then but clearly, I was wrong."

I lean forward. "He told me I was an exception."

Simon twists his face. "Oh god, what an *ick*. Please tell me you're never gonna talk to him again."

I stare at the floor.

Simon leans forward. "Eric . . . *no*. You're going to see him again after that?"

"We haven't really talked since," I admit. "I figure he's really busy. But I don't know what to think. Maybe he didn't exactly mean it that way, you know?"

"What else could he have meant?"

I say nothing.

Simon lets out a breath and says, "Listen, Eric. I get it, okay? We've all been there. Met that toxic guy we hope will treat us differently. If I thought I could convince you otherwise, I would try. But I know there's nothing I can say. So unfortunately, this is a lesson you have to learn for yourself."

Alex walks in. We don't talk about Christian for the rest

of the shift. But I can't stop thinking about what Simon said. I know he's right, but it doesn't change the feelings I have toward Christian. I still want to see him again.

The sun is falling behind the theater. I'm standing outside the marquee, staring at the passing cars. *Haru.* It's been a week since we last saw each other. I've been waiting every night after work, hoping he'll show up again. I touch the paper rose in my pocket, remembering what he said. "*He can give you a real rose, while I can only give you a paper one.*" I wish I could tell him the real one has already withered away. What if that was the last time we saw each other? I shake that thought out of my head. He would never leave without saying goodbye, right?

Where did you go this time? There's still so much of the city I want to show you.

A wind blows leaves around me. I let out a breath when I realize he's not coming tonight. As I finally turn to go, my phone vibrates. There's a text from Christian.

> How have you been?
> Heading to the hotel rooftop with
> some friends if you want to meet
> Bring the jacket

I nearly trip on the sidewalk. Christian wants to see me? I read the message again, making sure I understand this right. I haven't heard from him in a week. Suddenly he wants to go out for drinks? He could have at least given me a few hours' notice. I stare down at my work clothes. I can't possibly show up looking like this. His friends might mistake me for the waitstaff. I glance at the time. Maybe I can pick up a new shirt on the way. The department store is only a few blocks from here. I look both ways before I hurry across the street.

The restaurant is crowded tonight. There's a line at the front, waiting to get inside. I'm wearing a gray sweater over my work shirt, with a few sprays of Tobacco Vanilla. I recognized the cologne bottle from Christian's bathroom. He texted back a moment ago, letting me know he has a table. I walk up to the hostess and give her his name. "Right this way," she says immediately.

I follow her out to the rooftop. Christian is sitting with a group of guys, lounging in wicker chairs. A champagne bottle leans inside an ice bucket. His blond friend Nick is here, too. It takes a few seconds for Christian to notice me. He takes a sip of his drink before rising from his chair.

"Glad you're here," he says, putting his arms around me.

"Thanks for inviting me. I brought your jacket."

He smiles. "Hold it for me, will you?"

"Yeah, sure."

Nick looks up from the table. "Eric, my boy!" he shouts. He pats the empty seat beside him. "Forget Christian and come sit with me."

I glance at Christian. He chuckles a little.

"It's alright," he says.

"Okay . . ."

I was hoping we'd sit together. But there's not a lot of space at his side of the table. So I walk over to Nick, taking the seat next to him.

Nick slides a glass in front of me. "You're a little behind, aren't you?"

"Behind on what?"

The table laughs.

Nick squeezes my shoulders. "Isn't he adorable? Let's get you a shot, shall we? I'll take one with you . . ." The second the waiter approaches, Nick holds up a glass. "Another round for us, please!"

I look over at Christian. He winks at me from across the table, holding up his drink in the air. He's sitting next to someone I don't recognize. This brunet guy, wearing a white polo and jeans. I wonder how they know each other.

Nick puts an arm around me. "Tell me, Eric, how's life been since I last saw you? Any wild stories at the box office? I want to know everything."

"Nothing crazy. Just applying to schools and stuff."

"Christian tells me you're taking a gap year," he says, nodding. "I hope you're using it to travel. I was in Portofino a few weeks ago. Have you been to Italy?"

"No, but I've seen *Luca*."

Nick laughs. "You're hysterical. Where did Christian find you?"

A second later, the waiter appears with two shot glasses.

Nick hands one to me, taking the other. He holds his glass up and says, "Cheers to good health."

Our shot glasses clink. I hold my breath as it goes down. It's like swallowing gasoline. There's a harsh aftertaste, sending a shudder through me.

"Terrible, isn't it?" Nick says.

"What *is* it?"

"Gin." He hands me some water to wash it down. "The first one is always the worst."

"It might be my last, too."

"That's what we all say." Nick laughs. "I love this sweater, by the way." He touches my arm, running his fingers over the fabric.

"Thanks . . . I think it's cashmere."

"Oh, I can tell. You'll *have* to let me borrow it," he says teasingly. Then his eyes brighten, as if remembering something. He picks up a small menu. "Goodness, you're probably starving. Let's get you something to eat. You're not vegan, are you?"

"No."

"I wouldn't judge you if you are."

"I'm not."

The waiter appears again. Nick puts in an order of calamari, along with some cocktails. A Negroni Sbagliato, one of his favorite drinks. Thankfully, they don't check my ID. The view of the water is beautiful tonight. But I keep looking over at Christian, watching him be extra friendly with the other guy. How come I've never seen him before? Nick must have noticed me staring.

Because he leans in and whispers, "That's our friend Zach, if you're curious. He's visiting from LA."

I look away. "Oh, I wasn't . . ."

"He's leaving this weekend, though," Nick adds.

"Are they . . . friends?"

"You could say that."

I'm not sure what to make of this. But I don't ask more questions. The waiter arrives with our drinks. Nick watches me take my first sip. It's on the bitter side, but slightly sweet, with the taste of grapefruit. The bubbles make it easier to drink.

"Better than the gin, right?"

"Yeah, it's not bad at all," I say.

Nick smiles. "I'm glad you like this one. You'll have to try the elderflower next."

I don't know why he's being so nice to me. But I'm enjoying this attention. The night continues like this. Nick orders us more drinks, touching my shoulders, talking about his recent travels. Meanwhile, Christian hasn't said a word to me since I got here. Why did he invite me here if he's more interested in someone else? I keep glancing at him, hoping he's going to call me over. At one point, he rises from the table.

"Where are you going?" I ask.

"Just the bar. I'll be right back."

"Oh, okay."

He gives me a pat on the back and disappears inside. As I turn back to the table, Nick puts his arm around me. "Don't worry about Christian," he whispers. "We'll have fun without him. Let's order you another drink."

An hour passes and Christian hasn't come back. I keep glancing inside, wondering if he's still at the bar. Another round of shots appears at the table. I don't even remember Nick ordering them. Despite my better judgment, I take the shot with him anyway. It goes down much easier this time. My tongue must be numb from the alcohol. That's when I notice the lights are spinning a little. I don't usually drink this much. I close my eyes for a second.

Nick touches my back. "How are you feeling there?"

"I should probably take a break . . ."

"You should have mentioned you were a lightweight," he says.

I glance around the table. It's only the two of us sitting here. When did everyone else leave? I turn to Nick, who is staring at me now. "Did I mention how cute you look in that sweater?" he asks, running a hand along my back.

"Thanks," I say, feeling my cheeks get warm. I don't know if it's from him or the alcohol.

"I'm glad I convinced Christian to invite you out."

I blink at him. "What do you mean?"

"I wanted to see you tonight," he says.

"Me? Why?"

"So I could do this—"

Nick leans forward, pressing his lips against mine. It takes my brain a few seconds to register the kiss. I pull away immediately. "What are you doing?"

"Kissing you."

"What if Christian sees?"

Nick arches his brow. "I don't know if you've realized, but Christian isn't coming back."

"But where did he go?"

"He left with Zach."

"How come he didn't say anything?"

Nick smiles. "Because you and I are having a good time." He leans forward to kiss me again.

I turn away from him. "Sorry." Then I rise abruptly from the table. "I have to go now."

"Where are you going?"

I don't answer this.

"Eric—"

Then I remember Christian's jacket. He forgot to take it with him. I grab it quickly as I head off, ignoring the calls from Nick behind me. I'm too dizzy to even hear what he's saying. The lights are harsh inside the restaurant, blinding me a little. I find the elevator and head outside again. All the street signs are a blur. I can't even tell where I'm going. *Which way did Christian go? I need to give him back his jacket.*

Maybe I should try calling him. I pull out my phone, bringing up his name. It rings for a while, but he doesn't pick up. I try a second time but still no answer. I put my phone away and look around. His building isn't too far from here. Maybe I should just drop it off at his place. As I turn the corner, someone appears beside me. *Nick must have followed me outside.* When his face comes into focus, I realize it's someone else.

"Haru . . . is that *you*?" I blink a few times, making sure I'm not seeing things. I step toward him, stumbling.

Haru catches my arm. "Careful there—"

"What are you doing here?"

"I was looking for you," he says.

We haven't seen each other in a week. I want to hug him tight, but it's hard to stand straight. The sidewalk feels like it's moving beneath me. Haru holds his grip, keeping me steady.

"You've been drinking," he says.

"I'm totally fine."

"How about we get you home." He wraps my arm over his shoulder.

But I slip away from him. "I'm going to Christian's place. I have to give him back his jacket."

"At this hour? You can do it tomorrow."

"What if he needs it tonight? I promised to give it back to him." I'm not sure if I'm slurring my words, so I try to speak slower. "I have to go see him."

"Does he know you're coming?"

I don't answer this. I just stare at the jacket.

A silence passes. Haru holds out a hand. "Let's get you home, okay? We can even put on a movie—"

"I don't want to go home. I need to give him back his jacket." Why doesn't he understand this?

Haru sighs. "Eric, you're drunk."

"I'm not drunk."

I walk away from him. But Haru steps in front of me, his voice more serious. "I think it's time to go home."

"What are you, my conscience? I told you, *I'm fine*."

"Eric . . ." he starts again.

But I don't want to hear it. I stumble down the block until Christian's building comes into view. Haru follows along, making sure I don't fall. Thankfully, it's the same doorman from last time. He just tips his head as I make my way to the elevators. I press the button and step inside. But Haru doesn't come in with me. He places both hands on the doors, keeping them open.

"You're not thinking straight right now," he says.

"Let go of the door."

Haru takes a step back. "If that's what you want."

Then the doors close between us. The next thing I know, I'm heading down a hallway to his apartment. I ring the doorbell and wait. There's no answer. Eventually I start knocking until someone opens it.

"Eric?" Christian stands in the doorway, looking at me. "What are you doing here?" His voice is sharper than usual. It sobers me up instantly.

"Uh—" I don't know what to say. I hold up his jacket. "You left your jacket at the rooftop."

Christian stares at it and back at me. "Why didn't you just text me?"

"I did, but you didn't answer . . ."

"So you came here anyway?"

This silences me. I'm not sure what I expected from this.

I wish I could turn around, pretend this was some misunderstanding. Then I hear another voice inside the apartment. I tilt my head to see who it is. It's Zach, the guy he was sitting with at the rooftop.

"I didn't mean to interrupt—"

"Did you need something else?"

The edge in his voice stabs like a knife. I don't know what else to say. "I'm sorry. I just wanted to see you, since we didn't get the chance to . . ." My voice trails off.

Christian rubs the space between his eyes. "You can't show up unannounced like this," he says. "We're not together, Eric. I don't know how to make that more clear."

"I know we're not," I say. "I just thought there was something more."

"Because we spent the night together?" He lets out a breath. "Listen, Eric. You and I had a good time. Let's just leave it at that, okay?"

"What are you saying?" I ask.

"That we shouldn't see each other again."

A silence as I take this in.

"I'm sorry if I—"

"I don't need you to apologize." He stops me. "I just need you to go. And you can keep the jacket. Now have a good night."

Then he closes the door.

I stand in the hallway for a moment longer. Then I head to the elevator and make my way back down. I leave the building, stumbling down the sidewalk. I'm not even sure where I'm going. I throw Christian's jacket into a bush as I turn the corner.

Haru appears again. I forgot he was out here. But I don't bother to stop for him. I just keep on walking.

"The train is the other way," he says.

"I'm not going home."

I can barely see what's in front of me. Tears form behind my eyes, making it hard to walk straight. The world is a gray blur. I wish Haru would stop following me. I don't want him seeing me this way. As I step off the curb, Haru appears in front of me.

He places his hands on my shoulders. "You're going to hurt yourself."

"No, I'm not."

"Do you even know where you're going?"

I try to step around him. But he blocks me again. Then he reaches into my pocket, grabbing something.

"What are you doing?" I ask.

"Taking your phone . . ."

"Give me that back—"

There's a slight tussle between us. Eventually, Haru hands it back to me. My vision is hazy as I stare at the screen. "Wait—what did you do?"

"I sent Kevin your location."

"*Kevin?* Why would you do that?"

"So he can come get you."

"I don't want him to come get me," I say, trying to undo the message. "I can't believe you did that!"

"I'm trying to help you."

"As if you care about me."

"Of course I do," he says.

"Then where were you all week?" I look at him. "I waited for you every day and you never showed up."

Haru doesn't say anything.

"Is it because I went with Christian that one time? Was that your way of getting back at me? And now you showed up, just because I'm drunk?"

Haru sighs. "I just want to make sure you're safe."

"I don't need you to do that!"

Suddenly, my phone vibrates. I squint at the screen. Kevin is calling me. I consider letting it go to voicemail. But I don't want him thinking something's wrong. He might end up calling my parents. So I take a deep breath and pick up the phone.

"Hello?"

Kevin's voice comes through. "Eric? Is everything alright?"

"Yeah, yeah, everything's alright." The words feel funny in my mouth. "What's up?"

"Are you . . . drunk right now?"

"No, I'm completely fine. I'm not drunk, like, at all."

Haru leans forward. "He's lying."

I pull the receiver away. "Haru, be quiet!"

"Who's Haru? Is somebody with you?"

"No, it's just me! Nobody else is here."

"Where are you right now?" Kevin asks.

I take a look around me. It's still hard to see clearly. "I'm not sure."

"I have your location. I'll just come pick you up."

"No, you don't have to! Kevin, I swear, I'm *fine*."

But Kevin ignores this. "I'm leaving right now. Promise you will stay there, okay?"

"Seriously, Kev—" I start.

"Please stay there."

"Okay."

Haru leans in again. "He's not going anywhere."

I push him away. "Will you stop?"

Kevin's voice comes through. "Stop what? Who are you talking to?"

"*Nobody!* Okay, bye—"

I hang up the phone and turn to Haru. "I can't believe you did that! Now Kevin's on his way here!"

"How else are you getting home?"

"I told you, I don't need anyone's help."

"You can hardly stand straight," he says, placing his hands on my shoulders, as if to steady me.

I push him off again. "You know what, Haru? You can't just show up whenever you want and tell me what to do, okay? I waited *all week* for you. I'm always waiting around for you. And you only show up when you feel like it."

"That's not true."

"Then where have you been?" I press my finger to his chest. "Where were you yesterday? And the day before that? You know how much I wanted to see you."

Haru lets out a breath and says, "If I could spend every day with you, don't you think I would? Maybe you shouldn't waste all your time waiting for me."

I can't believe he's saying this. Especially after disappearing on me. "I don't have to listen to this." I wipe a tear from my face as I turn to leave.

"Kevin told you to wait here."

"I don't care what he says."

"Eric." Haru grabs my hand. But I pull away again.

"Leave me alone!"

My voice echoes through the night air. I don't realize how sharp my words are until I feel the burn in the back of my throat. Haru stares at me in silence. As I walk off again, a knot of guilt forms in my stomach. *I shouldn't have yelled like that.* But the moment I turn around to take it back, he's gone. The street is completely empty.

"Haru? Where did you go?"

There's no answer. It's only me standing out here.

"I didn't mean that, okay?"

Nothing but silence. I look around.

"I said I'm sorry. Haru?"

I call his name for a long time. But Haru never answers. I sit on the sidewalk, hoping he comes back for me.

Seventeen

I'm half asleep when headlights appear down the road. Someone gets out of the car, approaching me. It's Kevin's voice that wakes me as he helps me up from the sidewalk. My legs feel like they're falling straight through the ground. I don't even remember the car ride, except when Kevin hands me a water bottle while the radio plays on low volume. There's no elevator in his building. We have to walk up five whole flights of stairs. I can barely hold on to the handrail, stumbling at every step. At one point, I must have given up because Kevin lifts me up and carries me the rest of the way there.

"We're almost there."

It's dark inside his apartment. Kevin turns on the kitchen light, scorching my eyes. I wander over to the sofa and lie down for a moment. The room keeps spinning, making me want to throw up.

Kevin hands me a glass of water. I don't know how thirsty I am until I finish the last drop and he brings me another glass. Kevin sets it on the coffee table and sits on the edge of the sofa. "Do you need me to take you home?" he asks.

"*No, I'm fine,*" I groan. The last thing I want is my parents making a fuss of this. I'm already embarrassed enough to have Kevin caring for me. The feeling of dizziness sets in again. "I just need to lie down and close my eyes for a second."

Kevin lays a blanket over me and refills my water. He leaves a light on in the kitchen before he disappears into his bedroom.

I roll on my side, pulling the blanket over my head, letting the rest of the world slowly drift away.

It's still dark out when I wake up again. For a second, I have no memory of what happened, where I am. My throat is dry as I reach for the glass of water. It's still too dark to see anything. A single dot of blue light blinks beneath a television. My vision is blurry as I push myself up and look around the apartment. I remember the last time I was here. Jasmine and I came to watch Korean dramas and we ate Chinese food on the floor. It feels wrong being here without her now that they've broken up.

What time is it? I should probably get out of here. I rise from the sofa, ignoring the pounding headache. The walls keep moving around me. I'm trying to leave quietly but I accidently knock something off the coffee table. Kevin must have heard it, because he comes out of his room as I'm putting on my shoes. There's just enough light to make out his silhouette in the living room.

"Are you leaving?"

"I have to go," I say.

"Let me drive you."

"No, that's okay."

"Wait—"

But I've already turned the knob and left through the door. I'm nearly tripping down the stairwell as Kevin follows behind, calling after me. But I don't answer him. I hurry out of the building, breathing in the cold air. Which way am I going again? A second later, the door swings back open as Kevin appears behind me.

"Eric, hold on," he says. "Let me drive you home."

"I'm not going home."

"Where are you going, then?"

Why can't he just take the hint? I turn to face him. "You don't have to keep following me."

"I just want to make sure—"

"I can take care of myself. Stop worrying about me. We're not even family."

I instantly regret these words. But I don't want to think about this right now. I turn away and make a run for it. Kevin tries to catch up to me. But I turn another corner and disappear down the road.

The streets are dark and empty. I don't know what time it is or where I'm going. I just cross my arms as I keep walking. I can hardly make out what's in front of me. As I'm wandering around, my phone goes off in my pocket. I squint at the screen. *Why is Jasmine calling me?* I thought she was too busy to talk to me anymore. I bet Kevin called her after I ran off.

She probably knows what I said to him. I don't want to pick up and have to explain myself right now. But the other part of me misses hearing her voice. So I answer the phone.

"*Hello?*"

"Eric." Her voice is calm in my ear. "Where are you?"

I look around. "I don't know."

"What do you mean you don't know? Are you by yourself right now?"

"Yes."

"Do you know the way back home?"

"I don't want to go home."

"What's going on?"

I don't answer this.

There's a brief silence. Then Jasmine sighs through the phone. "Alright, can you at least tell me what you see?"

I look around again. The streets are still a blur. But I can make out a few things. A few lights are on farther down the road. Is that a giant donut blinking above the storefront? That's when it hits me. "I think I see Lucy's Donuts."

"Okay, that's good," Jasmine says. "You've been there before. Do you remember the diner across the street? It should be open late."

"Yeah, I think so."

"I want you to wait for me there, okay?"

"*Wait* for you? What do you mean?"

"I'm less than an hour away," she says. "I'm going to meet you there. Just wait for me, okay?"

"Okay . . ."

"Promise me you'll stay there," she says.

"I promise."

"I'm leaving right now. Don't go anywhere."

I hang up the phone. As I'm standing there, the sidewalk starts moving again, making me feel like I'm about to fall. I stumble toward the diner, searching for something to tether myself down to.

The fluorescent lights are nearly blinding. I'm sitting at a booth in the corner, staring into my cup of water. The place is practically empty, besides an old man at the other end of the diner. A waitress brings me some coffee I didn't order.

"It's on the house, sweetie."

I take a sip and rest for a moment. I must have dozed off at some point, because someone taps my shoulder to wake me. Jasmine's face comes into focus as she slides into the other side of the booth. She's wearing the jacket again. The one I let her borrow. The lights reflecting off the window glass make everything around us hazy.

"How are you feeling there?" she asks.

I don't answer. But my head is pounding.

"Looks like you've had a rough night," she says.

"What are you doing here anyway?"

We look at each other. I know I should be happy to see her, but I remember she's still leaving.

"My flight is tomorrow," Jasmine says. "We're heading out of Rockford, so I'm staying at a friend's tonight."

"How exciting."

Silence fills the booth. Jasmine takes in a breath and lets it out. "If there's something you want to say to me, I think you should say it," she says.

"There's nothing to talk about."

"Then what's been going on lately? And why did you run away from Kevin?"

"I don't know what you're talking about."

She leans into the table. "I'm worried about you, Eric. Can you just tell me what's wrong?"

I'm not sure what she wants me to say. Maybe I don't even know the answer. Then it comes out of me. "I don't want you to go."

"Eric . . ." she starts.

"I think you should just stay."

"You know I can't do that."

My hand hits the table. "Then why are you asking me? Why did you even come here? Just to tell me you're leaving?"

"Don't be this way," she says, somewhat tensely. "It's not like I'm leaving you alone. You have plenty of people who care about you."

"I don't need anyone to care. There's nothing wrong with me."

"I didn't say there was something wrong with you. But you can't keep pushing everyone away." She reaches for my hand, but I pull away.

That's when I notice something strange. Right outside the window. White petals are falling from the sky like snow. I rub my eyes, wondering if I'm imagining this. Then the piano music starts to play, filling the diner. But I can't tell where it's coming from. *Does anyone else hear that?* It feels like I'm losing my mind here.

"What is it?"

Jasmine's voice pulls me back to the table. But I'm not sure what to tell her. I just shake my head and say, "It's nothing."

Jasmine squeezes my arm. "Maybe it's time to go home," she says.

But I'm not listening at this point. I can barely think straight. The room is spinning again. For some reason, the piano music keeps playing. Where the hell is that coming from? I swear it's following me around. I rise abruptly from the table. "I'm sorry, I have to go—"

"What— *Where are you going?*"

But I don't answer her. Instead I rush toward the entrance, hoping she doesn't follow me outside. The moment I push through the door, the diner vanishes around me as I find myself on a moving train car. It's as if I stepped into a dream or something. The floor rattles at my feet as I glance around, wondering what's going on.

A door clicks shut from behind me. I turn around just in time to see someone moving into the next car. It's the tousle of dark hair that makes me recognize him instantly.

"Haru?"

I'm not sure if I'm hallucinating. I follow him anyway and throw open the door, hoping to catch up in time. But the moment I reach the other side, he's already moved to the next car. *"Haru, wait!"* Why won't he slow down for me? No matter how many times I call his name, Haru never glances behind him. But I keep running after him, moving from one car to the next. This train doesn't seem to have an end in sight. It just keeps going and going. I'm scared I'll never be able to reach him. He's far too fast for me, slipping from my sight like mist.

"*Come back!*"

Then the train enters the tunnel, swallowing everything in darkness. That's the last thing I remember.

Eighteen

I wake up in Jasmine's room the next morning. The light from the window makes me squint. I touch my left temple, feeling an ache from the night before. How long have I been lying in bed? And where's my phone? I push myself up and look around the room. I must have wandered in here by mistake. There's something folded on the end of the bed. It's the jacket Jasmine borrowed from me. I stare at it for a moment. She must have returned it after bringing me home last night.

I don't remember what happened after leaving the diner. There's a slight pain in my left side, making it hard to sit up. Maybe I tripped on something and knocked myself out. That wouldn't be the first time that happened. I think back to my conversation with Jasmine. Wasn't her flight leaving today? Maybe that means she's already gone. I run my hand over the jacket and glance around the room. A bar of sunlight shines on her piano. If I close my eyes, I can see her sitting at the bench, playing one of her songs. But it's only me in here.

The house is empty this morning. No television on in the living room, no one washing dishes in the kitchen. Then I remember my dream of Haru. *Maybe he left something here for me.* But there's nothing waiting for me at my desk. I wish

I hadn't treated him the way I did last night. Especially when he was only trying to help me.

I stare at the paper star at the window. The one he made me a while ago. There are so many things I wish I could say to him. Hopefully I'll see him again soon. But Haru doesn't show up tonight. He doesn't come back the next day, either. Or the day after that. But I keep on waiting for him.

The next few weeks move by slowly. I go to work and back home and the day starts over again. I try to keep myself busy, working on college applications, watching movies on my phone until I fall asleep. It's been raining a lot lately. I always look to see if Haru is waiting across the street after work but he's never there. There's no folded paper waiting on my desk when I get home. I go to bed alone and wake up with no one beside me.

Sometimes I go looking for him. I head to Millennium Park and walk around the Bean at night. When it's pouring, I bring an umbrella and hope I find him sitting on one of the benches. Maybe if I wait long enough, he'll show up again. We can grab deep-dish pizza at Lou Malnati's. But the days keep passing with no sign of him anywhere. Every couple days, I go to the same café and sit at the same table where he first found me. But Haru never comes through the door. No matter how long I stay there.

What if I never see him again? I think back to the gallery opening, when we were sitting together at the piano. I should never have left him there. If I knew our time would be this short, I would have spent every second with him, memorizing the lines around his mouth when he smiles, or how his hair falls across his eyes when he's playing the piano.

I blocked Christian's number a few days ago. Not that I was expecting to hear from him again. I finally returned all the clothes I bought to impress him. I don't know what I was thinking pretending to be someone else. No matter how much I try to be one of them, I'll always be an outsider looking in.

Things felt easy when I was with Haru. I didn't need to change myself around him. I look down at the red bracelet we got together in Japan. I still wear it every day. He's never disappeared for this long before. A part of me wonders if he was ever here at all. Then I touch the paper flower I keep with me, reminding myself it was real. I just thought we had more time together. *Where did you go this time? Will I ever see you again?*

There's a stationery store near the theater. I stumbled upon it on my way home a few days ago. It's always closed by the time I get out of work. Sometimes I like to stop and look through the window. Everything inside reminds me of Haru. *"My family owns a shop like this in Osaka,"* he once told me. *"You don't find a lot of them around anymore. I always make sure to buy something, even if it's just a piece of paper."*

Another memory comes to me. *Haru holds his hand out at the train station; the piece of paper flutters between his fingers. "I wanted to give you this before you left," he says quickly. "So we can stay connected." Then the breeze picks up, pulling the paper into the air as the doors close between us.*

I wonder where I would be now if it never flew out of my hands. Maybe it's still floating around somewhere, waiting for me to catch it. As I think about what he might have written, an idea comes to me. I don't know why I didn't think of it before. The next morning, I return to the stationery store before work and buy some paper. At lunch, I find a pen and sit at the counter. Maybe it's my turn to leave a note.

But what should I say to him?

Dear Haru,
I'm so sorry. I never should have left you that night. I've replayed that scene in my head a thousand times imagining different endings. I hope you can find a way to forgive me. Until then, I'll be waiting every day.
 I hope you keep your promise.

 x Eric

I fold the note in half and tuck it into my pocket. Later that night, I watch a few video tutorials about how to fold a paper rose. Then I leave it on my desk with my note inside. I know it's not as pretty as the flowers that Haru folds for me, but I hope he finds this anyway. I fall asleep that night dreaming about him.

It's drizzling the next morning. I'm half soaked when I arrive at the theater. Alex called in sick, so it's just me and Simon at the box office. It's a typical afternoon, assigning will-call tickets while Simon gossips about the actors in the show. He says there's some new drama with the cast.

"*Maria's pregnant,*" Simon says, pausing for dramatic effect. "At least, that's what everyone thinks. Why else would she be missing for the rest of the show?"

"Who's that again?"

"She's Camille's *understudy*—" He throws a bag of chocolate-covered almonds at me. "How many times do I have to tell you this?"

I glance at the bag of almonds. "Where did this come from?"

"Don't worry about it. There's beef jerky if you want some." Simon sits on the counter and takes a sip of his iced coffee. "Anyway, back to the story. Now, you didn't hear this from me, but we think the father could be Philip."

"I thought Philip was engaged to Camille—"

He nods. "*Exactly.*"

I take this in. "How do you know all this?"

"What do you mean, I don't know anything," Simon says as he looks around the lobby, in case someone is listening. "I also don't know that Philip's car has been parked outside Maria's building all weekend. Keep in mind, this comes after rumors of them checking into the Waldorf together a few weeks ago. But that's not even the crazy part." Simon leans forward, keeping his voice low. "They found walnuts in Camille's chicken salad the other day, when everyone knows she's *deathly* allergic. I hear there's a police investigation."

I gasp. "Oh my god."

"I'm telling you, Eric, you can't write the stuff that happens around here." Simon takes another sip of his drink, crossing one leg over the other. "Which reminds me. What's the update with you and Christian?"

I sigh. "I told you, I blocked his number."

"I'm just making sure," he says, stirring his straw around. "I still can't believe you didn't keep his jacket. We could have sold it to one of those resellers." He shakes his head, sighing. "I also heard he's been making his rounds through the cast, if you know what I mean."

It stings to know this, even though we were never together. "Simon—I'm trying not to think about him, remember?"

Simon nods. "You're right, he's dead to us. We won't bring him up again. Unless he actually dies or something."

"I appreciate that."

"Who's the other guy on your mind?"

I look at him. "What do you mean?"

"You're clearly thinking about someone," he says. "I'm assuming it's another boy, the way you've been moping around here. Staring longingly outside, as if you've been stood up. I also saw you writing that love letter yesterday."

The paper rose for Haru. It was still on my desk when I left this morning. "It wasn't a love letter."

"Then who was it for?"

I'm not sure what to say.

"I'm being intrusive again?" Simon asks.

"No, it's okay," I say, shrugging it off. "It's just a friend of mine. From last summer. We talk here and there. But I haven't seen him in a while."

"Why don't you just text him?"

I wish it could be that simple, sending Haru a message. It's like he disappeared to another universe I can't reach. But I can't tell Simon any of this. "It's complicated." I sigh. "We didn't exactly leave things on the best note."

"Do you think you'll see him again?"

I stare at the floor. "I don't really know."

Simon doesn't ask more questions. He climbs off the counter, squeezing one of my shoulders. "I'm sorry you're going through this. We all do. But you'll find someone new."

I don't say anything else. Because I don't want someone else. I want to find Haru again. A moment later, the phone rings. I let Simon answer it and take my seat at the counter. The rest of the shift is pretty quiet. I glance at the doors from time to time, hoping to see a glimpse of someone familiar.

The sun is going down as I leave the theater. Simon invited me out with his friends, but I told him I had plans tonight. Truth is, I'm waiting outside for Haru again. What if he shows up this time and I'm not here? The sidewalk is glistening as the wind blows leaves everywhere. I stand under the marquee and stare at the blinking traffic. I know there are better uses of my time. But the thought of losing him makes me feel more alone.

The hours pass like seconds. Sometimes it feels like I'm

stuck in this spot while the rest of the world is moving around me. It looks like the rain might start up again. Maybe he's not coming back tonight either. As I finally turn to leave, the sound of a bell goes off, echoing through the air. *Could that be* . . .

I spin around as a bicycle zooms past me, splashing rain on my shoes. I look around for Haru, but he's not there. Of course that wasn't him. I should stop getting my hopes up. As I'm walking away, someone calls my name.

"*Eric.*"

I pause on the sidewalk. For a second, I think I've imagined the voice. It wouldn't be my first time hearing things. As I turn around, my heart stops. Haru is standing on the other side of the street, one hand in his pocket.

We stare at each other as cars pass between us. The moment the light changes, I rush toward him immediately.

"*Haru!*" I throw my arms around him, nearly knocking us both over. I don't even care if anyone is watching. "*It's really you.*"

"Did you miss me?" Haru says, pulling me into him.

More than you know. "Of course I did," I say breathlessly. Relief floods through me as I hold him tight. I can't believe he came back to me. I close my eyes for a second, letting the rest of the world curve away from us. "I looked everywhere for you. Where on earth have you been?"

"You were looking for me?" he asks. "Thought you might not have noticed I was gone."

"Why would you think that?"

"You told me to leave you alone, remember?"

I stare at him, wishing I could take it all back. "You know I didn't mean that—"

"It's alright," he says, quickly tousling my hair. "I know you didn't."

"Thanks for coming back."

Haru looks down, pressing his lips together. "Listen, Eric . . ."

"Wait—"

This is my chance to show how much I want to make it up to him. "I wrote a list of things we can do," I say, feeling my back pockets. "I have it here somewhere. I was thinking we could go to this music festival that's happening in the park. Oh, and there's a paper exhibit at this museum that I know you would love to see." *Where did I put that list?*

"We can't do that."

"Of course we can," I tell him. This is going to be a new beginning for us. This time I'll make sure to put him first. "I know it's raining a little, but they might be playing a movie in the park soon. Let's go—"

I take Haru's hand, turning toward the park. But his fingers slip through mine. I look back at him. "Is something wrong?"

"I can't go with you," he says.

"Why not?"

"Because I only came back to say goodbye."

Raindrops fall against my skin. "Goodbye? You just got here."

"I know that," he says, letting out a breath. "But I can't stay long."

"Then we can do something else," I suggest. "We don't have to see a movie if you don't want to. We can always do that when you're back."

"I'm not coming back."

I go quiet for a moment, unsure what he means by this. "What are you talking about?"

"I said I'm not coming back."

A chill goes through me. I wait for him to say more but he doesn't. "You're scaring me here. Is this about Christian? Because I don't even talk to him anymore. I promise I won't—"

"It's not about him," he says.

"Then what is it? Why are you leaving?"

Haru doesn't answer this, making my stomach sink. The rain continues to fall around us. He moves my hair out of my face and says, "I'm not mad at you, alright? But you know this couldn't be forever. Don't want to keep you from your life."

"But you're a part of my life," I tell him. "What are you trying to say?"

Haru lets out a breath. "You know we can't be together. That I would have to go eventually. I realized there are things I could never do for you. I'll always be a paper flower in your life, and you deserve a real one."

I love his paper flowers. Doesn't he understand this?

I let go of his hand. "Don't say that. I don't want you to go. I don't need anything else from you. Don't you care about me?"

Haru takes my face in his hands, raindrops bouncing off his skin. "In another world, I would spend every second with you. But I don't want you to live in that world. I don't want you to spend your life waiting for me."

There's a pain in my chest. I thought we had a second chance to fix things. He's been gone for weeks. Now he's come back just to say goodbye? I swallow my breath and say, "Okay, fine. If that's what you really think. You can go then."

"I don't want us to leave things like this." Haru reaches for my hand.

But I step away from him. "You're the one ending this," I remind him. "I guess I shouldn't be that surprised, though. That someone else in my life is leaving me." *I never thought it would be you.*

"I'm sorry," he says.

We stare at each other. At this point, I'm glad it's raining. So he can't see the tears coming down. "It doesn't matter. You can just go."

The streetlights come on, illuminating the trees that line the path. When I think there's nothing more to say, I turn around and head off. Maybe a part of me thinks Haru will stop me. But there's no hand on my shoulder, no voice calling after me as I'm walking away. I don't bother to turn around, checking if he's still standing there. Because there's nothing I can do to make him stay.

I only wish you'd told me sooner. So I didn't have to wait for you.

Nineteen

The next few weeks are pale and gloomy. I spend my days inside the house, staring at the walls, watching movies in my room. Long naps in the afternoons are a good way to pass the time. Haru hasn't shown up since we said goodbye. Not that I'm expecting him to anymore. I'll still find myself waiting up for him sometimes. It's hard keeping people off your mind when they've taken so much space in it. I've been trying to forget about him. I take all the things he's made me, place them inside a box, and shove it far back in the closet.

I'm focusing more on myself these days. I started working on college applications again and sent some of them out. I even applied to a few places outside of Illinois, one of them in New York City. I'm not sure what I'll do if I get accepted. But I won't have to decide for a few months anyway. The film scholarship has been on my mind. The one I told Jasmine about. The deadline passed a few days ago and I never submitted anything. But they just sent out an email, extending the deadline to next week. This gives me another chance to produce something. While I don't have time to go out to film anything, I have folders of unused videos I could potentially piece together into something interesting. I just have to come up with an idea. I spend the next few days working on nothing else but the scholarship.

It's cold out when I arrive at the theater. I see my breath in front of me as I push through the doors. I've been taking on extra shifts at the box office. It's become the most consistent thing that gets me out of the house. I like the monotony of answering phones, handing out tickets, watching people come in and out of the lobby. It's also the only time I see Simon and Alex, my necessary dose of social interaction for the week.

The lobby quiets down when the show starts. I'm sitting at the counter, staring out at the entrance doors. Sometimes I'll catch myself looking for him. I wish I could get him out of my mind. I know he won't show up again . . .

"Are you still looking for that guy?"

Simon's voice pulls me back.

I turn away. "Don't know who you're talking about."

"The guy you're always waiting for," he says, leaning against the counter. His blue nail polish shimmers in the fluorescent light. "I figure it's the same one. Is he still ghosting you?"

"He isn't *ghosting* me."

"Then where is this mystery boy?"

I let out a breath. "He's not coming around anymore."

"Did you two end things?"

"No, it's . . . hard to explain."

"Well, I have plenty of time." Simon takes a seat next to me and gets comfortable. "Start from the beginning."

"Sorry to disappoint you," I say, leaning back in my chair. "But there isn't a story. We were never really together, to be completely honest."

"Were you in love with him?"

The question surprises me. Maybe because I never asked it myself. I stare at my hands, thinking about it. "Maybe I was. We spent a lot of time together. He made me forget about everything else, you know? He would disappear a lot, but was always there when I needed him. He was like my best friend, too. It's hard to find people who you connect with like that." I go still for a moment. "I'm starting to think I just imagined it all."

Simon nods thoughtfully. "People come in and out of our lives, you know? Sometimes for the better, and sometimes you wish it happened differently. It's just the way it is."

"How do you deal with it?"

"I just cut my losses," he says with a shrug. "Move on to the next guy who will probably disappoint me, too. It's the circle of life. I mean, how long are you gonna cry over the same guy? Throw that dead fish back in the sea."

I say nothing.

"And that's what we have friends for, anyway," he adds, playfully hitting my shoulder.

I smile a little.

Simon rises from his chair. "At the very least, you have to stop moping around here," he says. "You're killing the vibe."

He grabs his phone from the counter. "Alex and I are going to a party tonight. It's at one of the crew's apartments in Hyde Park. You should come with us."

"I don't know if I'm up for that," I say.

Simon shakes his head. "It won't be like last time. My friend Scottie's at UChicago, so it's not all theater people. You don't need to dress to the nines. Unless you want to, of course. But there won't be any Christians there. As far as I know, anyway. I mean, what else are you gonna do? Stare longingly out the window all night?"

I let out another breath. I was planning to go home and watch another movie, maybe work on the film scholarship application. But Simon has already invited me out a few times. I don't want to keep saying no, especially when he's making the effort to hang out with me. It might be nice to take my mind off things for a couple of hours. "Okay, I'll come. But I probably can't stay too long."

Simon smiles. "Perfect. We can split an Uber."

We get off work a few hours later. I change my shirt and meet Simon at the corner, where the car is waiting for us. Alex texted us a few minutes ago, letting us know she's already on the way. It's still cold out, but I decide not to bring my jacket. I always end up forgetting it at these types of parties. The car drops us off in front of an apartment building that could be mistaken for a fraternity house. Ivy runs up and down the brick-red walls. I've never been to this side of Hyde Park before. We make our way inside and head to the second floor.

There's more people here than I expected. The place is dimly lit, strings of blue lights hanging along the walls. At least the music isn't too loud. Simon hugs a few people, introducing me to everyone.

"This is Eric. He works the box office with me."

I keep looking around for Christian. Thankfully, I don't see him anywhere. I can't really imagine him at a place like this. He's probably at some fancy cocktail bar, drinking with the other guy I saw him with. I push the thought of him out of my mind. A moment later, Alex finds us near the Ping-Pong table that doubles as a second bar. She sets her drink down and puts her arm around me.

"When did you guys get here?" she asks.

"A few minutes ago," Simon says.

Alex glances at me. "What's wrong, Eric?"

"Some guy ghosted him," Simon whispers.

"Again?"

"*Stop telling people that,*" I say.

Simon and Alex give each other a look. Then Alex takes my hand, leading me to the other side of the room. "I want you to meet someone," she says.

"Okay . . ."

A dark-haired guy wearing an olive shirt is standing near the television. Alex grabs his shoulder, turning him around to face me. "This is my friend Jacob," she says. "He studies film here, isn't that right?"

"Art history."

"Same difference."

He holds out his hand. "What was your name?"

"Eric," I say.

We chat for a few minutes. Jacob is a sophomore at UChicago. Alex leaves us to get a drink, and we continue talking about recent movies we've seen. He has a Canon 5D Mark II and his favorite movie is *Interstellar*. To be honest, it's not the most riveting conversation. Jacob seems like a nice guy, but there's just no spark between us. Like two ships docked at different ports. He must feel the same, because at one point he checks his phone and tells me he has to meet a friend.

I wander around the party to see if I know anyone. There's a make-your-own-cocktail bar in the kitchen. But I don't really feel like drinking anything. I find Simon in the corner of another room, sitting rather closely with some guy, whispering into his neck. I leave him alone and go looking for Alex. There are so many rooms in this dorm. I can't seem to find her anywhere.

Another slow song comes on. I stand near the doorway, watching people pair up as the mood of the room changes. I know I haven't been here very long. But maybe I can slip out without anyone noticing. Simon seems distracted enough. Even Jacob appears to have found new company. He's making out with some random guy on the sofa. I stand there for a few more minutes, pretending to check my phone. Then I decide it's time to go.

The moment I step out of the apartment, someone calls my name. But the voice isn't familiar. I turn around and see someone coming toward me. The second I recognize who it is, I go completely still.

Leighton steps out of the apartment, letting the door close behind me. His blond hair looks almost yellow in the hallway light. I don't remember the last time we saw each other. It must have been the week after Daniel's death. For a brief moment, I consider turning down the stairwell, pretending I didn't hear him. But it's too late.

"Hey, man," he says. "Surprised to see you here."

"Yeah, same to you."

We don't shake hands or anything. Even though we both knew Daniel, we've only met a few times.

"How have you been?" he asks.

"Alright," I say.

Then the door opens again as another guy comes out behind him. He has short red hair and wears a gray crewneck. He must know Leighton because he walks right up to him.

Leighton puts his arm around him and says, "This is my boyfriend, Max. He's a sophomore here."

I look at him. "Your boyfriend?"

"Yeah, this is his place." He points back to the apartment.

Of all the parties to show up to. The universe truly has a sense of humor. "How long have you been together?"

"Almost a year now," he says.

"A year?"

I take this in for a moment. Because that doesn't makes sense. Daniel passed away a year ago. Unless Leighton started seeing this guy right after that. But how do you move on from someone that fast? Especially someone like Daniel. The moment it sinks in, my stomach starts to turn.

"Have a good night," I say abruptly.

I head downstairs and throw open the door. The temperature must have dropped, because it's freezing outside. I can't believe I didn't bring a jacket. My body shivers from the cold. The train stop is seven blocks from here. I cross my arms as I make my way down the street. The thought of Leighton fills me with anger. How could he forget about Daniel already? He basically moved on to some other guy the next day. Meanwhile, I barely go a second without thinking about him. I still look through photos of him when I'm alone. It only goes to show Leighton never cared about him the way I did. But I guess none of that ever mattered. Because Daniel still chose him in the end.

A large bus pulls up along the sidewalk. But it's not the kind you wait at a stop for. Then the door slides open, music playing from inside. I watch as people step down in pairs, all of them dressed up for what looks like a formal. I'm about to walk off when two guys come out, holding hands, making me pause again. The one with wispy brown hair looks so much like Daniel, I think it's him for a second. I stand completely still as he passes me, going toward the doors of the building, imagining it's me walking next to him.

As they head inside, I find myself alone again. The street is quiet as a feeling of loneliness moves through me. I turn down the sidewalk, wishing I could disappear from this. To another timeline where Daniel was still alive.

My phone chimes in my pocket. There's a new text message. It's from a number I don't recognize.

Guess who
I'll give you a hint
It's your neighborhood-spidey
Nick

I stare at the message. Christian's friend Nick? I haven't heard from him since that night at the rooftop bar. How did he even get my number? Christian must have given it to him. I know I should probably block his number, too. But for some reason, I don't.

I'm not sure why I'm doing this, but I text him back instead.

hey!
what have you been up to?

Nick responds almost instantly.

waiting around for the chance
to see you again
Let's grab a drink tonight

I hesitate. Then I send him another text.

where did you have in
mind?

Nick sends me another text, along with a location ping. He wants to meet at a restaurant in Lincoln Park. The place is called Charles Tuesday. I think about Haru for a moment. He would disapprove of the decision I'm about to make. But he's not around anymore. So it doesn't matter. I put the location into my phone and head to the train station.

Twenty

Piano Sonata No. 11 is playing as I enter the restaurant. The place looks like where you'd host the after-party for the Met Gala. Chandeliers hang from an arched ceiling, illuminating the velvet furniture around the room. A woman in a cocktail dress directs me to the back, where Nick is already sitting at the bar. He waves me over as he rises to pull out my chair, kissing me on each cheek. "Sit yourself right here," he says, squeezing my shoulder affectionately. "I assume you want something fancy to drink."

I smile at him. "Yeah, that sounds good."

The bartender doesn't bother to check my ID. Something I noticed when I was around Christian was that you can get away with a lot of things when you have the pedigree. Nick is another example of this. He smiles warmly, taking a sip from his glass. His blond hair is brushed to one side, curling softly at the edges.

"You have to try this," he says.

"What is it?"

"A French martini. My drink of choice lately."

I take a small sip, tasting notes of raspberry. "Oh, it's pretty good."

"That's a Michelin star, coming from *you*," Nick whispers. He nods at the bartender, ordering a second one.

A server brings out a tray of hors d'oeuvres. Tuna tartare and cucumber bites.

"Ordered these just for you," Nick says, resting an arm on the bar. "You like salmon, right? I remember you telling me."

"Yeah, I do."

He smiles again, taking another sip of his cocktail. "Well, what have you been doing these days? I need to know every detail, starting with your love life."

I shake my head. "There's no love life."

"I find that hard to believe, looking like you."

I can't help smiling at this. The bartender returns, setting down the drink that Nick ordered for me. Nick holds up his glass and says, "Cheers to our reunion."

Our glasses clink. My drink is somewhat smoky, but the notes of strawberry make it easy to go down. "What's in this again?"

"It's mezcal."

"I honestly can't tell there's alcohol in it."

"That's how you know it's good," he says with a smirk. He tips his glass to the man behind the bar. "You'd be hard-pressed to find a better bartender than Arthur here."

"So you come here a lot?"

"It's my favorite bar in all of Chicago." He leans forward. "I do my best to gatekeep this place, so let's keep this a little secret between us." He winks at me. "I like this shirt you're wearing. What event are you coming from?"

"Just some party in Hyde Park. But I didn't stay very long."

"Well, I'm glad you ended up here," he says.

"Yeah. I'm glad you texted me."

He holds up his glass again. "Cheers to us."

We chat for a while, enjoying our drinks. Nick asks endless questions about me. The schools I'm applying to, the major I'm interested in, where I see myself in ten years. "Goldman Sachs would be a dream," I say as seriously as possible, making him laugh hysterically. I enjoy his story about losing his phone in Aspen during his annual ski trip in November. Every time I'm halfway through my drink, he orders me another one. The attention feels good, especially from someone like Nick. I'm honestly having a great night, even though my thoughts are getting fuzzy. Nick never takes his eyes off me, always asking if I need anything else. Maybe I was too quick to judge him last time. He makes me feel more special than Christian did.

About an hour later, Nick calls for the check. The bartender brings out a rose macaron, which he tells us is on the house. Nick offers me the first bite, then pops the other half into his mouth. I check the time on my phone. It's almost eleven thirty now. The restaurant looks like it's closing soon.

"Why don't we head back to my place," Nick suggests.

"Do you live around here?"

"Only a block away."

"Oh, that's convenient," I say. Almost like he planned it.

I wasn't expecting to stay out this long. I should probably take the next train home, especially when my phone battery is running low. But I don't want the night to end, either. Maybe I could hang out for another hour. I don't realize how tipsy I am until I rise from my chair. Thankfully, Nick is there to walk me to the door. The moment we step outside, I notice something in the air.

"*It's snowing,*" I say.

"Better hurry to my place for cover."

Nick lives in a townhouse on Burling Street. I follow him up the steps as he unlocks the door with a passcode. The place is beautifully decorated with modern furniture. It's nowhere near the size of Christian's, but you could definitely host a big party. Especially with the built-in speakers on the wall. Nick disappears into the kitchen as I take a seat on the living room sofa. A moment later, he returns with two glasses of wine.

"One for you," he says.

"I'm not really a wine person."

"It's a Malbec. You'll like this one."

I take the glass, despite my better judgment. Nick puts on some music and sits close to me on the sofa. I can see the snow falling outside the window. It's nice to be out of the cold. One touch of his phone turns on the electric fireplace. We talk for a while, adding songs to a playlist he starts for me. Nick tells me about his art pieces, most of which were gifted to him. He points to the painting behind us. "That was done by this artist I met in Verona a few summers ago."

"He just gave it to you?"

"I might have paid in other ways," he says through a smirk.

We both chuckle at this. Nick rests his arm behind the

sofa, inching closer to me. My face feels warm from the wine. Maybe I've had enough for tonight. I set the glass down on the coffee table. Then I lean back, feeling his arm around my shoulder. We look at each other. I can't deny how handsome he is, especially with those blue eyes. Nick runs a hand along my neck and whispers, "I love how soft your skin is."

"Thanks . . ." I breathe.

A smile rises across his face. Then he leans in to kiss me. His lips are sweet from the wine. I close my eyes for a moment, letting his hands pull me into him. I feel a rush of blood moving through me, the warmth of his body. Then his hands move down farther, slowly lifting my shirt . . . But I stop him there.

He looks at me. "What's the matter?"

"I wasn't expecting to . . ."

Nick kisses me again. I turn my face away.

"Maybe we shouldn't," I say.

"Come on," he says, leaning in again.

But I push him back a little. "Sorry. I don't know if I want to tonight."

"You're serious?"

He stares at me intently. Maybe he's expecting me to change my mind. But I don't say another word. Then he releases a breath, straightening himself up. He grabs his phone, turning off the music.

"Why don't you go then," he says.

"Uh, what?" I stutter.

"I said you should go."

I don't know what to say. It's still snowing outside. I haven't thought about how I would get home. "I'm sorry if I . . ."

"Just get your stuff." The warmth in his voice is gone. He's like a different person.

"Sorry," I say again.

I rise from the sofa, feeling light-headed. The room is twirling a little, making it hard to stand straight. I wish I didn't drink that last glass of wine. I shouldn't have had anything to drink at all. I grab my phone that's dead and look for my shoes. Nick opens the door as I'm still struggling with the laces. Then I step out into the cold.

"Thanks for inviting—"

The door slams in my face.

I stand on the steps for a moment. Then I turn around, facing the cold as I make my way down the street. Snow falls on my head and shoulders. I can't believe Nick threw me out without a jacket. I should have just gone home instead of coming here. I wish I'd never responded to him in the first place.

The streets are covered with snow. I'm not sure which way is home. My phone is dead, so I can't look up the nearest train stop. I've never been to this side of Lincoln Park. I can barely read the street signs. My vision is blurred from the tears that are falling. I don't know if I'm going the right way. I feel completely lost, wishing someone would come find me.

My body is trembling now. I don't know how far I've walked. But it feels like I'm about to fall over. The world is spinning around me, making it hard to keep my eyes open.

I stumble upon an empty bench in the middle of the park. The next thing I know, I've laid myself down, ignoring the snow. There's nothing I can do about it, anyway. At least the alcohol has numbed me from the cold. I can't feel anything except the emptiness inside me.

Where did you go, Haru? I wish I could see you one more time.

Streetlights swirl above me. I take a deep breath and finally close my eyes. The snow continues to fall, settling over me like a thin blanket. I feel my body slowly shutting down. I don't care what happens to me tonight. All I want is to fall asleep and disappear from the world. I'm tired of waiting for people who are never coming. As my mind slowly drifts off, everything around me fades to nothing.

The sound of footsteps wakes me up. For a second, I think I'm dreaming. Maybe a branch fell from one of the trees. Or maybe it's Haru, coming to find me. I open my eyes slowly. Someone is standing beside the bench. It's too blurry to make out a face. Then my vision clears, letting me see her perfectly. I rub my eyes, wondering what she's doing here. Jasmine's hair glows slightly from the light reflected off the snow. She's more slender than I remember, and her skin is pale. She doesn't say anything at first. She stares at me for a moment. Then she brushes snow off the bench and says, "Mind if I sit here with you?"

I push myself up, letting her take a seat beside me. It's silent for a moment, snow falling gently around us. I'm not sure how she found me. My phone is still dead. How would she even know I was lost? Isn't she supposed to be on the other side of the world right now?

"What are you doing here?" I ask.

"I came to see you," she says.

"How did you find me?"

"It wasn't too hard." She smiles at me, moving her hair behind her ear. "What are you doing, sleeping on a bench?"

"I got lost."

"How long have you been out here?"

"I don't know. A while."

"Need me to show you the way home?"

When I don't answer this, Jasmine leans back and takes a breath. There's a long silence. Then she says, "Maybe it's time you and I finally talk. You can't avoid it forever."

I say nothing.

"Why won't you just say it?"

I don't want to have this conversation. But maybe she's right. Maybe avoiding it is only making it worse. "Because I'm not ready to believe it," I admit.

"Believe what?"

"That you're gone, too."

The words echo through me. I never thought I'd say it out loud. Jasmine stares at me for a moment. Then she leans forward and says, "I'm right here . . ."

"No, you're not." I shake my head. "You're not here at all. You left just like Daniel did." There's a pain in my throat, making it hard to speak. "Why did you have to leave me? I don't have anyone left."

Jasmine takes my face in her hands and says, "I'm so sorry, Eric. For leaving you this way. You know that was the last thing I wanted to do. To have you go through this alone. I can't imagine all the pain you're going through. I know it seems unfair, losing the people you love. Losing me." She wipes a tear from my cheek. "But I need you to remember that you didn't lose everything. It may be hard to see now, but there is so much left for you in the world. So much to live for still. All the people who love you. You just have to let them in. You have a whole life ahead of you. Even if I'm not in it."

"But I don't want you to go," I say.

Jasmine takes my hands, holding them tight. "You have every right to go through this your own way. Even if that means living inside your head, pretending everything is alright. But you can't keep it bottled up forever. There comes a time when you have to look around you and face what's real. And I think it's time now."

I take this in. "It's easier to pretend . . ."

"I know it is," Jasmine says. "That's why I left those letters for you. So we can always stay in touch. Why haven't you read them yet?"

"Because I'm scared."

"Of what?"

"That reading them will make it more real," I manage to say.

Jasmine puts her arms around me. She wipes my tears off again. "I understand that. But I think it's time for you to read them now."

I swallow my breath.

"Promise me, okay?"

Tears are swelling behind my eyes. "I promise."

"I want you to do one more thing for me now," she says.

"What is it?"

Jasmine leans back, taking my face in her hands again. Her voice is strangely calm when she says, "I need you to wake up and go home..."

At first, I don't know what she means. Before I can say something, the night suddenly fades around me, blurring my vision. All I hear is Jasmine's voice, filling the spaces of my head as everything goes dark again.

I need you to wake up and go home...

I open my eyes and find myself alone on the bench. It's still dark out. My hands are cold as I push myself up slowly, holding in a shiver. I glance at the other side of the bench. The blanket of snow is untouched, as if no one had sat there. My breath turns to mist in front of me. How long have I been asleep out here? I stare at the bench for a long moment. Then I rise to my feet, slowly making my way to the train station.

I head straight to my room when I get home. Everything is exactly as I left it this morning. I remember my conversation with Jasmine. I think it's time I keep my promise. I turn on a single desk lamp, opening one of the drawers. The letters are all there, folded inside white envelopes with a flower embossed in the top corner. My name and the date appear on each one in Jasmine's handwriting. I'm sorry I put this off for so long. But it's always better late than never. I take a seat on the bed, finally ready to read them.

Dear Eric,
If you're reading this, I guess it means we didn't get our miracle. I'm sorry to start it off this way. I wish I could be there instead, sitting next to you. Sometimes life gives us battles that we end up losing. As much as we try to fight through it. I promise you I fought my hardest, okay? But this letter isn't meant to be about apologies or what could have been. The last thing I want is for you to be sad when you read this. That's not why I'm writing to you. I want to leave something behind that will give you a piece of joy. Something for you to look forward to, especially in the moments you're feeling down. Think of it as my way of popping into the world, just to say hi. That way I'm not completely gone, okay?

I know this isn't going to fix everything. I could write you a million letters, but it won't be the same as before. I know that. I also know life is going to throw more things at you, and I wish I could be there to shield you from all of it. Through all the heartbreaks and times you feel you're lost in the world. All the rejections and boys you'll meet who don't deserve you. The struggles we all deal with throughout our lives that sometimes appear much larger in the moment than they are. I would remind you how incredible you are, to never let anyone make you feel small and unworthy of love. I'm sorry you're losing an older sister who would do anything to protect you. That's why I asked Kevin to look after you when I'm gone. Think of him as an older brother, okay? He cares so much about you, and I hope you know that. In my absence, I hope you'll still spend time together. He might need you, too. So keep him close.

And no matter what, I want you to stay in touch with Mom and Dad. I know they're hard to talk to sometimes, but they just express their love in different ways. That is one favor I ask of you here. Sit down for dinner every once in a while, okay? It reminds them how much you love them. I don't want them to think they've lost you, too.

This also isn't the last letter you'll get from me. Don't worry about how or when they'll come. Just know that you'll be hearing from me again, okay? I love you so much, Eric. I wish I had told you this more often. You're the best brother I could have asked for and I'm lucky to have you in my life.

There's one more thing I want to give you. It's in my room. I need you to go inside and turn on the keyboard. There are a set of buttons from one to seven. You can listen to them in any order, just press play.

Love you always,
Jasmine

I take the letter to Jasmine's room. It feels strange to be in here again. I turn on a lamp and sit at the keyboard. I read over the letter one more time, following her instructions as I press play. A second later, her voice comes through.

"Hey . . . it's Jasmine. You're probably not expecting this, huh? That must mean you got my letter. Or maybe you stumbled on this by accident while playing in my room. Either way, I'm leaving this for you." A pause. "I'm sure things still hurt right now. So I thought about what I could give that would make it feel like I was still there. What's a piece of me I could leave behind? Then I remembered, the song I played for you. The one you inspired. You don't know this, Eric, but you've inspired a lot of my songs. I never got the chance to play them all for you. So I want to play them for you now. Who knows, maybe they'll inspire you the same way you did for me."

Another pause.

"Anyway, this is for you. I hope you like it . . ."

As I sit there, tears swelling in my eyes, piano music slowly fills the room. It's a familiar song, like the one that's been following me around everywhere. But this time, it's not in my head. The music is real. I can feel it moving through me. I close my eyes, imagining Jasmine's fingers dancing across the keys. For a moment, it's as if she's here in the room with me.

I'm so lost in the memories, I don't hear Mom and Dad come through the door. They must have heard the music from their room, wondering where it was coming from. When was the last time any of us woke up to Jasmine playing the piano? They don't have to ask what I'm listening to, or how I found this. They know this music the same way they can recognize her voice. Mom and Dad sit beside me at the keyboard. Dad places a hand on my shoulder, Mom resting her head against mine. No words are needed as we listen to Jasmine's recording, crying together for the first time.

I sit at my desk the next morning.

> *Dear Jaz,*
> I miss you. I think about you every day. I still wake up to the realization that you're not here anymore. That it wasn't some dream. That I can't call you up and ask what you're doing. That I'm never going to see you again.
>
> I know it's been seven months now, but I'm still not used to a world without you in it. It's hard to accept the reality that you're really gone. I still text you every now and then. I even imagine what you would write back. Sometimes I go to Uncle Wong's Palace and pretend you're there. That you're sitting right next to me. I always order the pineapple fried rice because I know it's your favorite. It makes me feel less alone when I talk to you, even though no one's there.
>
> You don't know this, but I was mad at you for a while. For leaving me when I needed you most. I had already lost Daniel out of the blue. Why did you suddenly have to go, too? It was like everyone I cared about was taken from me and I couldn't do anything

about it. I know it's not your fault. But some days it's easier to just pretend none of it happened. I even made up this story where you left to pursue your dreams in music. I preferred the alternate world where you still existed, even if we couldn't see each other. But I know I can't stay in this forever. I know you want me to keep living my life. I know you want me to be happy. Even though it seems impossible right now.

Thanks for writing all your letters. You don't know how much they mean to me. I'm sorry it took so long for me to read them. But I think you probably understand why now. I just wanted to pretend for a little longer. That's why I'm writing back so late. I just needed a little more time. Thank you for pulling me back to the world. I guess you're still there for me, even if I can't see you.

I'm lucky I had you in my life, too. You were more than a sister to me. You were my best friend. Will miss you forever.

Love always,
Eric

Dear Kevin,
I know it's been a while since we've spoken. I hope it's okay that I'm writing to you instead of calling. I'm sorry about what happened a few weeks ago. How I ran off when you were only trying to help me. I'm

sorry for the things I said, too. You didn't do anything to deserve that. I truly hope you can forgive me.

I wanted to talk with you about this in person. But I thought it would be easier to write it down first. The reason I didn't want to see you these past several months. Why I've been ignoring all your messages. The way I've been treating you lately. The truth is, seeing you without Jasmine only reminded me she was gone. If I'm being honest with you, that's something I still haven't fully accepted yet. I thought it would be easier to avoid if I avoided you, too. Because I've never known you without her. That was unfair of me, trying to erase you from my life. I guess I forgot that you also lost Jasmine. And maybe you needed me, too.

When Jasmine passed away, I wasn't sure if I'd ever hear from you again. So I was surprised when you kept reaching out. You've always offered to be there for me, even when I couldn't in return. That's why I'm writing to you now. To apologize for before. So I hope it's not too late. I hope we get a chance to talk again. And I hope you'll forgive me.

Anyway, I'm grateful that Jaz had you in her life. I know she truly loved you. Thank you for being a part of our family.

Love,
Eric

Dear Daniel,

I know you'll never read this, but I wanted to write to you anyway. It's been over a year now since you died. Your birthday passed a couple months ago. It was the first one I had to celebrate without you. Don't think I forgot about you, okay? I got your favorite cupcake from Lily's and brought it up to the rooftop like we always do. I even got you a present. It's that shirt from the Crying Fish concert. I'm sad you'll never get to wear it, though. It's still hard to believe you're not around. That we're not going to college together like we planned. I swear every guy who has your hair, or wears the same red sweatshirt, makes me forget you're gone for a second because I want it so badly to be you. We never got the chance to say goodbye. I never got the chance to say a lot of things. So I thought maybe I would say some of them here.

 I'm sorry about the way things ended between us. Those last few weeks where we stopped talking to each other. How could I have known that would be our last time together? I regret it every single day. Not putting things aside for once, hoping you would reach out to me first. It's probably not a surprise that I was in love with you. I was never really good at hiding that. And that I was hurt you found someone else and didn't tell me about it. I know that was selfish of me, though. I should have been happier for you. I shouldn't have let it change anything. I should have appreciated our friendship the way I do now. The way you always did, even at times when I didn't deserve you. But you were always there at the end of the day. Showing up unannounced sometimes. Inviting me to the dance at the last minute. I miss that about you. I'm sad we never got our first dance. But I'm truly grateful for everything else. You'll always be my best friend. And I'll never forget you, okay? I hope you don't forget about me, either.

Love,
Eric

Twenty-One

FEBRUARY
THREE MONTHS LATER

Yellow Mai flowers fill the house. It's the morning of the new year. The windows are opened wide, letting in fresh air. I'm standing on the front steps with Mom and Dad. We spent all last night cleaning, sweeping the floors of the house, making sure to take out the trash. Because for the next three days, you are not to throw things away to avoid the risk of tossing out good luck. Lunar New Year is full of traditions. That's why I brought everyone outside this morning. We weren't able to do this last year. I wanted to give my family a second chance.

Tết is a celebration of new beginnings. Reentering the house symbolizes a fresh start. The person who enters first is believed to have bearing on the rest of the year. Mom and Dad decided it should be me. Although I'm not the most superstitious, I always respect their traditions. I made sure to cut my hair a few days before. This sheds all the bad energy I've been carrying with me. I hope I bring our family some good luck this year.

Mom taps my shoulder. "Con đi vô nhà trước đi rồi ba mẹ vô sau," she says. *You go in first and we will go after.*

I nod. "Okay."

Sunlight floods the house as we come inside. The dining table is filled with fried spring rolls and bowls of fruit. I helped Mom make everything the night before. She lights some incense and places it at another table. The mantel is filled with photos of people we've lost over the years. To show our respect, it is custom to offer them the food first. I walk over and pick up an incense stick. Then I glance at Jasmine's photo on the wall. I'm still not used to seeing her up there. It's been almost a year since she passed away. There are still days when the thought of this fills me with sadness. Then I play some of her music, and it feels like she's there again.

In honor of Tết, I made sure to have all her favorite foods today. I looked up a recipe for pineapple fried rice. I even cut the pineapple in half to make a bowl like the restaurant. I got another letter from Jasmine this morning. I'm saving it to read later tonight. I have a feeling she's wishing me a happy New Year.

"Happy New Year to you, too," I whisper.

Sometime later, there is a knock on the door. Dad stands and welcomes Kevin into the living room. According to my mom, the first visitor of the year needs to be important to the family. People are not to come over without an invitation. It was my idea to ask Kevin to visit the house today. He's been over a few times in the last couple of months. It feels nice having him around again as another member of the family. The two of us have really bonded lately. He helped me a lot with college applications.

Kevin brings in flowers and sets them on the table. Mom

comes around, handing us small red envelopes with money inside.

I reach into my back pocket. "Oh, I have one for you, too, Kevin."

He smiles as he takes it. "Dinner is on you, then."

"Don't get too excited."

We laugh as we sit at the table together. There's probably enough food here to last us more than a week. Everyone makes sure to try the pineapple fried rice. Kevin says it's almost as good as Uncle Wong's Palace. "*Almost?*" I say back. Mom brings out rice and mung bean cake for us. We spend the rest of the day watching some shows in the living room. For the first time in a while, the house doesn't feel empty. Sometimes you have to stop and look at the people you have around you. I'm happy for this new beginning.

Each one of Jasmine's letters asks for some sort of favor. Little promises she has me make to bring more joy into my life. Some favors are small, like cooking dinner with Mom and Dad, remembering to call Grandma, taking a walk through our favorite park.

Other favors require more effort, such as focusing on college applications, setting new goals, or challenging myself to come up with new film ideas. At first, I was only doing them for Jasmine, but they've slowly become an integral part of my life. I've already received most of my decision letters, which include a few acceptances to schools in the area. The scholarship program I applied to a few weeks ago just announced that I'm a finalist, which my parents are really excited about. Since then, I've started a new film project inspired by the recordings Jasmine left me. I think it might be the best film I've made so far. I got an email from the Reels Fest a few weeks ago. It's an independent festival based here in Chicago. My film was chosen for the shorts category, along with three others in my age group.

The screening is tonight at the Music Box Theater. I'm sitting down for coffee, looking over the program. My name is on the fourth page, underneath the title of my film. *Hoa Nhài*. The screening doesn't start for a few hours, so I've stopped by the café beforehand. I'm trying not to think about people watching my film for the first time. I remind myself art is subjective; all that matters is I'm putting myself out into the world. It can't be bad if it was chosen by the festival, right? Hopefully, someone will be moved by it.

There's another reason I came to this café. It is the same one where I met Haru, when he reappeared in my life. I come here every now and then, taking a seat at the same table. It's a bittersweet feeling, looking at the empty chair. It's been several months since we've seen each other. I still think about him all the time. It's strange how people can come into your life and disappear from it. It makes you wonder if they were ever really there. I think about Jasmine's most recent favor. *Reach out to a friend.* I take the piece of paper from my pocket and place it on the table. It's been folded into the shape of a star. Just like the one Haru made me before. It took a while for me to learn it. Inside is a note, only a few words long.

You were always real.

I leave it on the table before heading out. I put on my coat and make my way to the train station.

The marquee shines neon red outside the theater. I head in a few minutes early and find my seat. Velvet curtains line the walls of the auditorium. The first few rows are reserved for filmmakers and volunteers of the festival. I keep looking around, wondering how many people are coming. My palms are sweating a little. I haven't shown my film to anyone outside of the committee. I'm nervous about how it's going to be received tonight.

My knee moves up and down as people start streaming in. I keep turning my head, looking to see who's here. I didn't send out too many invitations. Not that I know a ton of people. As I'm watching the doors, Mom and Dad come in and take a seat in the middle. I leave the reserved row and go kiss them both on the cheek. A few minutes after, Kevin arrives and sits beside them. The screening is about to start. As I return to my seat, Simon and Alex call my name from the other side of the auditorium, blowing kisses at me. I breathe some relief, knowing they made it in time. I offer a wave before taking my seat near the other filmmakers.

The lights dim, letting us know the screening is about to start. I take a few deep breaths, knowing mine is up first. When my name appears on the screen, I squeeze the armrest as everything around me fades away . . .

The film opens with a black screen, accompanied by the

sound of a single note held on a piano. As the same note is played over and over like a metronome, a child's voice begins speaking through it. The note slowly turns into a song as the film cuts to a nine-year-old girl opening presents on her birthday. It's a home movie I found of Jasmine. The quality is a little grainy. She's laughing as she plays with her toy keyboard for the first time. You can hear Dad's voice on the other side of the camera. Music continues in the background as we cut to the next scene.

Jasmine is eleven years old. She's putting on a mini concert in the living room. Her fingers are small against the keys of the piano. Mom is sitting on the floor with me on her lap. We watch Jasmine play for us until the film cuts to the next scene. The picture quality improves. Jasmine grows up to fourteen. She's playing her first recital now. We're in the great room of her piano teacher's house. You can tell she's nervous by the little mistakes she's making. I'm recording this time because Dad is at work. For some reason, I keep moving the camera to the cat sleeping on the staircase. Mom taps me and mumbles something inaudible. This gets a few laughs from the audience as the scene changes again. Jasmine is seventeen years old. She's at her high school music recital. The auditorium is filled with other students and their families. Jasmine plays the song beautifully. She is at her best in this moment. When she's finished, everyone rises to give a standing ovation as the scene ends. The screen is black for a moment. Music fading back to a single note being held on the piano.

When the next scene starts playing, the mood changes.

Jasmine is sitting in a hospital bed. She's staring absently out the window. Mom is recording on her phone as Dad comes through the door. He surprises her with her keyboard to help her feel more at home. He places it on the bed, asking her to play a song. Dad is speaking in Vietnamese, like he usually does. The subtitles read, *Play us a song. One more time. Mom wants to hear.* Jasmine smiles a little as she begins to play something. You can hear Mom holding back tears from behind the phone. When the song is over, Jasmine blows a kiss to Mom's phone and the screen goes black again. The music completely stops. There's a long beat of silence until an audio track comes on. It's Jasmine's recording she left me. Her voice plays over the black screen.

> *It's Jasmine . . . I know you're probably still sad about everything. So I thought about what I could give you that would make it feel like I was still there. What's a piece of me I could leave behind? Then I remembered, the song I used to play for you. The one you inspired. You don't know this, but you've inspired a lot of my songs. I never got the chance to play them all for you. So I want to play them for you now. Who knows, maybe they'll inspire you the same way you did for me.*
>
> *Anyway, this is for you. I hope you like it . . .*

As the song begins, a montage of scenes I filmed play across the screen. Flowers blooming in the botanical gardens . . . the sweeping skyline from the top of Willis Tower . . . water lapping against the rocks on the lakefront trail . . . crowds passing beneath the marquee of the Chicago Theater . . . cherry blossom petals falling from the trees in Jackson Park . . . a sunset I recorded through her bedroom window . . . images of a city we grew up in together.

The song ends and the screen goes black again.

An audio of Jasmine's voice comes on one last time.

I want you to promise something, okay? That you will live life to the fullest and put your stories out there, because they are pieces of you that the world should see. And even if you don't believe this yourself, I want you to know one thing. I am your greatest fan, and I am always rooting for you.

The film ends.

When the lights come on, half the auditorium is in tears. My heart is still racing as I'm facing the screen. The applause is louder than I anticipate, a few people rising from their seats. It's strange seeing a live reaction to something you've made yourself. A piece of you that's put on display. I finally glance behind me and see Mom and Dad crying, too. I smile back as I look around for the others, but it's hard to see past the crowd. There's Simon and Alex in the aisle, holding roses as they cheer for me.

The house is full, except for one empty seat beside me. It's reserved for someone who couldn't make it tonight. Someone who will always hold a special place in my heart. I close my eyes and think about Daniel. I made a promise to save the seat next to me for my "big premiere," as he called it. *I know you would have come if you could. I saved a seat just for you.*

I turn around again. As I glance to the back of the theater, the air goes still for a moment. Jasmine is sitting in the second-to-last row. She smiles as we look at each other. Then someone walks in front of her and she's gone. Just like that. I stare at the empty seat for a second, knowing how proud she would be. Then I turn back, smiling to myself a little. A part of her will always be around, fluttering like the paper wish in the air.

I stare at the screen one last time as I think of her.

You'll always be a part of my life. This story is for you.

Epilogue

TWO YEARS LATER

My pen moves across a piece of paper, signing a lease for a new apartment. I stack boxes in the middle of the room as sunlight streams from a single window. Subway trains pass back and forth like threads weaving through the city. It's the beginning of summer. I've started an internship in New York City, assistant to the marketing team of a small media company. It's not exactly the job I went looking for, but sometimes you learn to pivot in life.

I've been living in the city for two weeks. My days consist of sending emails and editing videos for our marketing campaigns. I think of it as another form of storytelling, meant for a different audience, challenging me to step outside of myself. Then there are other days when I'm carrying six iced coffees and a bag of sesame bagels up and down Fifth Avenue, trying to catch a meeting that's been moved to a different building.

Thankfully, I have a lot of free time on the weekends. I spend the afternoons exploring the city, trying food from different trucks, walking along the paths in Central Park. I bring my camera with me, filming random shots that I'll figure out what to do with later. It's become my creative process. Piecing together a story from the everyday, finding the heartbeat beneath it.

It happens to be the first week of July. This time of year always makes me think of the Star Festival. Someone once told me the story of Orihime and Hikoboshi. The two were separated after falling madly in love, and the couple is only allowed to see each other once a year. The festival was created to celebrate their love and reunion. Paper wishes flutter through my mind as I continue down the street, thinking about them.

I left my phone in the office this morning. I'm on my way back to grab it, carrying some mail in my hands. The subway is full this afternoon, packing people in like sardines. As usual, the Q is running a little late. I stare at the floor absentmindedly. Another train approaches the platform. As I lift my head, instantly, I see him.

Time freezes for a moment.

Haru is on the train, standing there, no more than a few feet away from me. His hair is a little longer than I remember. He's staring at his phone, unaware I'm on the other side, looking back at him. For a second, I swear I'm imagining this. That can't really be him, right?

Then the train starts moving.

A gasp escapes me as he disappears from view. I look up and down the platform, wondering where he's headed. My heart is racing fast. This is the R Line, heading uptown. What's the next stop again? If I run fast enough, I can catch up to it. I don't have time to look it up. I turn immediately, dashing out of the subway.

The streets are crowded. My body breaks into sweat as I'm running. The next stop is seven blocks from here. I cut straight through traffic, moving between passing cars. I need to get there before it leaves again. Hopefully there's some delay. Then I see the subway entrance. I hurry down, reaching the platform just as the train appears. The doors open. I look everywhere, wondering which car he's in. Is he getting off at this stop? I catch my breath for a second, feeling lightheaded, about to hop on the train.

And then I see him again.

Haru stands on the platform, looking right back at me. For a moment, the rest of the world curves away from us. A long silence passes as I take him in, wondering if he's really there or if it's all in my head again. So I don't say anything at all. Then Haru looks down, noticing something. He bends over to pick it up from the floor.

"You dropped this," he says, holding it out for me.

It's one of Jasmine's letters. It must have slipped out of my hands. As I reach for it, our fingers touch slightly. For some reason, he doesn't let go right away. He takes me in and says, "I don't know if you remember . . . but we've met before."

I swallow my breath. "Yeah . . . I remember."

He smiles. "It's been a long time."

"Too long," I say.

Haru glances at the envelope. He turns it a little, as if noticing the details. "You've been back to Japan since we met?"

I shake my head. "No, I haven't."

He turns the envelope to show me something. "This is from my family's store in Osaka. It's the same washi we use. The flower on the corner is ours."

Haru lets go of the envelope, allowing me to see better. "It's from my sister. She sent them to me," I say. "But she went there a long time ago. The summer before I visited."

"She must have stopped by the store," he says, placing his hands in his pockets. "If it was in the summer, maybe we met."

I never imagined this possibility. The two of them meeting long before. I stare at the letter and back at Haru. Maybe I've been given another chance. I wonder if he's thinking this, too. "Do you want to, uh, get coffee or something?"

Haru smiles again. "I would like that."

I can't believe this. *Here you are, right in front of me.* I manage to stay composed and say, "There's a place not too far from here. We could grab a bite to eat, too. How long are you in New York?"

"The whole summer," Haru says. "What about you?"

"Me, too."

The subway train roars in behind me, blowing air up from the tracks, ruffling our hair. The doors slide open, but neither of us gets on. We stand there, on the same side of the platform, looking at each other. The letter is held tight in my hand. My mind goes back to the beginning again.

I think I finally got my wish.

Acknowledgments

If you're reading this, it means this book is finally out in the world. What a journey this one was. They say your second book is always the hardest, and they are right. I have the scars to prove it. But I'm proud of the final story you're holding in your hands. You know you've truly thrown yourself into your work when the scenes you wrote feel more like memories. I wish I could say this is a story I wanted to write for a long time, but that's not the truth, Ellen. *When Haru Was Here* came to me very differently than my first book. That's because the conditions were different. With *You've Reached Sam*, I had the freedom to write as if no one was watching. It was only me and my imagination, staring up at a bedroom ceiling, dreaming of telling stories someday.

When it came to this book, there were some *constraints*. A second book typically has to be in the same genre, explore similar themes as the first. And this time there were deadlines, which I missed over and over again. There were also the expectations of the readers. The ones who loved Sam and wanted their hearts broken all over again. I know you guys want that gut-wrenching ending that sends you to my DMs, asking me to pay for your therapy bills. But the truth is, when

I signed up to write two books back in 2019, I had no clue what the second one would be about.

When it was time to start drafting, I threw out ideas off the top of my head until one of them resonated. It went something like, "The perfect guy walks into the coffee shop and sits down next to you—but nobody else can see him." I didn't know anything else except this: these two could never be together. There was something lonely about the idea, but also relatable. It made me think about the imaginary experiences we have every day. The ones we often keep to ourselves. It was a story I didn't know I needed to write until I reached the very end.

This book was a challenging one, and I lost count of the number of times I rewrote it. But it reaffirms something I've always believed to be true. Some of our best work is born out of constraints. *When Haru Was Here* is a story I hold close to my heart, and I hope it means as much to you as it does to me.

Anyway, let's get to the acknowledgments. As always, the person I want to thank first is my sister, Vivian. How did you find the time to help me with this book while working in big law? Elle Woods has literally nothing on you. Remember when we were little kids, talking about the stories I made up in my head? Now you're helping me put them out into the world. I think you were a famous editor in a past life. You are not only the best critique partner, you are my trusted lawyer, and also my biggest fan. I can't thank you enough for all you've done.

Thank you to Mom and Dad for the love and support

ACKNOWLEDGMENTS

throughout my life. You guys have believed in me since the beginning, and I'm grateful to have you as parents. Thank you to my brother, Alvin, for always pushing me to be my best. And to Grandma, for the sacrifices you've made for all of us.

Thank you to Thao Le at SDLA. To Andrea Cavallaro for taking this story overseas. Shout out to Jennifer Kim, too. Thank you to my editor, Eileen Rothschild, for helping and supporting queer stories like this one. You let me write through a lens we don't often get to see. Special thanks to the Wednesday team—Alexis Neuville, Brant Janeway, Meghan Harrington, and Lisa Bonvissuto. To Kerri Resnick for all the best cover ideas. And to Zipcy for illustrating them.

I'm lucky to have so many writer friends. Thank you to Julian Winters, who was there from the beginning. You read *Sam* first, and you read *Haru* first. Please move here so we can hang out all the time. Thank you to Adam Silvera for giving me so much advice. Of course, thank you to the besties, Chloe Gong and Alex Aster, for all the support, the coffees, the flowers, and the endless happy hours. Thank you to Roshani Chokshi for always picking up the phone. You are truly a lifeline and I owe you so much. Thank you to Jack Edwards for moving to the city and becoming my best friend. And thank you to Jolie Christine and Ariella Goldberg for your help along the way.

Most important, thank you to the readers. The ones who loved Sam first. You guys changed the course of my life. I hope you know this book is for you.